California
Summer

Also by Anita Hughes

Christmas in London

Emerald Coast

White Sand, Blue Sea

Christmas in Paris

Santorini Sunsets

Island in the Sea

Rome in Love

French Coast

Lake Como

Market Street

Monarch Beach

ANITA HUGHES

California
Summer

St. Martin's Griffin
New York

This is a work of fiction. All of the characters, organizations, and events portrayed in this novel are either products of the author's imagination or are used fictitiously.

www.stmartins.com

Title page art courtesy of Freepik.com

LIBRARY OF CONGRESS CATALOGING-IN-PUBLICATION DATA

Names: Hughes, Anita, 1963– author.
Title: California summer / Anita Hughes.
Description: First edition. | New York : St. Martin's Griffin, 2018.
Identifiers: LCCN 2017060312 | ISBN 978-1-250-16665-4 (trade pbk.) | ISBN 978-1-250-16666-1 (ebook)
Subjects: | GSAFD: Love stories.
Classification: LCC PS3608.U356755 C35 2018 | DDC 813/.6—dc23
LC record available at https://lccn.loc.gov/2017060312

Our books may be purchased in bulk for promotional, educational, or business use. Please contact your local bookseller or the Macmillan Corporate and Premium Sales Department at 1-800-221-7945, extension 5442, or by email at MacmillanSpecialMarkets@macmillan.com.

First Edition: June 2018

10 9 8 7 6 5 4 3 2 1

To my mother

And to the people of California and especially Montecito:
May there be endless beautiful sunrises and sunsets.

California
Summer

One

Rosie carried her overnight bag up the stairs and was greeted by the familiar mess of their kitchen. Ben had left the blender on the counter, next to a half-empty box of strawberries and a can of protein powder. Rosie imagined him wearing his Lakers t-shirt, his gray sweats with the barely legible Kenyon logo, sprinting out the door like a bullet.

When they arrived in Los Angeles eight years ago they rolled their eyes at people eating takeout from brown cardboard containers, at the Priuses gliding silently down Santa Monica Boulevard, at the young women walking dogs that were large as horses or small as silver quarters.

"Nobody has a normal dog: a golden retriever or a Labrador," Rosie observed.

"That's because we're in Los Angeles. The city is full of artists, musicians, writers." Ben held her hand tightly, maneuvering through the crowds on Venice Beach Boardwalk.

"And models, waiters, and pizza delivery boys with college degrees and unpaid student loans," Rosie replied nervously. She thought about their own newly minted degrees, the loan statements being forwarded to their studio apartment in Venice, the meetings where they had shown their student film and been politely told they had something, but it was rough. "Shine it up and let us take another look."

Now, two apartments, one surprising success on the indie film circuit later, they owned matching Honda hybrids, belonged to the Save the Ocean Foundation, and shopped exclusively at Whole Foods.

"We're living the dream." Ben smiled when Rosie reported updates from their Kenyon classmates. Some worked in big corporations, others collected postgraduate degrees or took over family businesses in Ohio.

The ocean was just yards from their front door and she loved the sound of the waves crashing onto the sand. And she adored the secondhand bookstore that stocked a whole section of Ibsen and Pinter. But the studio executives in their three-piece pin-striped suits made her nervous. They treated you to a three-course lunch and then cut your budget so ruthlessly; Rosie wanted to run home and bury her head in a pillow.

Rosie wiped the kitchen counter and sorted through the mail Ben left on the table. Her mother still sent letters on creamy white stationery, though Rosie usually dashed off an email reply. There were two invitations to movie premieres and a note from Ben: *please pick up my tux at the dry cleaner.*

What should she wear to the premieres? Now that she held the title of "associate producer" on a studio picture her mildly bohemian wardrobe seemed wrong. She either had to buy vintage Galliano and Audrey Hepburn little black dresses, or brave the saleswomen at Prada and Pucci.

Rosie hauled her overnight bag to the washing machine. The title of "associate producer" puzzled her. She accompanied the location scout on trips to find the perfect settings. She visited factories with the costume designer to choose the right fabrics. She sat in meetings with the studio accountants and publicity team. She didn't seem to do anything by herself, but no one could do anything without her.

"Relax." Ben rubbed her temples as they lay in bed at night. He turned Rosie on her stomach and pressed his thumb on the small of her back. Ben knew her body as well as she did. In college, people had said they were mirror images of each other. They wore their wavy brown hair in the same off-the-shoulder style. They both had hazel eyes and freckles on their cheeks. They dressed in unisex t-shirts, often trading clothes. Rosie strolled campus wearing a Bob Marley t-shirt and had to admit she never listened to his music when a Marley buff tried to engage her in conversation.

Now Ben kept his hair in a crew cut and Rosie straightened hers and wore it halfway down her back. Ben dressed in sports shirts and slacks, and Rosie stuffed her side of the closet with cotton dresses. But when they ran on the beach, they shared a similar gait. They ordered the same smoothies from Jamba Juice. They both opened the Sunday *New York Times* at the same page and read the book reviews from back to front.

"Your job is to organize people and you're brilliant." Ben pushed his thumb harder into her spine. Rosie could feel her body melting and goose bumps popped up on her skin.

Ben's job was easily defined. He was the director. His name was stenciled on the back of his chair, it was ironed onto a t-shirt the cast gave him on the first day of shooting, it was printed on his parking space at the studio lot: BEN FORD, DIRECTOR.

Ben wore the t-shirt for a week straight. He marveled at it over breakfast. "Not assistant director, not second director: director," he said, chewing a mouthful of eggs. He wore it when he Skyped his best friend in Atlanta. He wore it under his dress shirt when they had dinner at CUT with Erin Braun, their lead actress, and her race car driver boyfriend.

Their hands were poised on the first rung of success; they just had to climb the ladder. Sometimes it was the best feeling in the world and sometimes it scared her to death.

Rosie separated the whites from the darks and added laundry detergent and fabric softener. Her feet hurt from two days of trekking around horse farms. Her arms were sunburned because Ben hadn't been there to remind her to reapply suntan lotion. She wanted to stand under the jets of their high-tech shower and climb under cool cotton sheets.

The bedroom was messier than the kitchen. Two days' worth of t-shirts, running shorts, polos, and slacks lay in a heap on the floor. Ben joked that when they bought a house it would have his and hers walk-in closets. His would be accessed by a special code so Rosie couldn't pick up his sweatshirts and socks. He liked that she kept the bed perfectly made, heaped with pillows, but he missed the masculine squalor of his dorm room.

Buying a house in the Santa Monica hills was on the wish list they tacked to a bulletin board in the bedroom. After the movie wrapped they had three goals: get married, go to Africa, and buy a house. Sometimes they changed the order.

"We shouldn't wait for our honeymoon to go to Africa," Ben pondered aloud, eating waffles in bed on a Sunday morning. "We could get married in Africa, on a wild animal reserve."

"We could buy a house first," Rosie offered, sipping fresh-squeezed orange juice. "And get married in our garden, overlooking the Pacific."

Recently they had a small argument over their wish list. Ben scratched out "house in Santa Monica hills" and replaced it with "house in Beverly Hills."

"Why would we want to live in Beverly Hills?" Rosie frowned when she saw the new entry.

"Movie people live in Beverly Hills or the Hollywood Hills." Ben shrugged, taking off his running socks.

"That's why we like Santa Monica," Rosie replied. "It has writers and artists and regular families with two kids and SUVs."

"If we want to get a bigger deal next time, we need to move in the right circles." Ben sat on the bed and put his arms around her. "Would a house above the Hollywood sign be so bad? With an infinity pool and our own orange grove?"

"I'd settle for an orange tree." Rosie grinned, closing her eyes and imagining a low modern house with floor-to-ceiling windows.

"I want to give you an orange grove and a rose garden and a fountain filled with goldfish." Ben pulled her down on the bed.

"I'm not very good with goldfish," Rosie giggled, feeling his mouth on her breast.

"Then we'll hire someone to take care of them," Ben mumbled, his fingers caressing her thighs.

Ben's clothes were scattered on the floor and Rosie threw them on the bed. She began separating dry cleaning from laundry, but suddenly she froze. The bed was unmade, the sheets twisted and hanging on the floor. Ben never made the bed. Sometimes Rosie made it while he was still in it. She folded her side and plumped the pillows against the headboard. She hated to come home to an unmade bed; it made her feel as if she hadn't showered.

She stepped back and studied the sheets closely. Ben's t-shirt against her cheek smelled of his deodorant. A pit formed in her stomach, opening wider like a chasm.

Ben's habits were as familiar to her as the inside of her underwear drawer. He screwed on the toothpaste cap so tight she had to run it under hot water to unscrew it. He tore off the cover of magazines and folded the corner of every page. He pulled the sheets around them at night as if he was protecting them in a cocoon. But when they had sex, when he covered Rosie's chest with his own smooth, compact body, when he opened her legs and plunged into her, he pushed the sheets fiercely off the bed. After, when they were both sweaty and spent and tasting of each other, he wrapped his body around hers and they slept uncovered, all night.

Rosie sat at the edge of the bed, trying to think. Had they had sex before she left? Could she have left Ben in bed, the sheets crumpled on the floor, and slipped off in the morning on her trip?

Her heart hammered in her chest and she blinked to keep the fear from forming into tears. Ben had an early call Tuesday morning. She remembered because it was such a glorious feeling to lie in bed, alone. She felt like she was back in college with a late-morning class, stealing an hour to read Donna Tartt's *The Secret History*.

She had made the bed and packed her overnight bag. Ben's drawer was full of fresh socks and she counted that he had enough clean t-shirts. The towels were stacked neatly in the laundry and the bathroom was filled with fresh, fluffy linens. She even rescued her favorite stuffed animal, Taffy the Penguin, and propped him on Ben's pillow: to keep him company while she was gone.

Rosie surveyed the bed and a hollow feeling formed in her stomach. The pillows were scrunched and there was an open *Rolling Stone* on the bedside table. The sheets formed a knotted column like a snake. She pictured a girl with bouncing breasts and tousled hair, arching under Ben's compact form.

Over the years they had very few fights. Ben was like a sleeping giant. He never raised his voice. He hardly ever disagreed with her. Sometimes he would wrinkle his brow, make her repeat what she said, and then calmly refute her argument.

Ben wanted to drive straight out to Los Angeles after graduation. Rosie thought they should get real jobs and save money before they embarked on their dream. Rosie wanted to call their company "Benny and Rosie Films." Ben thought they needed something slicker: "Benjamin Rose Productions."

Once or twice a year, something would set Ben off. Rosie didn't like a scene, after Ben spent days and nights in the editing suite. Ben favored the Beverly Hills Hotel for their anniversary dinner and Rosie preferred a quiet meal at home. His face would close up and he would throw on his running shoes and burn off his frustration on the pavement.

Even when he darted out the door, saying she didn't understand how hard he worked, Rosie knew he'd come back. They were best friends, lovers, and partners. They spent all day together on the set, sending telepathic signals. When they were apart, they called each other ten times a day, hugging their phones to their cheeks.

"Are you sure you want to set the fourth scene on a horse farm?" Rosie had asked the day before, standing in the middle of a paddock. "They're full of flies and manure. I don't think Erin is going to find it romantic. Maybe you should have her meet her lover at a lake or on a tennis court?"

"I want a stampede of horses," Ben said into the phone. Rosie imagined him with one eye squinting into the camera. "I want dirt, open fields, a majestic mountain in the distance."

"I guess that means you won't settle for a 7-Eleven on the other side of the stables?" Rosie laughed, walking through caked mud back to her car. "I'll call you when we get to Long Meadows."

Even when they couldn't talk to each other—when Ben holed up with writers and came home late wired on coffee and donuts, when Rosie flew to San Francisco or Dallas to meet investors—she felt like Ben was by her side. She saved up stories of obese oilmen wanting a stake in the movie, of San Francisco socialites demanding their daughter Chloe or Prudence have a small part in exchange for financial backing. When they lay in bed, toes touching, fingers massaging each other's backs, Rosie knew no one would ever come between them.

But the sheet lay in a heap of beige cotton. It spoke louder than a vague Facebook reference, louder than a magazine gossip column. Ben had had another woman in their bed. He had pushed aside the pillows. He had pulled the woman into the center of the bed. He had made love to her.

Rosie heard the screen door bang shut and the ice maker making a spitting sound. She noticed Ben standing in the hall and watched him strip off his t-shirt and throw it in the direction of the washing machine. He strode towards the bedroom, a glass of orange juice in one hand, and a smile spreading across his face.

"You should have texted me you were home." Ben put the glass down and planted an orange-juice kiss on her mouth.

"We beat the traffic," Rosie said grimly. "Made it in record time."

"You smell like hay and horses." Ben nuzzled the side of her neck. "Let's go out for sushi. I want to hear about every horse farm from here to Bakersfield."

"I was about to jump in the shower." Rosie pulled her eyes from the crumpled sheet. She looked at Ben: his long nose with a slight bump in the middle, his hazel eyes flecked with yellow, the dimple at the corner of his mouth. She tried to squelch her rising panic, to imagine this was an ordinary evening: shower, dinner, and bed.

"I'll join you." Ben casually stripped off his sweats. "I had the executive producer crawling around the set with a calculator. He was tallying how many Starbucks the crew drank during each take. Christ, next he'll be adding up toilet rolls."

"The sheets," Rosie said numbly, pointing to the floor.

"I'm a hopeless case." Ben grinned. "I meant to make the bed, but I just didn't have time. I'll turn over a new leaf when the movie wraps. I'll serve you breakfast in bed for a month."

"Ben!" she yelled as he headed for the bathroom.

"What's up?" He turned around, crossing his arms over his naked chest.

"You had a woman in our bed," Rosie said. Her teeth were chattering, a chill ran up her spine.

"What are you talking about?" Ben replied guardedly. He flicked an imaginary hair from his forehead.

"The sheets were at the edge of the bed. You had sex with a woman in our bed."

"Rosie, you're crazy." Ben stood beside her. There were beads of sweat on his shoulders.

"When we have sex you kick the sheets off the bed," Rosie said in a strangled voice, her eyes brimming with tears.

"I had a nightmare." Ben shrugged, a smile playing on his lips. "Something to do with Erin getting a cold sore as big as a pizza. I must have kicked them off during the night. I'll help you make the bed." He reached down and grabbed a side of the sheet.

"Ben!" Rosie screeched. "We've slept together for ten years. We've shared a single bed, a bunk bed, that king bed at the hotel in Sundance. You never kick the sheets unless we have sex. Tell me who she is or I'm leaving."

"Let's go to Johnny Rockets and share a burger and a shake. I'll explain everything if you just give me a chance."

"I want to know her name."

Ben dropped his hands to his sides. He sat on the bed, drumming his fingers on the mattress. He looked up at Rosie, his eyes bright and clear.

"Mary Beth Chase."

"Mary Beth Chase the producer? Mary Beth Chase the Hollywood vixen who wears La Perla in public and has her own bungalow at the Beverly Hills Hotel. Mary Beth Chase who is at least ten years older than you and has had more boy toys than other women have handbags?"

"She's none of those things." Ben kept his eyes on the floor. "She went to Wesleyan. She's whip smart and she's had five blockbusters in a row. People don't like women with balls, they just want to cut them down."

"And you want to screw them!" Rosie stormed. She paced the bedroom like a wounded lion. She couldn't look at Ben. She couldn't look at their matching chests of drawers, at the framed poster of their movie, at the picture of them taken at Sundance, arms around Robert Redford.

"She's been plying me with dinner and drinks for weeks. I didn't want to tell you till things were finalized, but the studio wanted to bring her in as executive producer. She knows how to steamroll a movie. Her productions bring in bigger numbers than anyone's besides Jerry Bruckheimer's."

"You went to bed to close a deal!" Rosie exploded. "Is this the Playboy Mansion? Are you Hugh Hefner?"

"You don't know how sorry I am. It just sort of happened. She wanted to see a clip of our indie. I brought her home to get the DVD. You were away. We sort of moved from the sofa to the bedroom."

"Stop!" Rosie screamed. "You threw away ten years of our lives so your movie could make a few more zeros."

"Rosie, I've loved you since we were juniors at Kenyon. I

couldn't have made it through Senior Seminar without you." Ben ran his hands nervously through his hair. "When we moved to LA, I thought about running home every night for a year. But I'd look at you in bed, and even asleep you had confidence in me."

"Don't!" Rosie yelled. Tears rolled down her cheeks. She felt like she was swimming underwater and someone had removed her snorkel.

"We've grown apart," Ben said slowly. "I feel like I'm not running fast enough because I'm waiting for you to catch up. You don't want a mega successful movie; you don't want a Beverly Hills estate. You cringed when I wanted to check out Maseratis."

"You lied to me, and when you got caught you said it didn't mean anything." She turned on him. "Now you think we're growing apart. Which is it?" she demanded. "Because I want the truth."

"I don't know what I want," Ben said lamely. "You're always the one who figures out what we want, but that doesn't seem to be working anymore."

"I want us," Rosie whispered. She was going to throw up or pass out: crumple into a heap on the sheets.

"I'll tell you what I do know." Ben was like a windup toy that suddenly sprang to life. "I want this movie to be the biggest thing since *Mission: Impossible*. I want to make a sequel every year and have houses in the Hamptons and Hawaii. You might see that as selling out but I see it as seizing an opportunity."

"I'm not against those things." Rosie's words came out between sobs. "We always said we'd be the next Tom Hanks and Rita Wilson. We'd show Hollywood we were made of Teflon."

"I think we should take a break." He looked at Rosie.

"We work together every day," Rosie replied frantically. She was like a woman in a magic show, sliced down the middle. Half of her felt physically sick; she never wanted Ben to touch her again. The other half saw Ben walk out the door; watched his wide smile and his hazel eyes and his freckles disappear, and thought her heart was breaking.

"The studio would buy out your contract," Ben said slowly, as if he was figuring it out while he talked. "Maybe you could do theater. You've always loved Ibsen and Pinter."

"You're planning my life for me! I'm associate producer," Rosie sputtered.

"They gave you that title because they wanted me." Ben shrugged. "We were a package deal. I'll move out. You can take your time figuring out what you want to do."

"You sound like you're reading a script," Rosie yelled, pounding her fists on the bed. "Did Mary Beth Chase hire a writer for you? Are you going to use this for the big breakup scene in the movie?"

"Rosie, let's not make it worse. We both need time to cool off. I'll go spend the night at the studio."

"You mean you'll drive to Mary Beth's bungalow!" Rosie was like a rocket breaking apart. She grabbed her overnight bag and pulled open her chest of drawers. She jammed in underwear, bras, t-shirts, shorts, socks, and leotards. She went to the closet and yanked out a bunch of cotton dresses. She gathered her makeup bag, the paperback books on her bedside table, and the slippers she kept under the bed.

"Where are you going?" Ben followed her through the hall into the kitchen.

"I'll post it on my Facebook status." Rosie dragged the bag down the stairs and flung it into the hatchback. She saw Ben in the rearview mirror. He was standing at the door in his boxers. She slowed down, thinking he'd run after her. He'd pound on the window and beg her forgiveness. He got caught up in the craziness; he'd do anything to win her back. Rosie idled the car at the red light and watched Ben pick up the newspaper from the porch and walk inside.

It was one block to the beach and she parked near the sand. The last surfers straggled in from the waves and a boy threw a tennis ball to his dog. She saw a young couple strolling hand in hand and all she wanted was to be walking along the shore with Ben and talking about their day.

The couple wore matching UCSB sweatshirts and denim cutoffs. He had an earring in one ear and she had a tattoo on her ankle. Their faces were so close together they walked like a monster in a fairy tale: two heads bobbing on top of one body. Rosie remembered when she and Ben used to bump into things; they were so deep in conversation they didn't notice where they were going.

They met on the lawn outside the dining hall. It was early fall; only the second week of classes, and the air was humid and thundery. Rosie lay under a tree, eating a peach and reading Mary McCarthy's *The Group*. She was feeling lost back on campus. Her best friend had transferred to Oberlin and her sophomore boyfriend hooked up with his high school sweetheart.

"Let me guess, you're enrolled in one of those lit classes where you've never heard of the authors and the books are so boring you can't stay awake." Ben sat on the lawn next to her. He looked vaguely familiar, as if she'd seen him at the back of a lecture hall. He had wavy brown hair and carried a backpack crammed with notebooks.

"Mary McCarthy is one of the best writers of the twentieth century." Rosie looked up. "Unless you're intimidated by female intelligence."

"I wouldn't have lasted two years at Kenyon if I was intimidated by intelligent women." Ben grinned.

Rosie liked his smile; it made his eyes crinkle at the corners.

"They grow like weeds around here. I'm Ben Ford, we were in a film seminar last semester."

"Rosie Keller." Rosie shook his hand formally.

"Are you a film major too?"

"Theater," Rosie replied.

"You should switch," Ben said decisively. "Do you want to influence three hundred people in one badly heated space with terrible coffee and overpriced sweets, or millions of viewers all over the world?"

"Last movie I saw, the popcorn cost six dollars and the coffee tasted like turpentine."

"Movies transport you to another place. You can be in Egypt, on a canal in Venice, at the Great Wall of China, just by watching the screen."

"I've read Chekhov, Ibsen, Pinter." Rosie ticked the names off on her fingers. "I've never read a great screenwriter."

"But have you seen *The Godfather, Apocalypse Now, Midnight Rider, The Sting*?" Ben leaned close. He smelled of sweat and ink.

"I am a Hitchcock fan," Rosie conceded.

"He's my idol." Ben's eyes sparkled. Rosie thought they resembled a kaleidoscope. "Which one is your favorite?"

"I'm half in love with Cary Grant," Rosie replied, folding the page of her book and placing it in her lap.

"Come with me." Ben grabbed her hand and pulled her up. He ran across the lawn, his backpack bouncing against his shoulder.

"Theater is two-dimensional," he continued as if they were paused in the middle of a discussion. "You're always wondering when the house lights are going to come on or whether it's still raining outside. Movies are like a magic carpet. The big screen takes you wherever you want to go."

They stopped outside a small building with no windows. Ben extracted a set of keys from his pocket and opened the door.

"Wait here," he instructed.

Rosie watched storm clouds gather in the distance. There was a faint rumbling of thunder. She wondered how she had never been to this corner of campus, and how she had not noticed this boy who was all frenetic energy and flashing hazel eyes.

Ben opened the door and drew her inside. They were in a small dark room with a screen on one wall. Rosie smelled garlic and butter, and there was a brown Indian blanket spread on the floor.

"Your magic carpet." Ben invited her to sit down. "Your gourmet snacks." He pointed to the bowl of freshly popped popcorn.

The screen went black and flickered onto the opening credits of *To Catch a Thief*. Rosie saw Cary Grant flirt with Grace Kelly. She watched them zip up hills of Monte Carlo in a tiny yellow car. She felt the glittering Mediterranean as if she was bobbing in a motorboat.

Rosie ate a handful of popcorn, feeling Ben's shoulder rub against hers. She could see the outline of his knees, his hands with long smooth fingers.

After *To Catch a Thief*, Ben put on *North by Northwest* and *An Affair to Remember*. Rosie forgot that it was dinnertime in the dining hall. She didn't hear the heavy raindrops falling outside. Ben took her hand and placed it in his lap.

"I see your point." Rosie grinned when the credits rolled and Ben flicked on the lights. He moved closer so their knees were touching.

"When I get out of here I'm going to drive straight to Los Angeles. I'm going to pound on Steven Spielberg's door and beg to sweep the cutting room floor."

"I don't think they have cutting rooms anymore."

"I'm not going to let anything distract me. I'd rather eat SPAM for a year than do anything other than make a movie."

"I don't think anyone eats SPAM either. Maybe canned tuna, or tofu and sprouts."

"I'm going to make the best damn film since *Titanic*, and it's going to play in every movie theater in America."

"I'll go see it." Rosie nodded, feeling his hand pressing hers.

Ben stopped. He looked at Rosie closely. He pushed his hair behind his ears and kissed her slowly on the mouth. He pulled back, studying her eyes, her nose, and her cheekbones. He leaned forward and kissed her again, putting his arms around her and scooping her up as if she were a doll.

"There's one thing movies can't make you forget," he said, tracing her lips with his thumb. "That you're sitting next to the most beautiful girl in the world."

The last ten years had passed so quickly, Rosie thought as she watched a familiar tall blond figure walk towards her on the sand. She wore a pantsuit with padded shoulders and a man's button-down shirt. Her hair was cut bluntly at her shoulders and her mouth was smeared with bright red lipstick.

"I've been combing the beach from Santa Monica to Venice." The woman sat down on the sand. "I was about to give up and grab a burger."

"How did you find me?" Rosie squinted through the tears. She sat hunched over, hugging her knees while her best friend rubbed her back fondly.

"I tried to call you but you've been out of range for two days. Then Ben called and told me you disappeared. I figured I better play lifeguard and rescue you."

"Ben called you," Rosie repeated, trying to stop shaking.

"He sounded worried about you, something to do with sheets and dirty laundry. He wasn't making sense."

"He made perfect sense when he told me we've grown apart and he was leaving. I beat him to it," Rosie sobbed.

"Neither of you is making sense and I'm starving. Let's go to World Foods and stuff our faces with tofu burgers. I never feel guilty there, even when I order fries."

"I'm not hungry." Rosie shook her head. She felt like her body was rooted in the sand.

"Then you can watch me eat, and you can tell me what's going on with Hollywood's most adorable couple," Angelica said and walked towards the parking lot.

"Ben slept with Mary Beth Chase, in our bed, while I was scouting locations." Rosie sat opposite Angelica in a booth at World Foods. Angelica was almost half a foot taller than Rosie. She had naturally blond hair that she sometimes dyed red or even black. Angelica was a chameleon. Even her eyes, a watery pale blue, seemed to change color depending on what she was wearing.

They met on the set of Ben's indie film. Ben was looking for a girl to play the role of a sophisticated young socialite. "Picture her as a modern Cornelia Guest," he explained to Rosie. "I want to cast somebody authentic. I'm sick of these actresses with hair the color of mayonnaise and breasts made of plastic. I want a real socialite: I want her to roll her r's and walk like she's balancing a dictionary on her head."

Ben and Rosie started hanging out at gallery openings in West LA. They lounged poolside at the Beverly Hills Hotel and snuck into the Polo Lounge. Ben spotted Angelica in a booth at Spago's. She was sipping champagne and rolling spaghetti into a ball on her spoon.

"That's the girl!" he said excitedly. "Look how she holds her fork."

"Her hair looks like she stuck it in a microwave." Rosie frowned. "I thought you wanted a sleek blonde with an elegant chignon."

Ben introduced himself as the producer of the film that would launch her career. Over German chocolate cake and a bottle of Veuve Clicquot, they learned that Angelica came from a wealthy Santa Barbara family. Her hair was actually straight and blond. Angelica believed in method acting and was auditioning for the movie version of *Hair*. "I want to show the director a white girl can groove," Angelica explained, licking chocolate from her fork.

Ben convinced her to take the role in his film instead, and Angelica and Rosie became fast friends. They both had schoolgirl crushes on Zac Efron and Leonardo DiCaprio. They both loved Mexican food; they both knew the lines of every song by Beyoncé.

"That doesn't sound like Ben." Angelica ate a handful of fries. "He's the last honest man in LA."

"He said I'm holding him back, that I don't want the big successful movie career." Rosie sniffled, stabbing a green salad. "I do want it. I love taking the bus tour of Beverly Hills. I adore beautiful rooms and green lawns and blue swimming pools. I saw *Remains of the Day* three times."

"I'm not buying his excuse." Angelica shook her blunt pageboy. "He saw a piece of flesh on his couch and he had to have her. Men see themselves in terms of the size of their penises. The more successful they become, the bigger they think their penises are. It's like looking in a fun-house mirror. When they think their dicks are enormous they have to use them."

Rosie shuddered, picturing Ben undressing another woman.

"Why the shoulder pads? I didn't know they were shooting a movie version of *Dynasty*."

"I'm channeling Katharine Hepburn!" Angelica exclaimed. "I got the role of Tracy Lord in the remake of *The Philadelphia Story*."

"Wow!" Rosie gulped her glass of water. "You're going to be fantastic. It'll be the movie of the year."

"They cast Dirk Graham in Cary Grant's role. Can you imagine me working with Dirk Graham? I wonder if he really went to Cambridge or if he practiced that accent with his acting coach. I could run my hands through his hair all day."

"You better not tell Matthew." Rosie frowned.

"Only on the set, when the director calls action." Angelica piled her burger with spinach and bean sprouts. "But a girl can dream. Matthew has been working seven days a week. I'm living with a ghost."

"He started a new job." Rosie pushed her plate away. "At least your boyfriend isn't replacing you with his boss."

"That's because Matthew's boss is a two-hundred-pound Lebanese who eats falafel at his desk. Matthew comes home smelling of cumin."

Rosie recoiled. She had seen pictures of Mary Beth Chase in *Variety* and *W*. She was six feet of curves and hair extensions. Her cheekbones were finely chiseled, and her lips were the color of cherries.

"We need to talk about you." Angelica dabbed soy sauce on her burger. "What do you want to do?"

"I know what I don't want." Rosie was having trouble swallowing. "I don't want to find a new job, I don't want to move, and I don't want Ben to have screwed another woman."

"I'm a lifesaver not a genie." Angelica squeezed Rosie's hand. "I can't make Ben's penis disappear."

"Maybe the studio doesn't want me," Rosie choked, the tears starting again. "Ben's the brilliant director, I'm just someone who can organize people."

"I wish you could stay with us, but we couldn't fit an extra plant into our place," Angelica said. "My mother keeps sending me checks but I keep sending them back."

"Half the actors in town get money from their parents." Rosie shrugged.

"If I accept their money, I'll get lazy." Angelica shook her head. "I won't get any roles, and I'll be living in my parents' guest cottage. My mother is smart as a fox."

"Your mother is wonderful." Rosie remembered driving with Ben to their estate in Montecito last Thanksgiving. Angelica's father was a famous record producer so Rosie had expected a mansion with miles of marble and glass. She pictured a movie theater with padded walls, a black granite kitchen, and rock stars wandering around in tight leather pants.

They drove up a long gravel drive and entered through wrought iron gates. The house was made of stone and covered in ivy. It had elegant bay windows, a peaked roof, and lawns that rolled down to a private lake.

Ben had whistled as he pulled up to the stone entry. He leaned close and whispered to Rosie, "This would be a great place to film a remake of *Rebecca*."

Rosie recalled the front hallway with its dark wood floors covered with oriental rugs. The walls were painted ivory and hung with framed photographs of Angelica and her brother, Sam. The living room looked like it belonged in an English hunting lodge. A stone fireplace took up one wall. Sofas were covered in floral chintz and brown velvet. Two Irish setters lay by the fireplace, lifting their heads when Rosie entered the room.

"Your house is beautiful," Rosie said to Angelica's mother, a statuesque woman with Angelica's Roman nose and white-blond hair.

"I expect it could use updating." Estelle shrugged. "It's been in the family for years. I'm afraid if I renovate, I'll dislodge the ghost of my grandfather. I'm positive he lives in the library; I hear him opening the brandy at night."

"I've never been in a house with ghosts." Rosie patted the Irish setter.

"Every house has a story." Estelle smiled. "But you can't learn all its secrets on the first visit. You'll have to come back."

"My mother is special," Angelica agreed. "But since I'm her only child in the same time zone, she calls me every day. I have an idea!" She gripped Rosie's hand tightly. "You can live in her guest cottage for the summer."

"In Montecito?" Rosie wiped her eyes. "I can't just run away."

"It would be perfect. Maybe when the movie wraps Ben will come to his senses. He's put you through hell, you need to pamper yourself. And you'll do me a favor. Once I get a paycheck for *The Philadelphia Story*, my mother will realize I'm serious about acting. In the meantime you can talk to her about her roses and feed the ducks in the lake. You deserve so much better, Rosie. Montecito is the ideal place to recharge."

"It's so removed." Rosie hesitated, thinking of the ninety miles of Pacific Coast Highway that separated Santa Barbara from Santa Monica. She wouldn't casually bump into Ben at Starbucks or run into him at Sprinkles.

"Ben needs to realize what he's missing. He'll wake up with Mary Beth's hair extensions on his pillow and wish he was lying next to you."

"I can't just quit the picture." Rosie shook her head.

"Take a leave of absence for personal reasons. It's written into every contract." She looked at Rosie and her eyes were dark. "He's an asshole and he doesn't deserve you."

Rosie picked up her phone. She wanted to call Ben and ask his advice. For the last ten years, if she couldn't decide between the butternut squash soup and the black bean chili she called Ben. If she wasn't sure whether to record *Homeland* or *Scandal,* she called Ben. But she couldn't call him. The Ben who made blueberry waffles on Sundays, the Ben who knew exactly how to touch her, the Ben who could whistle Frank Sinatra and knew every song by Muse had been replaced by a guy who screwed other women. A guy whose vision of the future included blockbuster movies, palatial homes, but not her. She put the phone down and set her mouth in a firm, straight line. "Call your mother."

Two

Rosie drove along the coast, keeping one eye on the ocean. Gazing at the Pacific, glittering like a diamond necklace, was the only thing that kept her from driving the car off the road. The ocean was what she loved best about Los Angeles: running on the beach, digging her toes into the sand, walking at sunset with a tall iced coffee. If she had to leave the scudding white sailboats and rainbow-colored surfboards, she'd stop living.

Ben hadn't put up any resistance to her plan, and neither had the studio. Ben stood in the bedroom as she packed, calmly encouraging her. She felt like she was already gone, like he was propelling her out the door.

"A change of scenery is the best thing." He nodded, his arms crossed over his chest. He wore a gray U2 t-shirt. He was freshly shaved; his hair slicked back, his eyes achingly hazel.

"You're the one who wants a change of scenery." Rosie stuffed her running shoes into a duffle bag. "You want a tall, curvy blonde instead of a small, mousy brunette."

"This isn't about other women," Ben said, as if he was talking to a child.

"Of course it is!" Rosie snapped. "For the last ten years you've been a film geek, content with your college sweetheart. Now that your name is on a director's chair, you've got a jet propulsion pack strapped to your back."

"We both need to see if we're in the right place." Ben put his hands on Rosie's shoulders. "Sometimes people stay together out of habit. I don't want that to happen to us."

"What happened to us is you slept with another woman." Rosie emptied her bedside drawer on the bed.

"You know I love you." Ben smoothed her hair with his fingers. "We just need to explore and be certain we want the same things. Maybe you can be part of the theater scene in Montecito. I've heard they have good summer stock."

"Stop patronizing me!" Rosie was trembling. She kept telling herself the worst was over, she couldn't love Ben anymore. But standing so close to him, she felt the air had been squeezed out of her lungs. "Go ahead. Screw every starlet in Hollywood. Rent a suite at the W, host all-night tequila parties."

"You know I'm not like that," Ben replied soothingly.

"You weren't like that." Rosie zipped up her duffle bag and stormed out the door. "I don't know who you are anymore."

Rosie's navigation system said it was only forty miles to Santa Barbara. Already the coastline looked more pristine. The urban beaches crammed with roller bladers and skateboarders and hamburger shacks gave way to miles of white sand. She glimpsed lines of surfers, families carrying buckets and picnic baskets. The harshness of LA slipped away: the traffic jams, the strip malls, the sense that you always had to be watching your back.

Her last meeting with the studio had been disconcerting. She spent a day rehearsing her speech; half hoping the producer would beg her to stay. She dressed in a yellow tunic and straightened her hair and applied mascara and lipstick.

"You're doing the right thing." Adam Stein nodded, sitting at his oversized desk. "This town can eat you up. Better to take some time off before you're forced to."

"I'll train my assistant to take over the things I was working on," Rosie said awkwardly. She had never been comfortable in Adam's steel and glass office. There were no plants, no pictures of Adam's girlfriend, no worn paperbacks on the shelf.

Adam was only three years older than Rosie but whenever she was near him, she felt like an intern. He wore Italian suits and monogrammed shirts. His walls were covered in movie posters, and scripts were piled neatly on his desk. She felt if she and Ben made a misstep, he'd pluck another script from the pile and suspend their production.

"If Lindsay Lohan had taken a summer off she'd still have a career. Even directors burn out, end up directing community theater in the Valley." Adam glanced at his Rolex as if the meeting was already over.

"I'll just be in Montecito; I can come in for a day or two," Rosie replied weakly. She wanted to tell Adam there was nothing wrong with her. It was Ben who was spiraling out of control, who had sex with another woman in their bed, who thought they needed some distance.

"Don't worry about it." Adam shrugged, standing up and walking towards the door. "We brought Mary Beth Chase on board, she's got an army of assistants."

Rosie left his office and drove out of the parking garage. She stopped in front of the Coffee Company and watched girls in mini skirts and four-inch heels balancing their bosses' lattes. Young men wearing narrow ties and khakis grabbed espressos and donuts and ran to production meetings.

On the passenger seat was a box with all her office supplies, her lists, and her notebooks full of memos. There was a dog-eared script, marked up with Ben's messy scrawl. She thought about Mary Beth Chase and her assistants. They would create spreadsheets on laptops and read *Variety* on their iPhones. They would wear Free People dresses and order lunch with some app like Door Dash.

The box spilled onto the seat, and she threw its contents in the garbage. She got back in the car and turned on the radio. Bono sang, "I still haven't found what I'm looking for," and she started sobbing.

The coastline as she approached Montecito was breathtaking. The Santa Ynez Mountains loomed to the north, studded with olive trees. Spanish-style houses climbed the hills, and blue and yellow beach shacks hugged the shore. The orange smog that marred the beaches of Venice and Santa Monica was replaced by a clean, white horizon.

Rosie turned onto Channel Road, feeling like a movie star. The Four Seasons stood before her, flags flapping in the breeze. She imagined pulling up to the double front doors with Ben at her side. The valet would greet them warmly and insist on taking their bags. The concierge would offer them a complimentary fruit basket and European bottled water and a dozen red roses.

They would stay in an oceanfront suite and sit on the balcony, sipping champagne. After the sun slipped past the horizon, they'd go inside and Ben would draw the curtains. He'd whisper, "Please forgive me," and pull Rosie down on the bed. Then he'd bury his face in her breasts and cover her with kisses.

*

Her phone lay on the passenger seat. Maybe she should call Angelica and tell her this was a terrible idea. How could she survive in a town where she knew no one? How would she keep busy so she didn't replay the image of crumpled sheets, of Ben shrugging nonchalantly, of her pounding her fists on the bed?

"It's like riding a surfboard," Angelica would insist. "When you fall off, you get right back up. If you don't, the next wave is going to pull you under."

It was easy for Angelica; she was an actress. Every time she accepted a new role she stepped into a different skin. One month she was a gangster's accomplice, packing a sawed-off shotgun, the next she was a nun, trying to save an alcoholic priest. Rosie had been the same thing since college: Ben's girlfriend and production partner. It might be simpler to drown in the ocean than try to be something new.

The car turned away from the coast towards the village. She hadn't eaten lunch and she was suddenly starving. She parked at the end of Coast Village Road. The air was cool, a light fog settling on the shops. She stepped out of the car into the wide, cobblestoned street, and felt like she walked onto a movie set.

Two-story brick buildings were covered in ivy; purple and white daisies lined the sidewalk. Almost every shop had a window box full of pansies and tulips and roses. Rosie breathed deeply, smelling the sweet, heavy fragrance.

If Ben was with her they would stop for pizza at the pizzeria or splurge on cheese fondue at the French Bistro. Afterwards they would visit a gallery or flip through secondhand books at the Front Page bookstore. But she couldn't finish a pizza alone and she needed at least one other person to eat fondue. Even looking at art or discovering books by herself didn't sound appealing. And the antique wedding dresses in the window of the Bridal Shop made her want to hop back in the car and keep driving.

Reluctantly, she entered a delicatessen with a soda fountain and cases of cold meat. There were twenty different kinds of cheeses, barrels of pickles, and sausages hanging from the ceiling. A sandwich board stood behind the counter, listing specialty sandwiches. Rosie scanned the selection: turkey club on a French roll, Canadian ham and Gruyère cheese, roast beef with horseradish and Bermuda onions.

She pictured Ben standing in their kitchen after a long day at the studio. He would assemble almost every item in the fridge: ham, Swiss cheese, mustard, pickles, mayonnaise, sprouts, lettuce, and tomatoes. He would carefully spread the mustard on a whole-wheat roll and build a sandwich as if he was constructing a pyramid.

When it teetered on the plate, dripping with juices, Ben would wait for Rosie to take the first bite. They would sit opposite each other and tell stories about the set, devouring the sandwich from both ends.

"Can I help you?" the guy behind the counter interrupted her thoughts. He wore a white apron over a navy polo shirt.

"I'd like a peanut butter and jelly sandwich on whole wheat," Rosie replied.

"This is a delicatessen." He shook his head. "We sell roast beef, turkey, ham, bologna, sausage."

"I'd really like peanut butter," Rosie pleaded.

"I can make you a salad sandwich or a cheese sandwich, but I don't have peanut butter." He turned back to slicing cheeses on a large silver machine. "I'm sorry."

Rosie leaned over the counter. "I lived with my boyfriend for eight years and he's allergic to peanut butter. I haven't had peanut butter since college. A few days ago he had sex with a woman in our bed. I'd give anything for a peanut butter sandwich."

The guy looked at Rosie as if he was afraid she was going to climb over the counter and make the sandwich herself. He took off his apron and folded it on the counter. "Wait here."

Rosie stood in the middle of the store, alone and embarrassed. She wanted to run away, or melt into the floor. The bell tinkled over the door and the guy returned clutching a jar of peanut butter.

"I'm sorry." She blushed. "I should have just ordered a turkey sandwich."

"My dad has owned this store for thirty years." He put on his apron and sliced a loaf of bread. "He's never said no to a customer." He wrapped the sandwich in white paper and handed it to her.

"Thank you." Rosie blushed deeper. "I didn't mean to blurt out my history."

"My grandmother wanted me to be a priest." He smiled. He had red hair and a face full of freckles. "Pretend you were in confessional. The sandwich is on the house. Come back when you're really hungry, and I'll make you a turkey club."

Rosie walked down the street and sat on a bench painted fire engine red. A few shopkeepers stood on the sidewalk, arranging baskets of flowers and racks of vintage dresses. She ate the sandwich quickly, the peanut butter sticking to the roof of her mouth.

A young woman wearing a long floral skirt and carrying a gold box sat on the bench. She had curly black hair and almond-shaped eyes. She opened the box and ruffled through the contents before handing the box to Rosie.

"Please have one, if I take the box home I eat them all." She smiled. "And then I hate myself in the morning."

Rosie glanced at the rows of chocolate truffles. "Is there a peanut butter truffle? I'm on a peanut butter kick."

"My favorite," the woman agreed. She extracted a truffle wrapped in gold foil. "I'm Rachel Gold: Gold's Chocolates." She pointed to the sign above the store behind them. "The greatest hazard of owning a chocolate store is disposing of leftover truffles."

"This is an interesting town." Rosie bit into the truffle. "The guy in the delicatessen made me a free peanut butter sandwich, and you're giving away truffles."

"Patrick." The woman nodded, nibbling a marzipan truffle. "He quit the seminary to take over his father's delicatessen. He must have sensed you needed help. He's always giving free food to Boy Scouts and Brownie troops."

"I sort of told him my life history," Rosie admitted. "Running away from a cheating boyfriend."

"That definitely warrants a complimentary peanut butter sandwich." Rachel finished her truffle and handed Rosie the box. "Take the whole box. It'll make both of us feel better."

"No, thanks." Rosie shook her head. "I can't seem to swallow anything. This is the first solid meal I've had in days."

"If you count peanut butter and jelly as solid food you are in trouble." Rachel looked at Rosie quizzically. "There are some great restaurants in town: Giovanni's, Trattoria Mollie's. You should drown your sorrows in fettuccini scampi and a classic red wine. I'll join you."

"I'm already late." Rosie glanced at her watch. "I'm staying with a friend's parents. They're expecting me for dinner, but I wanted to stop in the village. It's like a postcard. It feels like everyone is moving in slow motion."

"People aren't in a hurry in Montecito," Rachel agreed. "They just want to potter around the shops and buy engraved stationery and pieces of jewelry."

"It must be wonderful to own your own store." Rosie turned around and admired Rachel's storefront. The large window held an antique chest and GOLD'S CHOCOLATES was written in cursive at the bottom of the glass. The chest was laden with chocolates: truffles in gold boxes, jars of bonbons, chocolate fudge wrapped with gold ribbon.

"It has its challenges." Rachel shrugged. She had a heart-shaped face and a small snub nose. "Making sure the merchandise doesn't melt in summer, not letting children eat all the samples and complain to their parents they have a stomachache. But it's much better than the alternative."

"What's the alternative?"

"Gold's Department Stores: New Jersey's oldest family-owned department stores. Five stores in three cities, a new store opening in Teaneck soon." Rachel winced. "I used the money my father gave me to attend business school to open Gold's Chocolates."

"You started your own business," Rosie said. "He should be proud of you."

"He flew across the country to get his money back." Rachel grinned. Her teeth were white and very straight. "But he fell in love with Montecito too. They must put a secret potion in the drinking fountain. He said he couldn't blame me; he's been dying to escape New Jersey summers for years. I paid him back after twenty months."

"I'll have to find that drinking fountain." Rosie sighed. "I don't have a job or a boyfriend or a permanent home."

"Painful breakup." Rachel nodded knowingly. "The kind where your boyfriend takes your toothpaste, your friends, and your subscription to Netflix. I don't have the cure, but I can help ease the suffering."

"I'm not much of a drinker." Rosie shook her head. "And I'm not cut out for wild sex and all-night partying."

"Good, because you won't find any of that in Montecito. Even the owls go to bed at nine p.m. Drive down to Butterfly Beach to watch the sunset." Rachel pointed in the direction of the ocean. "I promise you'll feel better."

"Butterfly Beach," Rosie repeated.

"It's the only west-facing beach in Santa Barbara County." Rachel stood up. "The sunsets are like a Monet painting, and you'll have it all to yourself. You can cry your eyes out."

"Thank you." Rosie dusted chocolate from her shorts. It was getting chilly, and she wore a thin cotton shirt and denim shorts she had pulled on this morning.

"Here's my card." Rachel reached into her pocket and handed her a gold business card. "Come by tomorrow and sample my peanut butter brittle."

Rosie got back in her car and drove towards the beach. She couldn't remember chatting with strangers in Santa Monica. People in Los Angeles hid behind dark sunglasses and scrolled through their iPhones while they walked. She blinked away tears, feeling lonelier than before. She was like one of those people on daytime television, spilling their guts in front of the audience.

Rosie crossed the highway and pulled into the parking lot. It was so beautiful; she couldn't drag her eyes from the horizon. The sun lowered itself into the ocean, turning the water a deep, mysterious blue. The sand turned pink, glittering with shells. The seagulls stood still; even the sand crabs stopped moving.

She eased the car into a parking space and heard a crunching sound under her wheels. The end of a surfboard was sticking out under her car, like the Wicked Witch's red shoes in *The Wizard of Oz*.

"Oh my god!" she gasped, jumping out of the car. "I ran over a surfboard."

"My surfboard." A man of about thirty appeared in front of her. He had white-blond hair that curled over his ears. He wore black board shorts and his legs were covered in sand.

"I was watching the sunset." Rosie looked down in horror. "I'm so sorry."

The man leaned down to inspect the board. His shoulders were muscular and his back was smooth and brown.

"Don't worry about it." He stood up and smiled. He was a head taller than Rosie, with blue eyes and a dimple on his chin. "It's just a ding."

"I'll p-pay to get it fixed!" Rosie stammered.

"I shouldn't have left it on the ground." The man shrugged. "But the beach usually empties out at sunset; just us diehards left, catching the last perfect wave."

"I feel like an idiot." Rosie thought she was about to burst into tears.

"I'm Josh." He put out his hand. "Come and have some chips and salsa. My friends and I are terrible company, ten minutes with us and you'll stop feeling guilty."

Rosie followed him onto the sand. She didn't feel like making conversation, but she'd feel worse driving off, as if she had committed a hit and run. Josh loped ahead. He had long legs and knobby knees covered in scrapes.

"I'm guessing you're not a native." He passed her a bag of chips and a plastic container of salsa.

"I'm staying with friends for the summer," Rosie replied. She shielded her eyes and watched the sun melt into the sea. The pastel colors were prettier than any painting, and the water was a sheet of glass.

"You picked the right time of day to arrive." Josh scooped salsa onto a handful of chips. "Butterfly Beach at sunset is like finding the pot of gold at the end of the rainbow."

"It's so peaceful." Rosie breathed deeply. "I haven't been anywhere this peaceful."

"I'd introduce you, but I don't know your name." Josh moved towards the circle of surfers.

"Rosie Keller," Rosie answered. "I better go. I'm supposed to arrive for dinner."

"Where are you staying?" Josh asked.

"My friend's parents have an estate in Montecito." She ate a chip. "I'm hiding out in their guest cottage for the summer."

"You don't look like a killer." Josh frowned, handing her a can of Coke.

"Movie producer, actually." Rosie sipped her Coke. She hadn't had a soda in years. She and Ben drank lattes or smoothies in the morning and a bottle of white or red wine with dinner. Sometimes she'd have a martini or a glass of champagne at a cocktail party or a movie premiere.

"Ah, the Los Angeles hamster wheel." Josh nodded. "Montecito is full of Hollywood refugees, but they always go back. Some kind of magnetic pull from Ferraris and Rolexes."

"Are you sure I can't pay to fix your board?" Rosie asked.

"You could come watch us surf sometime, when you're not hiding out," he offered.

"I'll think about it." Rosie blushed. "I better go. Thank you for the chips and soda."

"Be careful driving," Josh said and smiled. "There are some crazy drivers out there. They'll run over anything."

Rosie backed out of the parking space and took the road through town. She drove past Italian trattorias and French cafes. It was Saturday night and couples were strolling along the sidewalk, choosing where to dine. She watched them consult wine lists and study menus.

It reminded her of a dinner they had in Hollywood after they returned from Sundance. Ben was all wound up. For a week straight he had been eating in the kitchen standing up, reading the paper while pacing the living room. They even made love in the shower, because Rosie couldn't drag him into bed.

Rosie and Ben met Angelica and Matthew at Spago's. It was expensive and old guard, but Ben wanted to make a statement. Ben was flattered when the hostess led them to a front booth, and speechless when Matt Damon walked over and shook Ben's hand.

"Matt Damon," Ben murmured after Matt returned to his table. "If God struck me down, I'd die happy."

"He's been this dramatic all week," Rosie giggled to Angelica. "You'd think he parted the Red Sea instead of winning an award at Sundance."

"It's our town," Ben said earnestly. "I have three offers to direct: MGM, Universal, and Sony."

"I got a call from Nicole Kidman," Angelica chimed in. She wore a black wig and a gold snake around her neck. "She's thinking of remaking *Cleopatra*."

"I was wondering why you're wearing a reptile." Rosie laughed. They had split a bottle of champagne and she felt light-headed and silly.

"A year ago, I couldn't get Nicole's third assistant on the phone," Angelica gushed. "I owe everything to Ben and Rosie."

"To Ben and Rosie." Ben refilled their champagne flutes. "May we never see the inside of a Domino's Pizza carton again."

"May our names go up above the Hollywood sign." Angelica raised her glass.

"May Angelica make enough money so I can retire," Matthew piped in.

"Admit you dig being an accountant." Ben punched Matthew's shoulder good-naturedly. "It's okay to be boring."

"Not everyone can be a creative genius like you and Angelica," Rosie protested.

"I love you Rosie Keller." Ben kissed Rosie sloppily on the lips. "Without you I'd be nobody."

Rosie drove towards the mountains. The estates were so vast; each one took up its own block. She pressed the button on a tall wrought iron gate and waited. The gate swung inward and she drove inside, feeling like she was being swallowed up, like the world would keep turning without her.

"There you are." A tall figure stood on the porch. Estelle's white-blond hair fell softly to her shoulders. She wore a navy silk dress with a Peter Pan collar. A strand of pink pearls hung around her neck. "I told Oscar I was waiting ten minutes and then I'd call the Coast Guard. I thought we might have to fish you out of the ocean."

"I'm sorry, I stopped at the beach to see the sunset." Rosie stepped out of the car and Estelle kissed her on both cheeks, holding her chin as if to make sure she wasn't broken.

"Then all is forgiven," Estelle said brightly. "Nothing is more glorious than the beach at sunset. If I could move this house, I'd place it right on the sand."

"But it's so beautiful here." Rosie stood on the porch, listening to the frogs. She could see the outline of the lake and the giant oak trees bending over the lawn. The house was lit by strings of fairy lights and the curtains blew through open windows.

"You're right. I'd never move a hair of this house." Estelle opened the front door. "I'm going to be buried in the garden next to Daisy. She was my first Irish setter, when I was a little girl."

"You've lived here since you were a child?" Rosie followed Estelle inside. She forgot how large the entry was. The ceiling soared above her and an arch led to the hallway. She could hear her footsteps on the wood, and her words echoed in the hall.

"Everyone thinks Oscar bought the house with all that music money." Estelle led Rosie into the dining room. "But my grandfather built it for his wife. He imported teas and spices from Asia. He installed a telescope on the top floor so she could see when his ship returned from China."

"That's a lovely story." Rosie sighed, admiring the long cherry table and glass chandelier.

"I'm famished," Estelle announced. "We'll tinkle the bell and let Oscar know you're here."

The table was set with crystal wineglasses and sterling silver flatware. There was a purple orchid and candles flickered in gold candelabras. Platters held bunches of grapes and baskets were heaped with freshly baked bread.

"I hope you didn't go to this trouble for me," Rosie said uncomfortably, sitting in a high-backed velvet chair.

"I know young people like to eat takeout in front of a television." Estelle rang a silver bell. "But I much prefer a beautifully set table."

Oscar had thick sandy-colored hair and blue eyes. He wore a white V-neck sweater and pleated slacks and carried a scotch glass in one hand.

"My wife is thrilled Angelica sent you," he said in a deep voice like an opera singer's. "Now she has someone to share her roses with."

"My roses are going to be so happy to have a young person around," Estelle agreed. She had large brown eyes rimmed by thick lashes. Only the lines around her mouth hinted at her age.

"I should be jealous," Oscar said affectionately. "Her roses get more attention than I do."

"Everyone must have a passion," Estelle insisted, popping grapes in her mouth. "I'm lucky to have three: my husband, my children, and my roses. Tell us about yourself, Rosie. What do you love?"

Rosie tried to swallow. A month ago the list would have rolled off her tongue: fresh hot cinnamon buns, movies at the foreign cinema in West LA, eating at the salad bar at Whole Foods. And doing anything with Ben. Solving the Sunday crossword puzzle in bed together, fishing off the Santa Monica Pier, climbing to the top of Dodger Stadium.

"I love to read, and sometimes I like to cook," Rosie said finally.

"We'll have to introduce you to new things. On Sundays we have tennis parties, and on Monday evenings our neighbors join us for bridge and a swim. Tuesdays, Oscar has the men over for cigars. And we have pool parties almost every day, nothing planned, people seem to just show up." Estelle beamed.

Estelle paused as a man wearing gray slacks and a white shirt brought out plates of sirloin tips, scalloped potatoes, and baby peas and onions.

"Morris, this is Rosie, a friend of Angelica's," Oscar introduced them. "Morris was part of a boy band I brought over from England years ago. He hated being onstage, and he's been our butler ever since."

"Pleased to meet you." Morris nodded. He had straight black hair and small black eyes. When he smiled he revealed slightly crooked teeth.

"Did you bring a tennis racket?" Estelle inquired. "If you didn't, I'll rustle up one of Angelica's."

"I don't actually play." Rosie sipped a glass of water, her mind reeling. It was too much: British butlers, tennis courts, swim parties. She glanced down at her cotton shirt and cutoff shorts and felt embarrassingly underdressed.

"We have all summer to teach you." Estelle scooped potatoes with her spoon. "It's a shame Angelica's brother, Sam, isn't here. He's an excellent player and terrifically handsome. We'll send over Hans from the club. He looks quite striking in his tennis whites."

"Estelle, dear," Oscar said over his glass of wine. "Rosie might like to relax."

"Angelica told me about Ben." Estelle turned to Rosie. "I thought you'd like to meet new people. We're actually quite boring in June. It's just neighbors and old people like us. July Fourth is when Oscar has his big 'music' party."

"Estelle believes every marriage should be a fairy tale." Oscar squeezed Estelle's hand. "We've been married for thirty-five years."

Rosie pushed the potatoes around her plate and listened to Estelle reel off the amenities of the house: a billiard table in the library, backgammon and chess in the morning room, a vegetable garden, and an orchard where Rosie could pick her own oranges.

"Give them to Morris and he'll make your orange juice and bring it to the guest cottage." Estelle put her napkin on her plate.

"It all sounds wonderful." Rosie sighed. "I've been up for so long, I'd really like to go to bed."

"But we haven't had dessert," Estelle protested. "We have pavlova, with fresh strawberries and kiwi."

"Estelle, dear." Oscar squeezed his wife's hand. "The pavlova will keep till tomorrow. Why don't you show Rosie the guest cottage?"

"Of course." Estelle stood up, smoothing her skirt. "I'm being rude. You must be exhausted. I'll tell Morris to bring your bags from the car."

Estelle disappeared into the kitchen and Rosie was left at the table with Oscar. She tried to think of something to talk about: the state of the record industry, Oscar's recent trip to South America. But her head felt heavy and her eyes started to close.

"Please don't mind Estelle." Oscar smiled. His face was lined and very tan. "She wants everyone to love this house as much as she does."

"It's quite amazing," Rosie replied, struggling to keep her eyes open.

"I have a very special wife." Oscar nodded. "But she needs to let people move at their own pace. Take your time getting your bearings; we're here when you need us."

Rosie blinked and looked at her plate. She hadn't imagined the estate would be so grand, or Angelica's parents would be so welcoming. She felt like she had left the frantic rush of Hollywood and stepped into a storybook.

Rosie wanted to tell Oscar how glad she was to be here. She wanted to say she had never visited such a quaint village or stayed in such a gracious home. But all she could think was how desperately she wanted to be in their apartment in Santa Monica, folding laundry and doing dishes. She wanted to listen to Ben sing in the shower, knowing when she climbed into bed, he'd run his hands down her spine and pull her against him.

Three

When Rosie woke in the morning, she couldn't remember going to bed. She recalled Estelle's singsong voice instructing her on towels and sheets, but she didn't remember climbing under the covers. The whole day was a blur. If she closed her eyes, she might be back in Santa Monica. She pictured jumping out of bed, grabbing the remains of Ben's strawberry smoothie, and rushing to the studio.

There was a knock on the door and Rosie pulled on her robe. Sun streamed through the French doors and Rosie glanced at herself in the mirror. Her face was free of makeup and her hair was frizzy from the humidity. She opened the door and found Morris carrying a silver tray and a folded newspaper.

"Mrs. Pullman thought you might be hungry." Morris placed poached eggs, a stack of toast, and a glass of orange juice on the table. There was a yellow rose in a crystal vase and sterling silver flatware wrapped in a linen napkin.

"I, um," Rosie mumbled.

"I can ask Peg to make scrambled eggs if you prefer," Morris suggested.

"Peg?" Rosie asked, rubbing her eyes.

"The cook. Her eggs are works of art," Morris replied. He had a soft, buttery accent and pale, papery skin.

"I'm sure they're great." Rosie looked around the room for the first time. The floor was covered in a floral rug and the windows were hung with white tulle curtains. There was a love seat upholstered in a bright floral pattern and a rolltop desk in the corner. "I feel like I'm in a remake of *Arthur*."

"The Pullmans like the finer things, but they're generous people." Morris smiled.

"I've never had a butler," Rosie said awkwardly.

"Try the eggs with a little ketchup." Morris unfolded the napkin. He popped open the ketchup and buttered the top slice of toast.

"Thank you," Rosie replied, inhaling the scent of butter and fresh bread. "And thank Peg and Estelle."

"You can thank Mrs. Pullman." Morris picked up the empty tray. "She's in the rose garden."

Rosie took the plate of eggs and toast and sat in the middle of the bed. Through the window she could see rolling green lawns and hear the buzz of a lawn mower. The bed was heaped with pillows and the comforter was soft as cotton candy.

The first bite of eggs melted on her tongue; Rosie closed her eyes and imagined she was staying in a luxury resort. Any minute, Ben would return from the spa and they'd take a bath together. She pictured soaping his back, feeling his hands searching for her under the bubbles. He would kiss her and neither of them would want to get out.

Rosie's phone rang and she started, pulled from her fantasy.

"I tried calling last night, but my mother said you were asleep," Angelica's voice came over the line.

"You didn't tell me your parents live like this." Rosie sat back against the pillows.

"Has my mother been boring you with her roses?" Angelica asked.

"Butlers and cooks and sterling silver flatware at breakfast," Rosie continued, buttering another slice of toast.

"Morris is a rocker who didn't want to go home," Angelica replied. "His parents were going to force him to become a chemist. Peg has been the cook since I was born, she's part of the family."

"Angelica, no one lives like this," Rosie protested, noticing the Tiffany lamp on the bedside table.

"My parents do, and so do all their neighbors in Montecito," Angelica assured her. "You need to heal. Let them take care of you."

"I'm not an invalid," Rosie mumbled and slumped deeper into the pillows.

"Take a bubble bath, catch up on your reading," Angelica said.

"Do I have a choice?" Rosie sighed, glancing at the paperback books on the bookshelf.

"It's one summer," Angelica retorted. "I'll come up next weekend. I'll bring hummus from Whole Foods and all the Hollywood gossip."

"Have you heard from Ben?" Rosie hesitated. For some reason she sucked in her breath and her hands turned clammy.

"I have to go." Angelica ignored her question. "I'm having my first costume fitting for *The Philadelphia Story* tomorrow and I have to wash my hair. As Katharine Hepburn would say: chin up."

"I'm so glad I'm best friends with Katharine Hepburn." Rosie put the toast on the plate. "I'll see you next Friday."

Rosie finished her breakfast and glanced around the cottage.

There was a Seurat painting above the fireplace: all pale pinks and blues. She imagined waking every morning and sitting at the roll-top desk, sipping tea, and gazing at the lawn. She'd wear the yellow fluffy robe she found in the closet and her skin would be smooth from a night facial mask.

Rosie glanced at the screensaver shot of her and Ben on her phone. They were at a friend's wedding, clowning around in a photo booth. Their heads were pressed together like Siamese twins: the same green eyes, the same freckles on their cheeks. Rosie grabbed the phone and threw it across the room, flinching as it clattered on the wood.

"Fuck you," she said aloud. "I'm going to make a list of things to do." She found a yellow pad and sat at the desk. "I'm going to plan my life without Ben Ford."

She watched a hummingbird peck at the feeder on the porch. Its wings buzzed at lightning speed, its small beak working furiously. Rosie scratched away at the piece of paper, numbering her to-do list like she used to do at the studio: Buy a turkey club sandwich from the guy at the delicatessen. Try Rachel Gold's peanut butter brittle. Help Estelle in her rose garden. Drive to the beach and watch the sunset. She remembered the detailed lists she used to make. Adam always praised her for keeping so many balls in the air.

"I'll ask Peg if I can borrow a dozen eggs and learn to juggle." Rosie sighed, tearing the sheet of paper and crumpling it in the garbage. "Because Rachel Gold has plenty of customers and the sun is capable of setting without me."

Rosie stood up and looked at herself in the mirror. Her hair was tangled and there were deep shadows under her eyes like face paint. "I could become a clown and perform at children's parties. Ben and Mary Beth will get married and hire me for their daughter's first birthday. It'll be held on the Venice boardwalk and I'll wear a honking nose and a rainbow-colored wig."

Rosie walked into the bathroom and slipped off her robe. The floors were creamy white marble and the walls were painted eggshell yellow. There was a glassed-in shower and a white porcelain tub. Rosie filled the bath and poured in a bottle of lavender bubble bath. She waited until the water was steaming hot and climbed in.

"Mary Beth and her minions will run the movie like a military operation, and I'll sit in the bath and get wrinkled toes." Rosie let her tears fall into the bathwater. "Because no one cares what I do; I am completely superfluous."

Rosie opened her eyes and saw the sun setting over the lawn. She glanced at the crystal clock on the bedside table. She had been asleep for six hours, ever since she crawled out of the bath and into bed. The remains of breakfast sat on the table: two pieces of toast and a half-eaten egg. Her shirt and shorts were tossed on the rug; a yellow towel was draped on the side of the bed.

She sat up and groaned. She'd never spent the day in the same room as stale breakfast; she'd never let towels and clothes pile up on the floor. She imagined Morris knocking to clear the dishes and leaving silently when there was no answer.

Rosie got up and opened the window. A soft breeze blew in from the ocean. She heard voices and saw groups of people standing around sipping cocktails. There was a croquet game going on and somebody playing a saxophone, or maybe a clarinet. She heard glasses clinking and one woman proclaim shrilly: "Duck pâté is not the same thing as foie gras. Don't they teach you anything at culinary school?"

Rosie rifled through her duffle bag for a pair of pants and a shirt.

She was suddenly starving, but she couldn't face a lawn full of guests talking about polo and liver pâté. She would sneak around the side of the house and find the kitchen. She'd make a stack of peanut butter and jelly sandwiches and run back to the cottage.

There was a knock on the door as Rosie combed the tangles out of her hair. She threw the towel in the bathroom, and smoothed the comforter on the bed.

"Come in," Rosie called, hoping Morris wouldn't think she was a terrible sloth.

"Dear, I was afraid you drowned in the bath." Estelle stood at the door. "We haven't seen you all day."

"I almost did," Rosie mumbled. "I've been asleep for hours."

"I'm sure you needed it." Estelle walked inside. She wore an ivory hostess gown with a thin gold belt. Her hair was teased into big curls and diamond earrings twinkled in her ears. She wore coral-pink lipstick and a dusting of powder that made her cheeks glow.

"I feel so lazy," Rosie said. "I'll take the dishes to the kitchen, and I can put the towels in the laundry if you show me where it is."

"Dear." Estelle put her hand on Rosie's. "You're not here to do dishes, you're here to mend."

"I was going to help you in the garden," Rosie said lamely.

"We have a few friends over. We played tennis and now we're having cocktails, mostly older couples but quite fun. One of our neighbors was a sitcom writer for years; he keeps us in stitches. Come join us."

"I'm not really dressed." Rosie shook her head.

"You're thirty years younger than us, you would look good in a potato sack." Estelle laughed. "We keep ourselves together with a lot of paint and wired lingerie."

"Maybe tomorrow night." Rosie bit her lip.

Estelle sat on the corner of the bed, twisting the rings on her fingers. "Everyone gets their heart broken. That's how you know you have one."

"You sound like the Wizard of Oz." Rosie smiled.

"When I was twenty-one I was so unlucky in love, I wanted to drink a vial of hemlock." Estelle looked at Rosie.

"You and Oscar have been married thirty-five years." Rosie tried to do the math in her head.

"It was before I met Oscar. I went back east to college, to Penn," Estelle continued. "At first I was terribly lonely, then I met a boy from Boston, Theodore Strand. He was from an old Boston family and his father imported whisky. We were perfect for each other! We wanted the same things: a big house, lots of children, a litter of Irish setters." Estelle paused. Her cheeks were flushed and Rosie thought she looked like a teenager.

"Theo was going to come home with me the summer after graduation and ask my father for my hand. But he didn't return to school after Christmas break. His father decided he should transfer to Boston University and go to work in the family business. I took the train to Boston and showed up at his door. I thought I could transfer too, or drop out. Why did I need a degree if we were going to get married?"

Rosie sat on the bed next to Estelle. She smelled her perfume, a deep floral scent.

"Theodore's father answered the door. They were having dinner and Theo was seated next to Primrose Scanlan, his prep school sweetheart. They got engaged over the break and the families were celebrating. I took the train back to Penn, packed my bags, and flew to California. I didn't leave my room for a month."

"But I'm not a girl of twenty-one," Rosie replied. "Ben and I have been together for ten years. We think alike, we look alike;

we even bought each other the same cards on our anniversary. Hollywood separated us. Ben thinks he needs to hitch himself to a big blond producer to get to the top."

"I am sorry. Maybe you're right." Estelle patted Rosie's hand. "Men do act without thinking."

"That's the polite way of putting it." Rosie laughed for the first time in days.

"Let yourself have a good cry and then have some fun. Play tennis, swim in the pool, roll on the lawn like Angelica and Sam did when they were kids."

"I'm cried out." Rosie sighed. "I should be thinking about a job."

"You should be thinking about what you love," Estelle instructed. "The rest will come. Peg made scrumptious spinach crepes and Morris opened a Kenwood pinot noir."

"I didn't do a very good job of her poached eggs." Rosie glanced at the plate.

"I must go." Estelle got up, adjusting her earrings in the mirror. "Oscar will start singing and everyone will go home. Sometimes he forgets that being able to recognize talent doesn't mean he has talent. His voice could scare the animals."

"How did you and Oscar meet?" Rosie asked.

"I'll save that story for a morning in the rose garden." Estelle opened the door. "You have to meet my tea roses."

Rosie watched Estelle cross the lawn and join her guests. Estelle took a puff of Oscar's cigar, her earrings glittering like fireflies. She linked arms with a tall brunette and the two women disappeared into the house, like schoolgirls at a birthday party. Oscar passed around a box of cigars, and the men stood in deep discussion, smoke rings spiraling in the air.

Rosie slipped out the door and crept along the side lawn, following the brick path to the house. Rabbits darted across the grass and she heard the hum of sprinklers switching on in the dark. She was afraid Oscar would spot her and drag her into conversation. She couldn't smile at these sleek, elegant people without remembering the Hollywood parties she attended with Ben, where they floated along, arm in arm, trying to remember names.

Rosie ducked into the back of house and found herself in a mudroom. There was a row of rubber boots, and jackets and raincoats dangling from hooks. She opened the heavy wood door and discovered a kitchen that belonged on the set of *Downton Abbey*. The floor was dark wood, so rutted and worn that in some places it sloped downwards. The ceiling was low and hung with steel pots and pans. There was a long table in the center of the room piled with folded laundry. Rosie expected a maid wearing a ruffled cap and apron to walk in and light the stove with a match.

She opened cabinets and drawers and found every kind of condiment. There were racks of spices, bottles of olive oil, jars of pickles, and fresh jams and jellies.

"Are you looking for something?"

"I'm sorry." Rosie blushed. "I shouldn't have let myself in."

"Make yourself at home." Morris waved his hand. "But you're missing a feast on the lawn."

"I was craving peanut butter," Rosie admitted, closing the cabinets and standing awkwardly near the sink.

"Have a seat." Morris pointed to the table. "I may be British, but I make a better peanut butter sandwich than Carol Brady."

"You watched *The Brady Bunch*?" Rosie smiled.

"Every kid in Britain watched *The Brady Bunch*." Morris pulled a jar of peanut butter from a drawer. "Why do you think I came to America?"

Rosie sat silently while Morris prepared a peanut butter

sandwich. She admired a ceramic vase that held yellow sunflowers and bunches of purple daisies.

"Mrs. Pullman loves flowers." Morris put the plate in front of Rosie and sat opposite her. "If you want to tell me why you're not sipping pinot and eating spinach crepes, I'm a good listener."

"Ben and I wanted a kitchen like this," Rosie said almost to herself. "Where we could curl up by the fire with a good book and a bottle of wine for hours."

"I'm guessing Ben is the reason you're here," Morris prompted.

"Angelica is my best friend." Rosie ate a bite of her sandwich. "She suggested I stay in Montecito with her parents for the summer. The house is beautiful and Estelle is like a fairy godmother."

"But you want to turn around and run home to Santa Monica," Morris finished her sentence.

"I have nowhere to run." Rosie sighed. "Ben thinks we need a break. He wants to conquer Hollywood without me."

"Then do something you love without him," Morris said.

"Estelle told me the story of her first love and her broken heart." Rosie smiled. "I guess I'm a cliché."

"Not a cliché." Morris shook his head. "We all have a Dear John letter tucked away. Mine was from Neil Friend."

"Neil Friend, the singer?" Rosie's eyes opened wide.

"He was the lead singer of our band. Before that we were boys in Cambridge, falling in love by the river. Oscar discovered us and launched us in America. He rented the band a house in Hancock Park. We felt so posh, sitting by the pool sipping bubbly. We signed a record contract, starting playing gigs. All of a sudden girls were camped out on the sidewalk, tossing love notes on the lawn." Morris paused, running his hand through his spiky black hair.

"One afternoon I came back from the shops and found Neil in bed with Amber Waite. I'll never forget the sight of his white buttocks poised above her tan flesh. I'd never seen a naked woman up close; I don't think Neil had either. Amber was the lead singer of one of Oscar's girl bands. They met at a party." Morris went to the fridge and got a bottle of milk. He poured two glasses and handed one to Rosie.

"We had a huge row. Neil said being seen with a hot girl was good for his image. We could still be an item 'behind the scenes.' I tried for a while. Our record was on maximum rotation. It was pretty cool shopping at Vons, hearing your song on the radio. But Amber kept popping up at the house, swimming naked in the pool. I couldn't tell what was real: Neil and me or Neil and Amber. I quit the band. I was going to go home to England, take over my father's pharmacy. But I realized I'd rather throw myself in the Thames. Oscar let me stay here while I decided what to do."

Rosie put down her sandwich, imagining a young, skinny Morris holed up in the guest cottage, crying over his failed love affair with Neil Friend.

"I slouched around eating Weetabix and watching *Ab Fab* and decided I wanted to be a butler. I love ironing and shining shoes and keeping a big house shipshape. I thought about getting a position at a country manor in Surrey, but my parents would die of embarrassment. So I became Mr. and Mrs. Pullman's butler. I'm happy as a kitten with a bowl of warm milk." Morris sighed. "It still hurts when I hear Neil on the radio. He's got a huge career as a solo artist."

"*Be My Friend* is one of my favorite albums," Rosie admitted.

"Neil's been engaged to women a couple of times." Morris shrugged. "But he still wears his pants pretty tight."

"I've been in the Hollywood goldfish bowl for eight years." Rosie picked at her sandwich. "I don't know what else to do."

"Where are your parents?"

"They're both engineers at Kennedy Space Center. I don't think I'm trained to build a rocket," she said and laughed.

"You could go back to school or set up your own production company?" he suggested.

"I had enough school. I've studied every film from Charlie Chaplin to Chris Columbus," she winced. "I couldn't open another company; we're Rosie and Ben, like peanut butter and jelly."

"I prefer peanut butter with bananas," Morris said mildly.

"Yuck." Rosie frowned. She threw the rest of her sandwich in the garbage. "I guess I'm not ready to give up on Ben and Rosie. Is that stupid?"

"Being stupid is part of life." Morris put his glass in the dishwasher. "You can always join me for an *Ab Fab* marathon."

"I might take you up on that." Rosie smiled and moved to the door.

Rosie walked slowly back to the cottage. The party had moved to the tennis court. Two couples played doubles under the lights. The other guests mingled on the sidelines, cradling glasses of wine. What would it be like to own a house with grounds so large you couldn't see the road? There would be closets full of tennis whites, and she would spend her afternoons perfecting her serves. Ben would come home from the studio and they'd play a hard match, then retreat to the terrace to drink martinis and eat prawn cocktails.

What if Ben was right? Maybe she was holding him back. Ben could be the most brilliant director since Coppola; Rosie was just someone wearing a suit who wrote lists and checked off boxes.

An idea bubbled in her head, and she strode to the cottage. She would call Ben and tell him she didn't want to produce anymore. He could work with Mary Beth Chase or any other hotshot producer; she'd stay home and be the perfect hostess wife. She imagined decorating their Bel-Air mansion, enrolling in a Cordon Bleu cooking course, learning floral arranging and feng shui. She'd make friends with the wives of the studio heads and get her hair done at Salon by Maxime on Rodeo Drive.

Rosie slipped into the cottage and grabbed her phone. She'd call Ben right now, before she lost her nerve. She could forgive him for cheating. It wouldn't happen again, because they'd live the way Ben wanted: in a mansion with three cars in the driveway and a personal trainer who jogged with him after work.

Ben's phone rang five times and went to voicemail. Rosie paced the room, hugging the phone to her chest. She picked up the house phone and dialed Ben's number again, willing him to answer.

"This is Ben, who's this?"

"It's me, Rosie. I'm calling from Angelica's parents' house," she answered, as if she left on a short trip and was calling to tell him she arrived safely.

"Rosie," Ben said pleasantly. "How are you?"

"I'm great." Rosie started pacing again. "I have a fantastic idea."

"I'm in a meeting, can I call you back?" he urged.

"It's Sunday night," Rosie said flatly.

"I'm at Pizza Joe's with a few of the writers. We're tweaking tomorrow's scenes."

"It's really important." Rosie tried to keep her voice light and cheerful. She knew how much Ben loved sitting with writers, massaging the script until it sang.

"I want to talk but you know what Sunday writing sessions are like. This is really important," he said pleasantly. "We're doing a major rewrite of the scene at the stables."

"You're right, I am holding you back," Rosie blurted out. "You should work with Mary Beth or anyone great. I'll stay home and manage our social life. We'll get a house in Beverly Hills or Bel-Air. We could rent for a year until we find something we love."

"Rosie, please," Ben begged. "They're waiting for me."

"We'll be the Hollywood power couple," Rosie surged on. "We'll lease you a Porsche or a Mercedes, we'll host dinners and pool parties."

"I promise I'll listen to you but they're making motions for me to get off the phone," he cut in. "Can we schedule a time to talk?"

"Please, Ben." Rosie tried to keep her voice steady. Her eyes glistened and she squeezed the phone. "I forgive you. I know how much you want to make it big and I do too. We could be really happy."

"I'm swamped for the next four weeks," he said gently. "How about I come up on July Fourth? We can talk then."

"July Fourth?" Rosie gulped, thinking of the long weeks of June stretching in front of her. "Sounds great. The Pullmans have a big party, come for the whole weekend."

"I have to go, Rosie. See you then."

Rosie hung up and stared out the window. The crickets were chirping and the sprinklers were going full blast. She moved to the desk and scribbled on the yellow notepad. She'd ask Morris for tips on running a big house. She'd get some recipes from Peg and ask Estelle for advice on being the perfect hostess.

Rosie pictured herself lean and tan, wearing a silk sarong over a bright yellow bathing suit. She'd have metallic sandals on her feet and a gold charm bracelet around her ankle. There would be a crystal bowl of margaritas and their friends would be splashing in the pool.

Rosie put the pen down and climbed on the bed. She was too excited to sleep. The remote was on the bedside table and she flipped through channels. There was a Hitchcock marathon and they were playing *The Birds*. It was one of her and Ben's favorite movies. They used to clutch each other's arms and watch Cary Grant protect Tippi Hedren from the crazed flock of birds. The final credits came up and she lay against the pillows. Eventually her eyes closed and she fell asleep.

Four

The next morning, Rosie made her bed, fluffing the comforter and plumping the pillows. She flinched slightly when she smoothed the cotton sheets, imagining the crumpled sheets in their bedroom: Ben and Mary Beth naked and sweaty, Ben attempting to pull the sheets around them, falling asleep with his hand on Mary Beth's breast.

Her stomach heaved as if she had been punched in the gut. She blinked, trying to erase the image. She remembered the day they bought the bed. They finally had a bedroom big enough for a king bed, and they drove to Restoration Hardware to admire the different styles.

"Our IKEA days are over," Ben said grandly, fresh from winning the prize at Sundance. "We are going to splurge and buy the biggest bed we find."

"It doesn't have to be the biggest," Rosie giggled, sitting on the corner of a sleigh bed with a dark wood headboard.

"You don't know what I'm going to do to you." Ben kissed her neck and touched her blouse. "I might need a very big bed for what I have planned."

"Wait till we get it home." Rosie laughed, removing his hand from her shirt.

"This is LA." Ben leaned close. "No one will notice a little heavy petting."

"Ben!" Rosie shot off the bed, blushing at the salespeople.

"They're just jealous," Ben scoffed, taking her hand and leading her around the store.

"This one." Rosie paused in front of a king-sized bed with a white frame. It had seashells carved into the headboard and a pale blue comforter. The pillows were gold and pink, and the sheets were smooth beige cotton.

"I like it." Ben nodded.

"It feels like we're shipwrecked on our own island." Rosie lay on the bed, staring up at the ceiling.

Ben lay beside her, his leg pressed against hers. He picked up the price tag and whistled.

"Is it too much?" Rosie sat up. "Maybe we should buy a queen-sized bed."

"Nothing is too much for something that's for both of us." Ben pulled her back down. "Investing in a bed is investing in our future."

Ben handed over his new American Express and scribbled his name as if he was signing an autograph. They drove home, grinning and giddy, and ate a picnic of sourdough bread and ham and Swiss cheese on the bedroom floor.

"It's going to take up the whole room." Rosie laughed, spreading a blanket where the bed would go. "We'll have to walk sideways to get to the bathroom."

"Then we'll have to stay in bed longer." Ben grinned, nibbling a strawberry. "On Sunday mornings I'll make you waffles. We'll stay in bed all day."

"That's very tempting." Rosie ate a sliced peach, wiping her chin with a napkin.

"You're sexy when you eat peaches," Ben murmured, taking the peach out of her hand.

Ben pushed aside the plates and tugged Rosie's shirt over her head. He slipped off his pants, and played with the zipper on her shorts.

Rosie started pulling off her shorts but he stopped her, leaning down and whispering, "Let me."

She lay back on the blanket, waiting as he pulled down her panties, as he stroked her lightly between her thighs. She tried to pull him on top of her but he held back, leaning down and covering her stomach with kisses. Her eyes closed and she felt him kiss his way up to her neck.

"I love you, Rosie," he moaned. "You make me feel like I can do anything."

"I love you too." She opened her eyes and looked up at Ben's familiar features and felt a heady blend of closeness and passion.

Rosie's legs fell open, her body arched up to meet his. She found his mouth and covered it with hers. Ben lowered himself on top of her, his chest hard and smooth, and slowly entered her, pushing her against the floor.

Rosie clung to Ben's back, feeling him push deeper, open her wider. The waves built, lifting her out of her body, making her cry out. Her fingers dug into his shoulders and she waited for the shuddering to stop and the dizzying feeling of release to subside.

When they were both sweaty and spent, Ben pulled her against him and hugged her tightly. His mouth nuzzled her neck. She heard the soft sound of his breathing, and thought they didn't need a king bed, they were happy with a blanket on a hardwood floor.

*

Rosie gazed out the cottage window, thinking of the dozens of times they had made love in their bed. Was all that fun—Sunday morning picnics, ink stains from the crossword puzzle, sand everywhere from wanting sex so badly they fell into bed before they showered—washed away by one afternoon?

Rosie walked to the desk and scanned her to-do list. She glanced at her reflection in the mirror, added some blush to her cheeks, and went to find Estelle.

"You look lovely this morning." Estelle beamed, screening her eyes from the sun. "Our climate agrees with you."

"I'm feeling a little better." Rosie smiled. "Morris has been so helpful, and the guest cottage is gorgeous. It's like staying in the middle of an English garden."

"Did I go overboard on the floral theme?" Estelle asked. She was hunched over her roses, a pruning shear in one hand. She wore a wide, floppy hat, a white shirt, and slim blue pants. Her hands were protected by gardening gloves and she wore ancient sneakers on her feet.

"I love all the colors." Rosie shook her head. "It's hard to be miserable when you're surrounded by pinks and yellows."

"Wait till you meet my roses." Estelle straightened up. "I planted some African buds that are just opening. They're like the inside of a candy store."

Rosie followed Estelle around the rose garden, learning the names of the different roses. Estelle talked earnestly about Bourbon Roses, David Austin English Roses, climbing roses, and miniatures. She recited names and facts like a scientist, her voice growing more animated.

"Did you know there is every color imaginable except blue?" Estelle asked. "They haven't been able to create a blue rose. Maybe that's why blue is a sad color. These are my hybrid tea roses." Estelle led Rosie to a rosebush with tall stems and satin buds.

"There are many varieties of hybrid teas." She leaned down and picked one for Rosie. "This is a Cary Grant, and over there is a Henry Fonda. My favorite is the Elizabeth Taylor. Aren't the colors exquisite?"

"I didn't know roses had names." Rosie sniffed the bright orange bud.

"They have names and feelings." Estelle nodded. "When I ignore them they close up and when I give them love they blossom. Oscar gave me my first rose, an Estelle."

"An Estelle?" Rosie repeated.

"A variety of the hybrid tea is called the Estelle. Isn't that marvelous? Oscar discovered it and gave me a single Estelle when he proposed. How could I say no?" She laughed. "Oscar and my roses have kept me very happy."

"I'm going to give Ben another chance!" Rosie exclaimed. "I'm going to quit producing and manage our social life. I'll throw fabulous parties with specialty cocktails and learn to play tennis."

"Did Ben ask for another chance?" Estelle inquired, fixing the brim on her hat.

"I called him last night." Rosie squinted in the sun. "He was working but he said he'd come up to Montecito in July. We'd talk about it then."

"What about you." Estelle crouched on the dirt. "What makes you happy?"

"I want to be a perfect hostess like you," Rosie said, feeling like a child admitting a crush on her teacher. "You make it look easy."

"That's because I love what I do," Estelle answered. "Every morning I wake up and think about my roses. I wonder which ones will be flowering today, which ones need extra sunlight. You don't have to have a job necessarily, but you need something that's yours."

"I've been too busy to think about anything like that." Rosie sighed.

"Do you like gardening? Singing? Painting?" Estelle prompted.

"I have a brown thumb," Rosie giggled. "I killed the sprouts we grew in our window box. And I can't sing. Not even my parents could sit through my rendition of "The Sound of Music." I've worked beside Ben since we graduated."

"Rosie, dear." Estelle brushed the dirt from her pants. "I'm an old woman but I still believe in passion: passion for my husband, for my children, but also for what's mine. I've loved this house since the day I was born. I've walked every inch of the grounds, discovered birds' nests and acorns stashed by squirrels. When we got married, Oscar was away all the time. Either he was in Los Angeles recording with his bands, or he was traveling to Japan, England, and Australia. That's when I fell in love with my roses. If you're not passionate about something, the man you love won't be passionate about you."

"I can learn something new," Rosie insisted, tears springing to her eyes.

"It's got to come from the heart." Estelle patted her chest. "It can be something simple: running or cooking."

"I jog to stay fit, but I don't know how anyone truly loves running," Rosie groaned. "I do like to mess around and make things in the kitchen. In college I was famous for my guacamole."

"Then start there." Estelle nodded. "You have to have something that's completely yours. You can't wait for a man to come home and complete you."

"It's been a long time since I tried my recipes." Rosie wavered. "Ben and I worked so late every night, we usually threw together a sandwich or ordered gourmet pizza."

"You can use our kitchen as a laboratory," Estelle offered. "Peg will show you where the utensils are. If there's anything you need, Morris can get it for you."

Rosie stared at the pink and purple rosebuds until they became a blur. Suddenly she couldn't see herself standing in a vast marble kitchen, waiting for Ben. She couldn't picture him stepping out of a Maserati, wearing an Armani suit and carrying a case of Penfolds Sauvignon Blanc. Instead she saw herself in Estelle's guest cottage, thumbing through paperback books and watching movie marathons on the flat screen. Ben had slept with another woman and Hollywood seemed a million miles away.

"I promised I'd tell you the story of how Oscar and I met." Estelle brought her out of her reverie.

"I'd love to hear." Rosie smiled weakly.

"Oscar's father was my father's chauffeur," Estelle began. "Oscar grew up in this house too, in a flat over the garage. He is five years older than me so our paths rarely crossed. I remember him as a skinny boy with long hair and round glasses like an owl. He got a scholarship to UCLA and started getting a name in the record business. It was luck in the beginning. He knew a few guys in a band, liked their sound, and sent tapes to every record company in Los Angeles. He's always been stubborn," Estelle said fondly. "His father got sick at the same time I came home from Penn. Oscar drove up every weekend to visit him, and we had dinner together on the lawn. It was as if we just met: his hair was cut short and he wore contacts instead of glasses. He seemed very elegant and mature.

"We realized we loved the same things: grand houses, people, parties, fine wine. He was just getting a taste of that life. His first band was a success and all the doors were opening. Sometimes I worried he'd be swept away by the glitz of the music business, but he came up every Friday until he proposed." Estelle paused, twisting her gold wedding band. "At first my parents were hesitant and my friends shrugged him off. Oscar didn't have the right breeding. But he won them over. And we've been lucky. Two beautiful children, Oscar's career, good friends."

"It reminds me of the movie *Sabrina*," Rosie said dreamily. "Audrey Hepburn is one my favorite actresses, and Humphrey Bogart and William Holden were so dashing and handsome."

"Sometimes love appears in the most unlikely places." Estelle stood up and brushed off her pants.

"You think I should give up on Ben?" Rosie asked, standing up beside her.

"I don't know Ben well enough to tell you what to do," Estelle responded and looked at Rosie. "I just know as selfish as it sounds, you have to put yourself first."

Rosie walked slowly to the house. She tried to recapture her resolve, her certainty that she and Ben would be together. The house seemed foreign in the daylight. The roof was slanted like a witch's hat. Ivy climbed the walls, and downstairs the French doors were flung open. Rosie heard music and the sound of a vacuum cleaner droning like a bee.

Rosie opened the door to the kitchen and smelled tomatoes and garlic. The kitchen looked exactly as it had last night. A fresh pile of laundry lay on the table and a large pot simmered on the stove.

Rosie remembered the box-like kitchen of her apartment at Kenyon. Her roommates couldn't understand why she would rather cook than eat at Peirce Hall, with its soaring ceilings and stained-glass windows. But Rosie loved the way cooking slowed down her thoughts, made her concentrate on what was in front of her instead of what was running through her head.

She didn't like to bake. Cake batter made her feel sick and the smell of raw eggs clung to the counters for days. But preparing simple recipes—pasta in a red sauce, split pea soup, and tortillas with black beans—was satisfying. When Ben came to her dorm to watch old movies, they shared spaghetti marinara and a bottle of cheap wine.

Now Rosie stepped into the pantry and scanned its contents. She discovered jars of marmalade and blackberry jam. Glass canisters held macadamia nuts and cashews. There were bowls of golden raisins and fat figs and dates.

"So you're not a ghost," Morris said behind her.

"Estelle said it was all right for me to use the kitchen." Rosie blushed, turning around.

"I didn't think you were stealing the peanut butter." Morris set a basket of oranges on the counter. "I'm glad to see you outside the cottage."

"Thanks for babysitting me last night," Rosie answered. "And for making such a great peanut butter sandwich."

"I can make you another," he suggested, pointing to the jars of jam.

"I was going to try one of the recipes I made in college," Rosie explained, waving at the canisters on the shelves.

"Excellent idea." Morris nodded, slicing oranges. "Do you have the ingredients you need?"

"I had two roommates my junior year. Becky was from Hawaii and Lucinda was from East LA. I know how to cook fish and anything that involves tortillas, beans, and lettuce," she replied. "Estelle thinks if I do something I enjoy I'll be happier."

"And if you're happy, the cheating boyfriend will come back?" Morris looked up from the juicer.

"I do sound like a cliché," Rosie groaned. "I realized I don't have to be Ben's production partner. I can keep house and throw parties and make sure we're friends with the beautiful people."

"You are the beautiful people," Morris said. "If Ben doesn't recognize that, he may not be the right guy."

"I'll start with guacamole," Rosie said brightly, as if she didn't have a care in the world. She was going to stop wallowing and move forward. She would make the guacamole. Then she'd find Angelica's tennis racket and bang some balls on the tennis court.

"I have to take Mr. Pullman his orange juice." Morris poured the orange juice into a crystal glass. "He's on a conference call with a metal band in Stockholm. Peg is at the market. If you need anything, ask me."

Rosie opened the fridge. She took out avocados, tomatoes, a Bermuda onion, and a container of cottage cheese. She searched the pantry for cumin, cilantro, and garlic. She had two secret ingredients: cottage cheese that gave the guacamole a creamy taste and Hawaiian sea salt. Becky had introduced her to pink Hawaiian sea salt. The grains were like delicate crystals, and Becky used to eat them from the palm of her hand.

"What are you doing here?" a male voice said behind her.

Rosie jumped. A jar of garlic cloves fell to the floor, smashing into tiny pieces.

"You scare easily," the man said. "You wouldn't make a good thief."

Rosie crouched down to pick up the garlic. The man wore blue jeans and a blue t-shirt. He was tall, with thick shoulders and long legs. He had blond hair and blue eyes so pale they were almost gray.

"You're the surfer." Rosie blushed, standing up. "I ran over your board."

"I hope the Pullmans haven't hired you as a cook." Josh bent down to scoop up the glass. "You could be dangerous with a knife."

"I'm staying in their guesthouse; I'm friends with Angelica," Rosie said. "What are you doing here?"

"I work here." Josh took out a large plate of lasagna and put it in the microwave. He poured a glass of milk and sat at the table. "Do you want some? I can heat up another plate."

"You're going to eat all that?" Rosie frowned.

"Surfers are always starving," Josh admitted, wiping his mouth with a napkin.

"Are you Oscar's assistant?" Rosie asked curiously.

"I'd be a lousy assistant." Josh shook his head. "I'm a terrible typist and I don't have all the latest apps on my phone. I take care of his classic car collection."

"Classic cars?" Rosie sat down opposite him.

"You haven't seen Mr. Pullman's collection?" Josh put down the glass of milk. "He's got a few cars that Jay Leno would drool over. He just bought a mint-green '56 MG that purrs like a kitten."

"Angelica told me about Estelle's rose garden, but she didn't mention classic cars."

"Mr. Pullman doesn't collect so he can brag at cocktail parties," Josh said, buttering a loaf of sourdough. "He really loves cars. If he wasn't so busy with his bands he'd be in the garage with me, tinkering with a Fiat or an Alpha Romeo Spider."

"Driving in a convertible looks so exhilarating. I loved Grace Kelly in *To Catch a Thief*." Rosie sighed. "She zipped through Monte Carlo in a gorgeous European sports car and it seemed so romantic."

"That was a '53 Sunbeam Alpine Mark I." Josh nodded. "It's in a car museum in Paris. Mr. Pullman tried to buy it a few years ago but he was outbid."

"You're a walking car encyclopedia." She grinned.

"I've been rebuilding classic cars since I was fourteen." He shrugged. "The more love you give them, the more they gleam. If you're a movie producer"—Josh looked at her thoughtfully—"why are you hiding out in the Pullmans' guest cottage?"

"You remembered." Rosie pictured the pink-and-orange sunset at Butterfly Beach.

"I have a memory like an elephant." Josh finished the lasagna and took the plate to the sink. "It's a curse."

"Sometimes I think I forgot everything I studied in college." Rosie sighed.

"I remember the first time I rode a surfboard, I was ten years old. I was at the beach with my sister. She was eight, with her own wet suit and foam board. She convinced me to try it and I paddled out—it seemed forever, though it must have been fifty feet. The ocean was pale blue and so calm I felt like I had slipped into another world. Then this big wave appeared and tipped over my board. I was so scared I inhaled a gallon of seawater. By the time I swam to shore, I was shivering and covered with seaweed. I didn't go back in the ocean until I was twelve."

"Bad experiences help you grow," Rosie replied.

"That's existential babble." Josh took a plate of brownies from the fridge. "I had a philosophy class where the professor insisted if you hadn't felt pain you weren't fully alive. I've had my toe almost ripped off, fifteen stitches in my leg, and my heart broken twice. I'd be fine without any of those experiences."

"Where did you go to college?"

"UC Santa Barbara." Josh ate a wedge of brownie, the crumbs falling onto the counter. "Four years of World History and surfing. I lived two blocks from the beach and surfed every day. I liked learning about the human condition, but I realized I never wanted to wear a suit or sit at a desk."

"At least you're earning a living doing what you love," Rosie replied.

"I work at the Classic Car Showroom in town and I take care of a few private collections on the side. Mr. Pullman's collection is my favorite. He just got a 1953 Rolls-Royce Phantom that's a gem. Can I show it to you?"

Rosie glanced at her onions and avocados and tomatoes. "I was about to make guacamole."

"The garage is right out back." Josh sliced another brownie. "You've never seen an interior like this. It's like the inside of a British drawing room, with a humidor for cigars."

Josh led Rosie down a cobblestoned path to the garage. She followed him into a dark space and waited while he fumbled with the light switch.

Rosie blinked under the suddenly bright light. The room was bigger than a hotel ballroom. The floors and walls were a pristine white. Every inch of space was filled with cars. The cars were colors Rosie had never seen: burnt orange, sapphire blue, powder pink, and emerald green. Chrome bumpers twinkled like diamonds, and polished leather made the room smell like lemons. There were convertibles with wide runners, station wagons with wood sides, a vintage Ford with red seats and a gold-plated steering wheel.

"Here she is." Josh led Rosie to a silver Rolls-Royce with a creamy white interior. "She's a replica of the car Queen Elizabeth drove through London after her coronation. They only made eighteen of them."

Rosie sat in the backseat, admiring the gleaming wood and the supple white leather. The bucket seats curved around her body and the windows were covered in gauze curtains.

"It's gorgeous," Rosie murmured, leaning back against the headrest.

"Some people think cars are all about speed: Ferraris and Maseratis and Lamborghinis." Josh climbed in next to her. "But they each have their own personality. The Rolls-Royce Phantom is a grand duchess. The backseat is big enough to have afternoon tea."

"It looks like it was built yesterday." Rosie ran her hands over the soft white upholstery.

"I spent the last week making her shine." Josh hopped out and opened Rosie's door.

"I like this one." Rosie walked over to a bright orange two-seater with oversized oval headlamps.

"A 1961 MG." Josh nodded. "I'm restoring one at home. She has the most beautiful curves. I fell in love with her at a car auction."

"You sound like you're describing a woman," Rosie giggled.

"A car is easy, it can't break your heart." Josh frowned. "I stay away from women. I'm a confirmed bachelor."

"The only confirmed bachelors I know of are Zac Efron and Leonardo DiCaprio," Rosie said. "Even most movie stars get married or are in serious relationships. Everyone needs love."

"I wake up every morning and run to the ocean: water calm as glass, sun hovering over the horizon." Josh rubbed the steering wheel. "I love women in the abstract. I love their shape and their hair, but they don't make me happy."

"There are lots of happy couples," Rosie protested. "Look at Oscar and Estelle."

"Once in a while two special people find each other," Josh admitted grudgingly. "But they're the exception. I studied history and women are the root of most problems: Helen and the Trojan War, Antony and Cleopatra, Napoleon and Josephine, Romeo and Juliet."

"Women wouldn't be the problem if men didn't spend so much time obsessing over them," Rosie corrected. "And Romeo and Juliet weren't real, it was a play by Shakespeare."

"The outcome is the same." Josh shook his head. "Most love affairs at best cause heartache and at worst start wars."

"What about children?" she wondered aloud.

"My sister will have children and I'll be the coolest uncle. I'll take the kid surfing and let him sit in the driver's seat of a '67 Mustang."

"I can't imagine not wanting to get married and have children," she said earnestly.

"Everyone's different," Josh responded. "If you're a movie producer, why aren't you in Hollywood producing?"

Rosie blushed and walked to a wooden station wagon with bench seats. "This belongs in one of those old surfing movies like *Endless Summer*."

Josh opened the driver's door so Rosie could peek inside. "Why are you hiding in the Pullmans' guest cottage? Did you kill someone on the set?"

Rosie looked at Josh. His face was tan and unlined. His nose was slightly crooked, and his eyes seemed to dance. "I found out my boyfriend had another woman in our bed. At first he tried to lie about it but when he got caught he said it didn't mean anything." She took a deep breath. "Then we started arguing and Ben thought we should take a break. He is the director." Her voice wobbled. "Angelica suggested I get out of town and stay in Montecito with her parents for the summer."

"I'm sorry," Josh said.

"Ben got sidetracked." Rosie gulped, tears springing to her eyes. "We've been together for ten years. We both needed time to rethink the relationship. He's going to come up in July and we're going to see where things are headed."

"You sound like one of those relationship therapy workshops," Josh mused. "I like to keep life simple."

"How would you know what it feels like to be cheated on?" Rosie fumed. How dare Josh analyze her reactions; they barely knew each other. She opened the garage door and darted across the lawn. Ducks bobbed on the lake, and she ran until she reached the cottage. From now on she would keep her worries to herself. She went inside, closed the curtains, and buried her face in the pillows.

Five

Rosie stood in the Pullmans' kitchen and tasted the guacamole. The last two days she had spent blending and mixing. There was no Hawaiian sea salt so she substituted a coarse salt from Mexico. But it didn't add the same sweet and tangy flavor. The guacamole was creamy: light and fluffy from two scoops of cottage cheese, but it lacked the zing that made it special.

The end of her little finger had a spot of guacamole and she tried it again. Diced onions and chopped tomatoes were arranged neatly on the marble counter. Two mixing bowls stood side by side. Rosie wore a light cotton dress and had an apron tied around her waist.

After Josh showed her Oscar's car collection she lay awake for hours. Josh's words stung and she ruminated about the tragic love affairs in cinema: *Doctor Zhivago*, *Casablanca*, and *An Affair to Remember*. She thought of the heartbreaking novels she read: *Madame Bovary* and *Anna Karenina* and *Love Story*. She wanted to call Ben, just to hear his voice, but she knew if he answered she would start crying.

She finally fell asleep and when she woke it was late afternoon.

People splashed in the pool, and she could hear Estelle's voice asking for lemonade, Oscar calling for more ice. She sat up and saw Morris crossing the lawn carrying a tray of sandwiches.

Her robe lay on the bed and she pulled it on and stood by the window, watching Oscar and Estelle greet their guests. Estelle wore a green cotton caftan and Oscar wore navy swimming trunks and a white polo shirt. They linked arms; their heads pressed together, their laughter wafting across the lawn.

"That's going to be Ben and me," Rosie said aloud. She rummaged through her bag and found a cotton dress that was not too crumpled. She brushed her hair, dabbed bronzer on her cheeks, and walked briskly to the kitchen.

Since then she had stopped only to walk around the grounds in the evening. She loved the sound of the crickets at dusk, and the frogs croaking in the grass. Last night she sat by the lake, throwing bread crumbs to the ducks, humming Ben's favorite Coldplay songs.

"How's the chef?" Morris put a laundry basket full of shirts on the table. "Ready for your cooking show debut?"

"Hardly." Rosie grinned, wiping her hands on her apron. "I need Hawaiian sea salt, it doesn't taste the same without it."

"May I?" Morris put a spoon into the mixing bowl.

"Angelica and Matthew are coming up for the weekend." Rosie waited for Morris' verdict. "I want to make dinner, and I want it to be delicious."

"You mean you want to impress Angelica so she tells Ben you've become an incredible chef, and you look beautiful and tan and he should hightail it up here and claim you." Morris put down the spoon.

"I want to prepare gourmet food Ben will be proud of," Rosie corrected. "Then we can host intimate dinners and invite A-list actors like Ryan Reynolds and Blake Lively."

"So you think I should have worked harder to keep Neil," Morris chided. "If only I had done my butt exercises every day and worked on my tan, he may have picked me over Amber."

"I'm not doing this just for Ben," Rosie insisted. "I like to cook. It keeps me occupied."

"It's Peg's day off and Mr. Pullman wants salmon for dinner. I've got a pile of shirts to iron and shoes to shine." Morris picked up the laundry basket. "Would you mind going into the village and picking up some fish?"

"I'd love to." Rosie placed the mixing bowls in the fridge. "I'll see if I can find Hawaiian sea salt."

Rosie parked at the end of Coast Village Road and grabbed her purse. The sidewalk was packed with tourists wearing Montecito t-shirts and licking ice cream cones. Rosie stopped in front of a shoe store and admired red and black Gucci sandals in the window.

"Come in," the salesgirl beckoned at the door. She wore a white crocheted dress and silver sandals.

"I'm just looking." Rosie shook her head. She had never indulged in designer footwear. Her shoe collection consisted of flip-flops, Keds, and a few pairs of presentable sandals and pumps.

"We just got a shipment from Milan," the saleswoman purred. "The Manolo Blahniks would look stunning with your coloring."

Rosie hesitated and followed her inside. The shop was like the inside of a jewelry box. The carpet was purple and the walls were covered in silver wallpaper. There were Bottega Veneta wedges in brilliant colors, Christian Louboutin stilettos, Chanel flats, and Tod's loafers in orange and green.

"Are you visiting?" the salesgirl asked.

"I live in LA." Rosie nodded, admiring Prada pumps. Even

when she was made associate producer she stayed away from designer shoes the other female executives wore. They were gorgeous, but they cost as much as her student loan payments.

"Everyone in Hollywood wants this shoe." The salesgirl brought out a box of Manolos. "They already sold out at Neiman's."

The sandals were gold with red and green jewels embedded in the leather. Rosie slipped them on, feeling like she belonged on a yacht in the Greek Islands.

"They're beautiful." Rosie walked gingerly around the store.

"Very sophisticated." The salesgirl nodded. "They dress up a pair of jeans or look stunning with a gold lamé dress and a Dior clutch."

Rosie stood in front of the mirror. She looked taller, sleeker, the jewels shimmering like a magic carpet. Even her eyes looked greener. She reached into her purse and froze. Did she really need a pair of Manolos, and when would she wear them? Then she glanced at the mirror again and took a deep breath.

"I'll take them." She handed the salesgirl the credit card she shared with Ben.

"Would you like the evening bag?" the salesgirl asked casually.

"No, thank you," Rosie replied, trying to make the pit in her stomach go away. She had never spent so much on shoes. She waited while the salesgirl slid her card, imagining Mary Beth Chase's shoe closet: racks of Versace pumps and Roger Vivier sky-high wedges. Mary Beth probably arranged her shoes by color and had separate shelves for her athletic shoes and winter boots.

Rosie ran out of the store before she could change her mind. She hugged the box to her chest, inching through the crowd. She stopped in front of a jewelry store that displayed gold earrings and diamond bracelets.

"I don't need any jewelry," Rosie said aloud. "But maybe a really beautiful dress."

Rosie kept walking until she found a dress boutique. She sifted through satin evening gowns and dresses with poufy skirts. There were cocktail dresses in every color and long sheaths with silver belts. Rosie spied a red silk dress with a heart-shaped bust and a flared skirt.

Rosie pictured wearing it to an intimate dinner at Adam's house. Ben would have on a white shirt and tan linen slacks. He'd wear Italian loafers and a Rolex Oyster watch. She took it to the dressing room and tried it on in front of the three-way mirror. She took the Manolos out of the box and slipped them on her feet.

"That dress is divine." The saleswoman appeared behind her. "Perfect for a cocktail party or a quiet dinner."

"I love the way it feels against my skin." Rosie stroked the fabric. "Like the wings of a butterfly."

"It's a great color on you." The woman nodded. "Not many people can wear that color."

Rosie flashed on Mary Beth's pale blond hair and creamy white skin. Mary Beth would look like a vampire in the red dress. She turned and smiled at the saleswoman.

"I'll take it." She nodded. "I'll wear it, actually, break it in."

Rosie breathed deeply, trying not to think what Ben would say when he saw the bill. She remembered the dozens of times they watched *Breakfast at Tiffany's*. Ben loved the scenes when Holly Golightly slipped on a black cocktail dress and a big white hat.

"Blake Edwards knew how to direct a woman," Ben would say, stroking Rosie's leg. "Most directors treat women like accessories, but he made them goddesses. Audrey Hepburn was a sprightly Aphrodite. You look like her, you know; you both have the same wide eyes and upturned nose."

Now Rosie walked briskly, swinging her bag against her hip. She passed a card store, an antiques store, and a florist with a window box bursting with chrysanthemums. She stopped in front of a chocolate shop with a chocolate treasure chest in the window.

"You look like you won the lottery." Rachel appeared at the doorway. "Or found a dreamy new boyfriend who showers you with riches."

"I was coming to say hi." Rosie grinned. "And try some peanut butter brittle."

"Did you find Butterfly Beach?" Rachel asked.

"It was the most beautiful sunset I've ever seen." Rosie nodded. "It was like a painter's palette left out in the rain."

"Come and see my shop." Rachel waved her inside. "It's not very big, but I love it."

The shop reminded Rosie of Miss Havisham's room in *Great Expectations*. An oriental rug covered the floor and oak shelves lined the walls. Every surface was covered with chocolates. There were tins of chocolate mints, jars of chocolate coins, boxes of truffles, and plates of nougats and marzipan. A chocolate dollhouse stood in the corner with miniature chocolate tables and chairs.

"I need a dessert for a dinner party." Rosie peered at a selection of cakes under the glass.

"My German chocolate cake is amazing and the chocolate torte is delicious," Rachel suggested, offering her a sample of the torte. "Entertaining a new man?"

"My best friend, Angelica, is coming up from LA." Rosie tasted dark chocolate and raspberries. "I think Ben and I may actually work things out."

"Really?" Rachel leaned over the counter. "When my boyfriend cheated on me, I cut up all his boxer shorts."

"Ben and I have been together for ten years." Rosie sighed, sampling a piece of peanut butter brittle. "I miss him."

"Love's a bitch." Rachel nodded. "I've been on a few dates with

Patrick. If my father found out he'd pack me up to New Jersey faster than the roller coaster at Atlantic City."

"Patrick in the delicatessen?" Rosie inquired.

"I've got a thing for red hair and freckles," Rachel answered. "But he's Catholic. My father would rather I stayed with Michael, who screwed two bridesmaids at his cousin's wedding. Michael is Jewish, and an accountant."

"I didn't know parents still thought like that." Rosie tried not to laugh.

"Thank god my father is on the other side of the country, but I swear he knows everything I do." Rachel rolled her eyes. "He wants his daughter to marry a good Jewish boy like in *Fiddler on the Roof*."

Rosie selected the German chocolate cake and Rachel put it in a box and added a pound of peanut brittle. "Good luck with the cheating boyfriend." She handed Rosie the bag. "I hope he deserves you. You look like a movie star."

Rosie carried two grocery bags into the Pullmans' kitchen. She had found Hawaiian sea salt at Montecito Natural Foods. She had spent a wonderful hour reading the labels of salts and spices from around the globe. From there she went to Village Meat and Fish and bought fillets of salmon, a pound of cod, and a bag of lemons.

"You leave looking like the girl next door and come back as Elizabeth Taylor." Morris whistled, coming through the French doors.

"Do you think it's too much?" Rosie made a small twirl. The red fabric spun around her waist and the gold sandals glittered under the lights.

"I never knew you had Elizabeth Taylor's eyes." Morris smiled. "And those sandals! I'd love a pair in my closet."

"Elizabeth Taylor had violet eyes," Rosie protested. "I've never bought anything so impulsively. Ben's contract is enormous, maybe I should have been wearing Manolos all along."

"Don't think about Ben." Morris unwrapped the salmon. "Wear them because they feel like sex."

"Yes, boss," Rosie giggled, opening her shopping bag. "I got everything I need for dinner tomorrow. I'm going to make fish tacos with guacamole and German chocolate cake for dessert."

"You're going to save me a slice." Morris peeked inside the cake box.

Rosie put the cod in the fridge. She placed the cake in the pantry and put the lemons in the fruit bowl. She walked over to Morris and kissed him briefly on the cheek.

"What's that for?" He rubbed his cheek.

"For talking to me when I was so depressed, and for saying I look like Elizabeth Taylor."

"That's great." Morris put the salmon in the fridge. "But I still want a piece of cake."

Rosie stood in the bathroom of the guest cottage, applying mascara. She wore a white tank top and white linen pants and the new gold sandals. Morris had insisted on pressing her pants and she had borrowed Estelle's curling iron. She brushed her hair and studied herself in the mirror. The circles under her eyes had disappeared and her arms and legs were tan. She rubbed pink lip gloss on her lips and went to wait for Angelica.

Crossing the lawn to the main house, Rosie wondered why she was so nervous. She and Angelica had spent countless nights eating ice cream straight from the carton. They suffered through Bikram yoga and kept each other on a five-day juice fast. But now Rosie had chosen her outfit as if preparing for a blind date. She took a long bath and spent an hour curling her hair.

In the years of their friendship, Rosie had always been part of Rosie and Ben. She had walked with the skip of someone in a bulletproof relationship. Angelica had the height, the pouty lips, and the glorious blond hair. She had parents with a magnificent estate and checks that appeared regularly in the mail. But she didn't have someone who loaded up their iPhones with exactly the same songs. She hadn't picked out the names of their children and the breed of their dog.

But now Rosie was a refugee in Angelica's parents' guest cottage and Angelica was channeling Katharine Hepburn. She hadn't talked to Angelica all week; they exchanged texts because Angelica was slammed with wardrobe fittings.

A sleek Aston Martin entered the gates. It was midnight blue with chrome wheels and a British license plate. Rosie squinted, thinking one of Oscar's singers had come to the house for a meeting.

"Rosie!" A tall figure waved from the passenger seat. She leaped out of the car and ran up the steps. Angelica wore pin-striped pants and a boxy navy jacket. Her cheeks were powdered and her eyebrows were plucked in a high arch.

"Where's Matthew?" Rosie hugged Angelica, smelling Chanel No. 5 and hair spray.

"In LA. Have you met Dirk? Don't you love his car!" Angelica waved her hand. "He had it imported from England; it drives on the wrong side of the road."

"Why are you with Dirk instead of Matthew?" Rosie said in a guarded voice.

"I'll explain in a minute." Angelica dragged Rosie towards the car. "I want you two to get to know each other. Dirk, say something so Rosie can hear your divine accent."

Dirk stepped out of the car and kissed Rosie on both cheeks. He had floppy dark hair and green eyes. His cheekbones were finely chiseled and his teeth looked perfectly capped. He wore a seer-sucker blazer and pleated navy trousers.

"Delighted to finally meet you." He nodded. "Angelica talks about you all the time. And this place is fantastic." He beamed at Angelica. "It reminds me of George and Amal Clooney's summer home in the Cotswolds."

"I can't wait to show you mummy's rose garden," Angelica squealed. "I'll get Morris to grab your bags. He's British too, you might know the same people."

Rosie followed Angelica into the house, suddenly feeling queasy.

"Angelica," she hissed, after Angelica sent Morris to collect the luggage. "Why is Dirk here and why did you call Estelle 'mummy'?"

"Dirk's accent is so dreamy, it's catching," Angelica giggled. "I've been saying 'let's take the lift' and 'open the boot.' I can't help it, it sounds so sexy."

"Come into the kitchen now!" Rosie demanded.

"We can't leave Dirk." Angelica wavered. "It wouldn't be polite."

"He can catch up with Morris." Rosie pulled Angelica's arm. "Unless Morris exposes him as not being British at all and having grown up in West Virginia."

"You're so tan and your hair looks great." Angelica followed Rosie into the kitchen. The counter was lined with porcelain plates and there was a wooden salad bowl and linen napkins. "It was a good idea for you to get out of town."

"You're not answering my question," Rosie repeated. "Why aren't you with Matthew?"

Angelica took out a compact from her purse and smoothed her hair. She picked a peach from the fruit basket and took a bite.

"I forget how lovely it is here." Angelica walked to the French doors. "The tennis court and the swimming pool. Morris at your beck and call. I'm cooped up on a soundstage practicing my vowels."

"I am grateful to you and your parents." Rosie nodded. "The house is gorgeous and your mom is wonderful. But why are you with that Pierce Brosnan wannabe?"

"Dirk is much more handsome than Pierce Brosnan ever was. Anyway, Pierce Brosnan is sixty!" Angelica turned around.

"C'mon, Angelica, you're a great actress on the screen but you're lousy at pretending in real life," Rosie prodded.

Angelica poured a glass of water and sat at the table. "I broke up with Matthew. I moved in with Dirk."

"You did what!" Suddenly Rosie was back in Santa Monica, discovering that Ben screwed Mary Beth Chase and wanted to take a break.

"Dirk understands me, we have the same goals." Angelica sipped her water. "*The Philadelphia Story* is getting pre-production buzz and everyone wants him for his next film."

"Are you listening to yourself?" Rosie paced around the kitchen. "What about the boyfriend who picked you up at midnight when you waited tables at Il Fornaio? The boyfriend you've shared a bed with for two years?"

"Matthew and I were never like you and Ben." Angelica looked at Rosie. "Matthew has been ignoring me for months. The only words he responds to are 'food' and 'sex.' Honestly, Rosie, he's plugged into his computer twenty-four hours a day."

"It's hard to compete with someone who ships his Aston Martin from England," Rosie grumbled. "Matthew probably feels inferior."

"All he had to do was talk to me," Angelica argued. "Suggest we walk on the beach or go out to dinner."

"Was it really that bad?"

"It really was," Angelica assured her, her voice getting thick.

"I'm not going to wait for Matthew to stop staring at a computer screen. I want to go dancing. I want to fly to Paris and stand at the top of the Eiffel Tower."

"Please don't tell me Dirk promised to take you to Paris," Rosie groaned. "That's the oldest Hollywood cliché."

"He's not going to take me to Paris," Angelica protested. "We're going together, after *The Philadelphia Story* wraps. We're equals, like you and Ben."

Rosie softened. She remembered what it was like to love someone who knew exactly what you were talking about. If Rosie complained Adam was being unreasonable, Ben would grin and say he'd handle him. When Ben stared at the dailies for too long, Rosie made him a cup of hot cocoa and told him to take a break. At night, they couldn't get enough of talking about changes in the script and wardrobe malfunctions. They lived and breathed movies and it was intoxicating.

"Let's join Dirk and have a drink," Rosie conceded. "We'll see if Dirk still has that British accent after his third martini."

They sat on the back porch, drinking dry martinis. Rosie passed a silver tray of asparagus crepes and crab cakes.

"What have you been doing up here?" Angelica asked Rosie. "You should get involved in the arts. Montecito has great summer theater."

"I've been here less than a week; I haven't done much of anything. I went shopping and tried a few recipes I learned in college," Rosie answered. "I don't want to do local theater. I'm going to play tennis and Estelle is going to teach me about roses."

"I wanted you to get away for the summer, not turn into Rachel Ray." Angelica raised her eyebrows.

"I've been thinking about what Ben said, that I'm holding him back," Rosie said cautiously. "Maybe I should concentrate on our social life; throw great parties, cultivate the right people."

"When did you talk to Ben?" Angelica stirred the olive in her martini.

"I called him last weekend. He was in a meeting but we're going to talk soon. He's coming to your dad's July Fourth party."

"I don't know if it's a good idea to base your future on Ben," Angelica said, nibbling a crab cake.

"I like cooking," Rosie protested. "And I've always wanted to play tennis."

"I used to play tennis with Ewan McGregor," Dirk broke in. "He's got a terrific serve."

"Dirk has only been in LA for a few years." Angelica glanced at Dirk, her eyes sparkling. "In England he knew everybody: Daniel Craig, Matthew Goode, Gerard Butler."

"What movies did you make in England?" Rosie asked, blotting her mouth with her napkin.

"I did theater, Royal Shakespeare," Dirk replied smoothly. "My signature role was Hamlet."

"Dirk had a huge following," Angelica said loyally.

"Performing onstage is a noble calling, but acting in movies allows for the niceties in life," Dirk ruminated. "I've got my eye on a yacht. I'm going to name her the *Angelica.*"

Rosie placed her asparagus crepe on her napkin, afraid if she put it in her mouth she might choke.

"The studio wants Dirk for the remake of *To Catch a Thief*," Angelica explained. "They'll be filming in the South of France."

"Really!" Rosie gasped. *To Catch a Thief* was her and Ben's favorite movie. They had dreamed of producing a remake. They spent hours debating which actors would be best for the lead roles.

"Nothing is final." Dirk shrugged. "I only wish my gorgeous Angelica would play Grace Kelly's role."

"They want someone more famous than I am," Angelica said hastily. "Katie Holmes or Kate Hudson."

"They don't have your poise or your beauty," Dirk replied gallantly.

Rosie got up to go into the kitchen. Suddenly she couldn't stand another minute of their mutual admiration society.

"I'm going to start dinner," Rosie excused herself.

"I'll come with you." Angelica followed her.

Rosie walked ahead, thinking the dinner party was a bad idea. The more Angelica and Dirk talked about Hollywood, the further away it seemed. She tied an apron around her waist and laid the tortillas on the counter.

"Are you okay?" Angelica stood behind her.

"I'm fine." Rosie blinked. "I'm making fish tacos."

"I didn't ask about the menu," Angelica snapped. "Why weren't you part of the conversation? You weren't listening to anything we were saying."

"I was preoccupied." Rosie avoided looking at Angelica. "I didn't want the guacamole to congeal."

"Rosie!" Angelica blocked her path to the fridge. "You were supposed to come up here and relax, and you're cooking and playing tennis."

"Ben is an amazing director, maybe the best of his generation. He should work with the biggest producers in Hollywood." Rosie chopped green onions.

"I'm not following," Angelica said, leaning on the counter.

"Ben and I could be happy if I back off from the studio and concentrate on our social life." Rosie added grated cheese and tomatoes to the tortillas.

"What about Mary Beth?" Angelica asked.

"I hate that he cheated on me." Rosie threw the cod on the

skillet. "Sometimes when I picture them together I can't breathe." She sprinkled the onions on the tortillas. "But it only happened once. Ben said we needed time to think and he was right."

"Did he say anything else?" Angelica inquired.

"What do you mean?" Rosie looked up from the tortilla.

"Did he tell you his plans after his movie wraps?" Angelica asked.

"Ben's still shooting." Rosie shrugged. "Then comes post-production. He probably hasn't thought about when he's going to get a haircut. You know how consumed he gets when he's on the set."

"Dirk and I had dinner with Ben the other night." Angelica sipped her glass of water.

"You and Dirk?" Rosie repeated. "You didn't tell me they had met." She took the cod off the stove and cut it in thin strips.

"Ben wanted to talk about his next picture," Angelica explained, putting her glass in the sink.

Rosie concentrated on her tacos. She added two scoops of gua-camole and a spoonful of shredded cabbage. She decorated each one with cilantro and added a dollop of sour cream. "What next picture?" she asked finally.

"Ben is going to direct *To Catch a Thief.*"

Rosie imagined going on location with Ben, staying at the Carlton InterContinental Hotel in Cannes. They would drive to Monte Carlo and gamble small amounts at the roulette table. If they won they'd treat themselves to a bottle of champagne and drink it on the dock, watching the yachts rock in their berths.

"I should call and congratulate him." Rosie set the fish tacos on three plates. "Dirk's right, you would be great in the Grace Kelly role. You could finally go back to your natural hair color and be a blonde. I'm surprised Ben didn't offer it you, he's your big-gest fan."

"I'm so sorry, Rosie." Angelica looked at her friend. "I dreaded telling you the whole drive up, I almost made Dirk turn around and go back to LA. You're my best friend in the world and I don't want to do anything to hurt you," she said lamely. "I'd give anything for someone else to have delivered the news."

Angelica's words were a dull roaring sound in her ears. Rosie stood in front of the stove, clutching the frying pan. Her chest tightened and her legs were wobbly.

"Did Ben offer you Grace Kelly's role?"

"I'm not going to answer that question while you're holding a frying pan," Angelica responded.

"Did he?" Rosie put the frying pan down.

"He did," Angelica admitted. "But I turned him down."

"Why did you turn him down?" Rosie whispered.

"We met Ben for dinner at the Beverly Wilshire the other night," Angelica answered. "Ben thought Dirk would be perfect for the Cary Grant role. He said they have identical profiles. And he begged me to play the Grace Kelly part. He thought I could capture her languid beauty and portray a proper blue blood."

"Who was Ben with at the Beverly Wilshire?" Rosie tried to swallow.

"He was with Mary Beth," Angelica said slowly. "Mary Beth is going to be executive producer. They've even formed a new production company: MB&B Productions. I couldn't say yes, Rosie. I wouldn't do that to you."

"Why didn't you tell me?" Rosie's throat was parched and she felt dizzy. "And how could he do that without asking me?"

They had never gone to the trouble of forming a corporation. They were Ben & Rosie. Why would they spend their time and money on attorneys and legal documents when they would be together forever? But neither of them made decisions about anything without asking each other's permission. Rosie wouldn't even try a new brand of cereal because Ben needed his bowl of Cinnamon Toast Crunch every night before bed, and Ben always bought Colgate toothpaste because Rosie hated anything with mint.

"I was going to tell you tonight," Angelica lamented. "I felt terrible but I didn't know you wanted to get back together with Ben. The last time we talked you wanted to kill him."

"For almost a week I've been waiting for you to come up here," Rosie said. "I thought we'd make s'mores in the fireplace and swim in the pool and stay up all night painting our fingernails. Now you show up with a British actor and tell me that my boyfriend has formed a new production company."

"I'm sorry." Angelica hugged her. "I can tell Dirk to sleep by himself and we can share the cottage. I'll borrow my mother's nail polish and we'll have Morris bring us Pop-Tarts."

Rosie sank into a chair and remembered the items on her to-do list in the cottage: learn the names of different varieties of roses; ask Morris how to pair wine with a meal. Everything she thought she and Ben would have together—the house in the Hollywood Hills, the vacation home in Palm Springs, the two children with brown hair and freckles—dissolved before her eyes.

Ben and Mary Beth would tour the South of France. Mary Beth would wear Oliver Peoples sunglasses and stilettos. They would sit at outdoor cafes and kiss over pain au chocolat and steaming espressos. At night they'd go back to their hotel suite and climb under sheets with ridiculously high thread counts.

"It's not your fault," Rosie said finally. "And you can't let Dirk sleep alone. He must look sexy in his boxers."

"Dirk is pretty hot in his underwear," Angelica acknowledged and touched Rosie's shoulder. "You're the best person I know. You're going to find someone new. I found someone."

"It's easy for you, but I'm different. You're blond and beautiful and have your name on a movie billboard." Rosie sighed, untying her apron.

"It's going to get better," Angelica assured her. "Let's have dinner, I'm dying to try your tacos."

The fish tacos were arranged on white porcelain plates. There were sterling silver salt and pepper shakers and crystal water glasses Rosie had dug out for the occasion.

Rosie threw her apron on the table. "I'm sorry, I'm not hungry." She ran out the door and across the lawn and didn't stop until she reached the cottage.

Six

Rosie dug her toes into the sand and watched the seagulls skim the waves. It was late afternoon and the tide was coming in. Families had packed up their coolers and gone back to their hotels to nurse their sunburns. A few swimmers paddled close to shore and a line of surfers waited at the break. The weather was cooling off and goose bumps crawled up Rosie's skin.

Rosie had been at Butterfly Beach since early morning. She woke up ashamed of her behavior. Angelica wasn't to blame for Ben's defection, and Angelica idolized Grace Kelly. She could reel off the titles of her movies, her charities in Monaco, the dates of her marriage and her death. Rosie should have thanked Angelica for turning down the role in *To Catch a Thief* instead of fleeing to the cottage.

In the morning, Rosie couldn't face Angelica and Dirk over poached eggs and bacon. She slipped on shorts and flip-flops and drove to the beach. A run would clear her head, and then she would go back and apologize. She'd force herself to eat lunch with Angelica

and Dirk without cringing at the way he flipped his hair or pronounced his vowels.

But once Rosie felt the spray of the ocean and saw the beauty
of the coastline, she couldn't drag herself away. The peace settled
over her like a fog. Angelica had left her a message but she'd answer it when she got home. All she wanted to do was walk the beach
and watch crabs bury themselves in the sand. The sun touched the
water and the horizon stretched out like a silk ribbon.

Rosie couldn't understand how Ben moved on so quickly. When
she thought about his new production company she couldn't breathe.
She felt foolish for thinking Ben's tryst was a single mistake. Rosie
had made the mistake of believing they could make it work.

Perhaps she should get a job in community theater like Ben and
Angelica suggested. She'd be the assistant stage manager at the
Montecito Playhouse. She'd stand in the back and recognize some
faces from Hollywood. Actors often came to Montecito to do summer stock. But producers who left Hollywood didn't go back. They
were replaced by an eager crop of film school graduates faster than
one could make the froth on a cappuccino.

Maybe Rosie could be a professional dog walker, lead German
shepherds and Labradoodles along the beach. Or she'd get one of
those telemarketing jobs where you worked in sweatpants and
watched *All My Children* on mute. She considered sending her re-
sume to other studios in Hollywood and her stomach lurched.
Everyone in town would know Ben Ford brushed off his college
sweetheart.

Rosie wished she had brought a sweater, but she didn't want to
leave until the sun set. A surfer dragged his board onto the sand
and peeled off his wet suit. He shook the water out of his hair and
walked towards the parking lot.

"I'd ask you to watch my board but you might let a horse run over it." The surfer smiled. His blond curls stuck to his ears and his knees had cuts and bruises.

"I didn't know horses were allowed on the beach," Rosie replied.

"They are, actually." Josh crouched on the sand next to her. "Riding on the beach at sunset is awesome."

"I've been here since sunrise," Rosie admitted, running her fingers through the sand. "It's so peaceful."

"You picked a great day." Josh nodded and perched on his surfboard. "No breeze, just enough of a swell."

Rosie sat awkwardly beside him. She wanted to apologize for running out of the garage, but she wasn't sure what to say.

"I wanted to say I'm sorry." Josh turned to her.

"I was about to say that!" Rosie exclaimed.

"Apologize for what?" Josh asked.

"For running out of the garage. Last night I ran away from Angelica before dinner. She and her new boyfriend came up for the weekend. I'm not behaving well in social situations." Rosie sighed.

"That's why I come to the beach." Josh chuckled. "It's hard to mess up when it's just you and the waves."

"You don't need to apologize." Rosie squinted into the late-afternoon sun. "I was angry but I'm beginning to understand."

"Understand?" Josh repeated.

"How you can have been burned so badly that you never want to start another fire."

"I was going to say I'm sorry for eating your fish tacos. I found them in the kitchen last night. Morris told me you made them after I ate the whole plate."

"We sound like Abbott and Costello." Rosie grinned, remembered the hours she and Ben spent doubled over with laughter watching Abbott and Costello movies. "I'm glad you liked them."

"They were amazing." Josh nodded. "I've taken surfing trips to Mexico where we lived on fish tacos for days. I've never tasted any that were so good. You should go pro."

"It might be my only talent," Rosie lamented. "I've been wondering if I should become a children's party planner or a dog walker."

"Dog walking would be dangerous." Josh shook his head. "You might run over a Shih Tzu."

"I didn't mean to run over your board." Rosie flinched. "And I did offer to pay to fix it."

"I was trying to make you laugh." Josh touched her arm.

"I got some bad news yesterday." Rosie stared at the waves. "Ben started a new production company with Mary Beth Chase."

Josh looked at Rosie. "Is she the woman in your bed?"

"Hair like Rapunzel, fake breasts, and lips of a blowfish." Rosie nodded. "Did I mention she has an MBA from Stanford, and more movie successes than any female producer in the twenty-first century? She's the woman with the golden fingernails."

"Sounds frightening." Josh's brows knit together.

"She's Ben's ticket to Space Mountain." Rosie dug her toes into the sand. "He's launched into the stratosphere."

"You two aren't going to work it out?" he asked.

"Ben can't separate the bedroom from the office." She sighed. "He wants a woman who can do everything."

"You'll find someone else," Josh assured her.

"I thought you didn't believe in love." Rosie frowned.

"It may not be right for me." He shrugged. "But it is for most people."

Rosie wrapped her arms around her chest and turned to Josh. "Tell me about the time you got your heart broken."

"I met Sally in a Political Science class at UC Santa Barbara. She was smart and loved the ocean. We surfed every day. We got serious senior year, moved in together, planned a trip to Thailand. One day I came home and she had signed us both up for the LSAT. She had written out a list of law schools. Michigan for Christ's sake! And New Orleans. I explained I didn't want to be a lawyer and I couldn't live away from the beach." Josh gazed at the ocean. "We had a huge fight and I offered to compromise. We could live in LA. She'd go to law school and I'd figure out what I wanted to do."

"What happened?" Rosie wondered aloud.

"She started surfing less and spending more time in the library. One afternoon I came home and there were two study guides in the kitchen. Sally admitted she was falling in love with a pre-law student in her Economics section." He paused. "They both got accepted to Northwestern and now they practice law in Chicago. They just got engaged; she sent me a wedding invitation."

"I'm sorry," Rosie murmured, remembering the pain of Angelica saying that Ben and Mary Beth started their own production company.

Josh blinked, turning to Rosie. "I'm starving. Want to grab a burger? I'm buying."

All she'd eaten since this morning was a bag of pita chips and an apple. "I'd love to, but you don't have to pay." She stood up, brushing the sand off her legs.

"Sure I do." Josh grinned. "I ate your fish tacos."

Rosie followed Josh's car into the village. They parked under an oak tree and strolled along the sidewalk. Josh wore a Billabong t-shirt and leather flip-flops. The hair on his arms was blond and a narrow scar ran up his leg.

"When I was a kid I used to walk into every store with a quarter." Josh waved at the shopwindows. "I'd ask each shopkeeper what I could buy and they thought I was so cute they gave me something for free." He stopped in front of a diner with striped awnings. "Then I had a growth spurt and it didn't work any-more."

"I didn't know you grew up here." Rosie followed him inside. The floor was black and white squares of tile and there were red vinyl booths. An old-fashioned cash register stood on the counter and there was a glass case filled with tubs of ice cream.

"Just down the road." Josh nodded, sliding into a booth.

"Do your parents still live in Montecito?" Rosie sat opposite him.

Josh scanned the menu and set it on the table. He looked up and his eyes darkened. "They're both dead."

"I'm sorry." Rosie's cheeks flushed and she put her napkin in her lap.

"We apologize a lot for two people who barely know each other." He smiled, changing the subject. "Montecito is a great town. You should stay here for a while."

"And do what, become a beekeeper?" Rosie glanced at her menu.

"There's nothing wrong with being a beekeeper," he answered. "You don't have to be a neurosurgeon or a rocket scientist to be happy."

"My parents are rocket scientists at Kennedy Space Center." Rosie grinned. "They didn't approve of my major, but they were happy when Ben and I won the award at Sundance."

"They're not going to stop being proud of you because you change careers." He signaled for the waitress.

"I don't really have a career. I assisted the casting director and the location scout. I consulted with craft services and sat in on bud-get meetings. I didn't have anything of my own."

Josh ordered a double cheeseburger and a chocolate shake and

Rosie asked for a Cobb salad and a lemonade. They talked about Josh's sister who was an artist in San Francisco and Rosie's brother who taught economics in Japan.

"I was the only one in the family who watched movies or read novels." Rosie sipped her lemonade. "At dinner my brother solved logarithms, and my parents discussed landing feasibility of the space shuttle."

"My sister and I were really close." Josh stirred his milk shake. "Every summer we'd have lemonade stands and build fortresses in the garden."

"Is she married?" Rosie asked.

"A long string of boyfriends." Josh waited while the waitress placed a burger and fries in front of him. "But she doesn't want to settle down. I keep telling her to hurry up and choose the right guy so I can be an uncle."

"Marriage is okay for everyone but you?" Rosie asked, pouring dressing on her salad.

"Yvette is a little complicated. She has that nomad's heart and fiery personality," he mused. "She's always the heartbreaker in the relationship."

"I'm surprised you eat burgers." Rosie thought about Ben and Mary Beth and suddenly wanted to change the subject. "I thought surfers subsisted on tofu and wheatgrass."

"I burn so many calories I have to eat nonstop." Josh wiped his mouth. "When my buddies and I go on surfari we can eat three dozen eggs and two pounds of bacon in one sitting." He added relish and mustard to his burger. "There's a taco stand in Encinitas that makes the best enchiladas. Nothing beats coming in from the waves and chowing down with your mates."

Rosie ate silently, wondering what she was doing sitting with a guy wearing board shorts and flip-flops at a vintage diner in

Montecito. She was used to eating a Whole Foods salad on the set. Sometimes she and Ben slipped out to the Coffee Company and sipped iced frappuccinos. If they ordered a burger at one of the outdoor cafes in Santa Monica it came with organic beef and artisan cheese and a kale salad.

"I have an idea!" Josh put down his burger. "You could open a fish taco shop in town. You'd have a line out the door, like at the cookie store or the gelato place."

"I'm not a chef." Rosie shook her head.

"They were the best fish tacos I ever tasted," Josh insisted. "What's your secret?"

Rosie blushed, picking at crumbling blue cheese. "I use a few special ingredients in the guacamole."

"It would be a blast to have your own shop." Josh dipped his fries in ketchup. "I'm saving to buy the Classic Car Showroom when my boss retires."

"I wouldn't be good at it," Rosie answered. "I've never been my own boss. I'm better at taking commands than giving them."

"It beats dog walking." Josh ate a mouthful of French fries. "Or hiding out in the Pullmans' guest cottage."

"I'm not hiding," she bristled. "I'm taking a break and figuring out what to do."

"You're smart and young and have a college degree. You can do anything." Josh finished his burger.

"Everyone wants to give me advice: Ben, Angelica, Estelle. I don't need more advice." Rosie rose unsteadily to her feet.

Josh stood up and put his hand on Rosie's. His hands were bigger than Ben's, and his fingernails were perfect half-moons.

"I'm sorry." He smiled. "Sit down and finish your salad."

"I hate salads." Rosie's mouth trembled. "All I ate in LA was salads: spinach salad, goat cheese salad, chicken Caesar salad."

"Excuse me," Josh called the waitress. "Could you take these plates away and bring us a banana split with two spoons."

"I haven't eaten a banana split since I was twelve." Rosie sank back into the booth.

Josh sat down and smiled. "Then you have a lot of catching up to do."

Rosie pulled into the Pullmans' driveway and noticed Dirk's Aston Martin parked by the steps. It was almost seven p.m. and Rosie would be late for dinner. The lights were on in the living room and she heard Dirk's British accent and Estelle's high, clear voice. There were the sounds of glasses clinking and music playing on the stereo. She parked by the garage and ran to the cottage. She couldn't join them wearing shorts and flip-flops. Estelle believed in dressing in the evening, even if it was just her and Oscar at the long dining room table.

Rosie thought about Josh as she searched her closet for a pair of slacks and a sweater. She had never met someone so comfortable in his own skin. At Kenyon everyone wanted to get PhDs or become artists or writers. In Hollywood people were obsessed with fame and climbing the entertainment industry ladder. Even those who worked on indie films had two mantras: "Sundance" and "Cannes."

Rosie glanced at her face in the mirror. She had new freckles on her nose and sun streaks in her hair. She couldn't remember ever not having a serious goal. In high school she was determined to get into a great college. At Kenyon she worked hard to get good grades. When she met Ben she stopped thinking about the future: all they had to do was keep moving forward. Now she was like a train that fell off its tracks; she didn't know how to get back on the rails.

"There you are!" Estelle greeted Rosie as she entered the living room. "Angelica was telling me about the lovely dinner you made last night."

Rosie glanced at Angelica to see if she was angry with her. Angelica wore a pleated linen skirt and a ruffled blouse. She sat on a chintz love seat next to Dirk, sipping a glass of white wine.

"The fish tacos were delicious." Angelica nodded. "We were hoping you'd make some for lunch but you disappeared."

"I went to the beach early." Rosie accepted a glass from Oscar and stood by the fireplace. "I was only going for a run, but I stayed all day."

"You must be starving," Estelle said. "When I walk the dogs on the beach, I could eat a whole box of donuts."

"Mother." Angelica rolled her eyes. "I've never seen you eat a donut in my life."

"I wanted to set a good example." Estelle's brown eyes sparkled mischievously. "But I keep a box of Dunkin' Donuts in the bottom drawer of the pantry."

"Dad, is she telling the truth?" Angelica turned to her father.

"Your mother has hidden talents and desires." Oscar smiled affectionately. "She's on the verge of inventing a new rose."

"That's fascinating." Dirk beamed. "I spent a lot of time at Vita Sackville-West's garden at Sissinghurst when I was performing at the Old Vic."

"I haven't invented a rose," Estelle scoffed. "I'm experimenting with a couple of varieties. I want a perfect peach rose, it would look so pretty in the drawing room."

Rosie listened to the conversation as if it was a symphony. The voices rose and fell; Estelle laughed, Angelica giggled, Oscar's voice boomed like a drum. Even Dirk chimed in now and then, reeling off facts about British theater. Rosie felt herself shrinking against the fireplace. There was nothing she could add to the discussion.

She didn't want to talk about Hollywood and she didn't know anything else.

"What do you think of Montecito village?" Estelle turned to Rosie. "Morris said you did some shopping."

"It's like a stage set. The storefronts are quaint and the sidewalks are perfectly scrubbed," Rosie said, and bit her tongue. She'd have to stop thinking in Hollywood lingo. "I ate at a diner that looked straight out of *Grease*."

"Sam's Shake Shack?" Angelica inquired. "We used to get milk shakes there after school."

"I ordered a lemonade, but Josh's chocolate shake looked delicious."

"Josh?" Estelle asked curiously.

"The guy who takes care of Oscar's car collection. We are sort of friends. I ran over his surfboard the day I arrived." Rosie blushed.

"Josh Fellows is still here!" Angelica exclaimed, tracing the rim of her wineglass.

"Josh is a good worker," Oscar broke in. "He treats my cars like priceless works of art."

"I thought he'd have moved on by now." Angelica shrugged and fiddled with her wineglass. "No one stays in Montecito their whole life."

"There's nothing wrong with staying in Montecito. I was born in this house." Estelle gave Angelica a sharp look.

"You're different, Mother," Angelica said patiently. "You're a Montecito institution. You have a gorgeous estate and award-winning roses. Josh stayed in Santa Barbara for college."

"How long have you known Josh?" Rosie turned to Angelica, curious why she had never mentioned him.

"He started working for Daddy when I was a freshman at USC," Angelica remembered. "I teased him that he was the only mechanic I knew who was born and raised in Montecito."

"Angelica," Estelle said pointedly over her wineglass. "There's nothing wrong with being a mechanic or a chauffeur if you love cars."

"Daddy, I'm sorry. I always forget your father was the chauffeur." Angelica blushed and looked at her father. "Gosh, I'm hungry. Can we take this conversation into the dining room?"

"Daddy and I are very proud of your success as an actress," Estelle continued tersely. "But we would be proud of anything you did if it made you happy."

"Okay, Mom, I understand." Angelica dropped her eyes to the floor. "Peg made Yorkshire pudding, let's eat."

Oscar led the party into the dining room and took his seat at the head of the table. Rosie was placed beside Dirk, and Angelica sat across from him. Rosie kept glancing at Angelica, wanting to drag her into the kitchen and talk about last night. She felt like she was in a play production of *Remains of the Day* and she didn't know how to get her best friend off the stage.

Morris served stuffed Cornish hens and glazed yams. There was Yorkshire pudding and raspberry pie with whipped cream. Rosie noticed Morris' British accent was more pronounced and he bowed every time he approached the table.

"What's your Fourth of July theme this year, Mother?" Angelica ate a forkful of pie. "I've told Dirk about your legendary parties: tennis matches and croquet on the lawn and music that plays all night."

The Yorkshire pudding stuck in Rosie's throat. She had pictured being with Ben on July 4th. She would wear her new red dress and gold Manolo sandals. Now she dreaded seeing him. What if he brought Mary Beth to Montecito and she ran into them in the village. And she couldn't bear listening to Ben talk about his and Mary Beth's new production company. It was better if she skipped the party altogether.

"It's going to be 1920s theme," Estelle said excitedly. "We're going to have a sixteen-piece band that plays Cole Porter and Louis Armstrong. Men will wear white tie and tails and women will wear those wonderful flapper dresses. I thought about hiring a juggler and maybe even a fortune-teller. It always makes people feel good to believe they have wonderful events coming in their future."

"You should ask Rosie to make her fish tacos," Angelica suggested.

"I couldn't cook for so many people," Rosie protested. "I haven't made the recipe in years."

"Of course you could if you wanted to. It would be fun," Estelle said to Rosie. "Peg can help you."

"Actually, I wasn't sure I'd go to the party," Rosie confessed, examining her fork. "You and Oscar will be so busy with your guests, I don't want you worrying if I'm having fun. I might stay in the cottage or there's a play at the Montecito Playhouse starring some actors I know. Maybe I'll go see it."

She had seen a flyer in the village, but she never considered seeing a show. But anything would be better than standing on the lawn with a cocktail and watching Ben's eyes light up if someone mentioned he was going to direct *To Catch a Thief*.

"You didn't want to have anything to do with local theater," Angelica reminded her. "Or is it a date? Are you going with Josh?"

"Josh and I are just friends," Rosie snapped. She put her fork down and took a gulp of wine.

"He is cute, if you're attracted to blond surfer types," Angelica said casually.

"I'm not attracted to anyone." Rosie glared at Angelica. "I just thought it might be a good idea. I don't want to be a burden and you're the one who said I should get involved in local theater."

"Don't be silly. We don't expect you to be the life of the party, but you must meet all our friends. And you can see a play anytime,"

Estelle said severely. "All of Oscar's wonderful music people will be there. You'll meet Ryan Addams and Colby Young."

"Colby Young! Well, that is great news. He's my favorite artist." Angelica beamed. "We can't wait."

Rosie sat silently at the dining room table while Morris served coffee. Suddenly tears sprang to her eyes. For the last week she had felt at home, but with Angelica and Dirk in the house, she was reminded she was a visitor. Angelica told her parents tales from pre-production of *The Philadelphia Story;* they talked about her brother, Sam, in Vermont, and their Irish setters, Rollo and Portia.

"Rosie," Estelle said when everyone finished their coffee. "Will you join me in the library, I want to show you something."

Angelica and Dirk went with Oscar to the garage to see his classic car collection. Rosie followed Estelle to a room with paneled walls and thick oriental rugs. A piano stood in one corner and two velvet armchairs faced the fireplace.

"You didn't look very happy at dinner," Estelle began, pouring two shots of cognac and handing one to Rosie.

"It's great to see Angelica," Rosie replied brightly. She took the cognac and stared at the amber liquid.

"Angelica told me about her dinner with Ben at the Beverly Wilshire," Estelle began.

Rosie glanced at Estelle, trying to keep her voice steady. "You mean the dinner with Ben and Mary Beth, the head of his new production company."

"I think it's time to immerse yourself in something new," Estelle continued, sipping her cognac.

"I am thinking." Rosie sighed. "I sat at the beach all day trying to figure out what to do."

"And?" Estelle perched on a velvet ottoman.

"Dog walker, telemarketer, children's party planner." Rosie slumped into an armchair opposite her. "Josh suggested I open a fish taco stand."

Estelle studied the flower arrangement on the piano. "A fish taco stand! That's very interesting. Not a stand, that's tacky, but a proper shop in the village."

"I could never do that. I'm not a chef." Rosie shook her head.

"Nonsense, don't say never. Angelica raved about your tacos. Even Morris said they were delicious. I've always thought owning one's own shop would be great fun."

"I wouldn't know where to start. I haven't done anything like that," Rosie argued.

"It can't be harder than running a movie set," Estelle suggested. "It would be a wonderful way to channel your energy."

"You mean it would be a way to stop thinking about Ben." Rosie grimaced.

"I know you don't want to go back to Hollywood." Estelle crossed to the window and looked out on the lawn. It was dark and the outdoor lights glimmered like fireflies. "I like having you here in Montecito. I'd be sad if you left."

"I'm just in Montecito for the summer," Rosie reminded her.

"You can stay in the cottage as long as you like." Estelle turned to Rosie. "But you need to occupy yourself, and you need to do something you love."

"I met a young woman who owns a chocolate shop," Rosie ruminated. "I could ask her how she got started."

"Gold's Chocolates?" Estelle inquired. "I adore her chocolate truffles. If you open a store, I'll be your first customer and I'll bring my garden club."

"I should go find Angelica." Rosie stood up. She wasn't ready to start planning a new venture. "I haven't been able to drag her away from Dirk all night."

"They do seem quite attached," Estelle said meditatively. "I really do think a fish taco store is a good idea. I can picture it: ROSIE'S FISH TACOS in red and white letters."

"I'll think about it," Rosie promised. "You wanted to show me something?"

Estelle smiled like a cat basking in the sun. "I did."

Rosie walked towards the garage. The farther she got from the library the more far-fetched Estelle's idea seemed. Rosie didn't know anything about running a store.

But she pictured the village of Montecito, the cobblestone streets and the oak trees hanging into the middle of the road. She would wear a red-and-white apron and there would be a line of sunburned tourists at the counter. When the shop closed she'd chat with the other shopkeepers, and when she went home she'd be too tired to think about Ben.

"There you are!" Angelica exclaimed as Rosie opened the garage door. "You keep disappearing."

"Your mother wanted to show me something," Rosie explained.

"Let's get out of here. Daddy has a 1963 Aston Martin Dirk is crazy about." Angelica strode towards the porch. "If he calls the car 'darling' one more time I'll be jealous."

Rosie followed Angelica to the back porch and they sat on a swing facing the lake. Crickets chirped in the dark and the stars were diamonds on a bolt of black velvet. The sprinklers came on and filled the air with a soft, white noise.

"I'm sorry I ran off last night," Rosie said, breathing in the scent of damp grass and flowers.

"I didn't mean to drop the atom bomb about Ben and Mary Beth," Angelica answered and leaned back in the swing.

"Ben seemed so happy to hear from me when I called him the other day." Rosie remembered his voice on the phone when she invited him to the party.

"I'm sure he was happy to hear from you. He has always loved you, Rosie, he just can't see straight." Angelica adjusted the ruffles on her blouse. "He's moving so fast climbing the Hollywood ladder. He's like a racehorse with blinders on."

"I don't want to think about Ben now." Rosie swung her legs in front of her. "I'm sorry I ragged on you about Dirk. He might be the greatest British export since Smarties."

"Dirk is gorgeous," Angelica giggled. "Sometimes I just want to sit and stare at his profile."

"He does look like Ewan McGregor," Rosie admitted. "And that cleft on his chin is dreamy."

"And he's so sophisticated," Angelica continued. "Matthew's idea of dressing up was putting on a clean t-shirt. Dirk wears linen blazers and shoes with tassels."

"Ben always wore the same pair of loafers," Rosie remembered. "He probably has a whole wardrobe of shoes now made of every kind of reptile."

"Rosie, you have to stop."

"I know you're right. I told you I didn't want to think about him." Rosie nodded. "I considered going to BA."

"BA?" Angelica asked.

"Ben Anonymous," Rosie joked. "Estelle wants me to decide what I'm going to do next and she's right; limbo is lonely."

"Dirk's place has an extra bedroom," Angelica offered. "It's the size of a broom closet, but it's yours if you want it."

"I'm actually considering not going back to LA." Rosie leaned back against the cushions.

"What are you talking about?" Angelica rocked back and forth on the swing. "Of course you're coming back! Los Angeles is a big city and Ben is one guy. You'll meet a new man the first night we go for cocktails at Chateau Marmont."

"I don't want to meet someone new," Rosie insisted. "And I don't want to work at a production company."

"What else would you do?" Angelica asked.

"Josh suggested I open a fish taco shop," Rosie said tentatively. "Your mother thought it was a good idea."

"In Montecito?" Angelica raised her eyebrows.

"Why not?" Rosie answered more stridently than she felt. "Estelle said I could stay in the cottage. There's plenty of money in our joint account. I could lease a space in the village, serve fish tacos, maybe lemonade and fruit drinks."

"Open a store in Santa Monica until you find a new film project," Angelica suggested. "Set it up and have some struggling actor run it when you go back to the studio."

"I don't want to hang out in Santa Monica or Venice or West Hollywood," Rosie insisted. "I like Montecito. Butterfly Beach is so peaceful: I'm not afraid of being run over by skateboarders or people on rollerblades, it's just waves and sand."

"You're thirty not fifty!" Angelica exclaimed. "You'll never meet anyone to date here. The tourists come in pairs and the men who live here have wives who'd demand big alimony if they got divorced."

"I'm not looking for a boyfriend or a husband," Rosie said, the idea of a fish taco shop becoming more real. She could smell cod sizzling on an industrial stove and see tacos wrapped in silver paper with her name scrawled in red letters.

"You're going to sink your time and money into tacos," Angelica challenged her. "All you'll end up with are calluses on your hands and the smell of fish in your clothes."

"I'll wear perfume," Rosie suggested. "And I'll lather my hands with skin cream at night."

"You promise you won't start wearing surfer t-shirts and flip-flops all the time?"

"Scout's honor." Rosie crossed her hands over her chest.

"My best friend is becoming a fishmonger and it's my fault," Angelica moaned.

"Maybe I'll be the next Casey's Cupcakes," Rosie offered. "She made a fortune on cupcakes and was featured on television."

"Casey sold cupcakes with flavors like amaretto truffle and chocolate velvet. Her stores were all pink and white and the cupcakes were presented in gorgeously decorated boxes."

"Then I'll be the Casey of fish tacos. Everyone loves fish tacos, it's bound to be a success," Rosie said with a lot more confidence than she felt.

Rosie searched the kitchen for a pen and paper. She wanted to write her to-do list while it was fresh in her mind. In the morning she would visit Rachel and ask if she knew any storefronts for rent. She felt like she was jumping off a high-dive board, but the rush was strangely exhilarating.

"I thought I heard someone in here." Morris came in from the hallway. "Angelica's boy toy asked for some Earl Grey tea."

"Dirk's not a boy toy," Rosie admonished him. "He's a Shakespearean actor."

"I'd like to get a look at his passport to see if he's really British." Morris sniffed. "I bet the closest he's come to performing Shakespeare is a high school stage in middle America." Morris took out the silver tea set. He found a tea towel and polished the teapot.

"Estelle said you tried my fish tacos." Rosie looked up from her notepad.

"I'm a big fan of tacos. Every night Peg makes me sausage rolls or meat pies." Morris filled the kettle with water. "She thinks I still miss British food. I don't have the heart to tell her I'd rather have a piece of salmon with steamed vegetables or a taco with guacamole and grated American cheese."

"Do you really think they were good?" Rosie asked anxiously.

"Best Mexican food I've had since the two days I spent in Puerto Vallarta." He nodded. He took silver dessert spoons out of the drawer and rubbed them with the tea towel.

"I'm thinking of opening a fish taco shop in the village," she said. "Estelle thinks it's a great idea. Angelica is positive I'm committing myself to a manless purgatory."

Morris waited for the kettle to boil. He put two cups and a jug of whole cream on the tray.

"Would I have been happier if I joined another boy band instead of becoming a butler?" He placed tea bags in the cups. "There were British bands arriving at LAX every day. Oscar could have fixed me up and I'd still be living the high life: Beverly Hills mansions, screaming fans, male models. Maybe I would have found a nice guy and settled down: an entertainment lawyer with blue eyes and curly black hair," Morris mused.

"You think I should go back to LA?" Rosie asked.

"I think there are no guarantees." He added a bowl of sugar to the tray. "But when I take Mr. Pullman his afternoon cocktail and he thanks me for keeping his day running smoothly, I'm happy. When I see a closet of shirts I've pressed and a drawer of shoes I've shined, I'm proud. When the Pullmans greet dinner guests and I know the table is set so perfectly they could entertain the Duke and Duchess of Cambridge, I've done a good job."

"You are a wonderful butler," Rosie agreed. "The Pullmans are the lucky ones; they are fortunate to have you."

"And when I make a pretty girl smile"—Morris picked up the tray and looked at Rosie—"I'm the King of England."

Rosie waited till Morris went upstairs. She poured herself a cup of tea and studied the sheet of paper. She wrote *Rosie's Fish Tacos* in large flowery letters and numbered the items on her to-do list.

Seven

Rosie stood in front of the shop's window and studied the white sign with her name in cursive letters. The lettering was the deep red of her favorite Bobbi Brown lip gloss. There was a heart over the "I" in her name and a red rose after the word "tacos."

"What do you think?" Rosie turned to Rachel, who was standing on the sidewalk beside her.

"I think you are too calm for someone who's never owned a shop before." Rachel wore a navy smock with a white apron tied around her waist.

"It still doesn't seem real," Rosie said. It had only been two weeks since she decided to open the fish taco shop and now she was standing in front of her own storefront. It was a tiny space three doors down from Rachel's chocolate shop. The floor was white-and-red linoleum and there was a white Formica counter where customers could stand and eat their tacos.

"You have two weeks till your grand opening." Rachel took a toffee out of her pocket and popped it in her mouth. "You could quit before it's too late."

"Josh is posting flyers up and down Butterfly Beach. He promised that every surfer within a twenty-mile radius is going to be at the opening."

"Is that why your smile is wider than my hips?" Rachel asked curiously. "Has Josh been helping you after hours?"

"Your hips are perfect," Rosie countered. "He has been coming around. I couldn't have done it without him."

The fish taco shop had taken shape faster than Rosie thought possible. Rachel had told Rosie about a soup and sandwich store that was closing. Rosie peeked in the window and saw iron pots and an antique cash register. There was a tiny storeroom and enough space behind the counter for one person to chop and cook. Rosie walked inside, smelled garlic and clams, and knew it would be perfect.

Rosie signed a year's lease and moved in at the end of the week. On her first morning she sat in front of her to-do list, sipping coffee and biting the end of her pencil. Her hands were clammy with fear and she wondered what she had gotten herself into.

"I didn't think you would take me seriously." Josh appeared at the door. He wore gray pants and a long-sleeved t-shirt. His hair was damp and there was blond stubble on his chin.

"Think I can't do it?" Rosie asked with more confidence than she felt.

"You survived Hollywood." Josh entered the shop and looked around. "This will be easier than making Play-Doh figures at preschool."

"The owner left the stove and the fridge." Rosie consulted her list. "But I've never been to the fish market and I don't know how to import Hawaiian sea salt."

"First you take this list and tear it up." Josh grabbed the piece of paper from her hands.

"Don't!" Rosie shrieked, spilling coffee on the counter.

"You tackle one thing at a time." Josh tore the paper into ribbons. He put one piece in front of Rosie and tucked the others into the empty cash register. "What does this piece of paper say?"

Rosie read aloud: "Buy cooking utensils, order signage, get business permit."

"You do those things, and when you're finished you get the next piece of paper." Josh pointed to the cash register. "If you do everything at once it's overwhelming."

"Okay." Rosie nodded, her shoulders relaxing. "Today I will buy cooking utensils."

Josh walked to the door. He turned around and his eyes were the color of cornflowers. "I'll come by after work and check you didn't do anything else."

Every day Rosie visited produce patches and fish markets and flower stalls. She drove inland to farms that sold tomatoes, avocados, and lettuce. The local dairy sold cottage cheese, and she found a wholesaler that imported Italian sodas. Each night she checked items off her list and added new treasures to the supply room.

Josh stopped by most evenings to check on her progress. Sometimes he brought dinner and they sat on boxes in the empty shop, going over her list.

"You don't have to do this." Rosie sliced pizza and poured glasses of orange soda. "Shouldn't you be surfing?"

"I surf every morning," Josh answered, unfolding his napkin. "I want to help; I don't want Hollywood to win."

"What do you mean?" Rosie sat opposite him. Her shoulders were sunburned and her calves ached from trudging through an avocado farm.

"People our age think they have to live in a city to be successful." Josh ate his pizza slowly.

"Like Sally, the girl from UC Santa Barbara?" Rosie asked.

"Even my sister ran off to San Francisco after high school." Josh nodded. "They don't believe you can be happy in a small town. I love Montecito, it has everything I need."

"Montecito isn't any small town." Rosie drank her soda. "It's Oz."

"I'm sick of those LA weekenders coming up here and flashing their Armani sunglasses and their platinum Amex cards." Josh reached for a second slice.

"I didn't know I was heading a cause," Rosie joked. "I thought I was opening a taco shop."

"It's going to be great." Josh smiled and something in Rosie felt brighter. "You're going to be the fish taco queen."

One evening they locked up the store and drove to the beach. It was too late to surf, so they sat on the sand and ate enchiladas from a Mexican restaurant on the Pacific Coast Highway.

"You have to sample the competition," Josh explained, laying nachos and salsa on a blanket.

"You know a lot about owning a business." Rosie dug her toes into the sand.

"I've been saving for my own business since I started working at the Classic Car Showroom." Josh ate a handful of chips. "Right after I graduated from UCSB."

"You've been saving for twelve years?" Rosie gulped.

"I'm not in a hurry." He shrugged. "But it would be great if the showroom was mine."

"I feel like one of those LA weekenders." Rosie blushed, scooping salsa onto a chip. "Flashing my money and buying a store."

"At least you're not wearing Armani sunglasses." Josh studied her in the fading light. Rosie wore navy leggings and a white cotton t-shirt. Her hair fell loosely to her shoulders and her cheeks were brown from the sun.

The breeze picked up and Rosie wished she brought a sweater. Suddenly she wondered what it would feel like if Josh put his arms around her. He was so different from Ben, with his blond curly hair and broad chest. Ben was lean and wiry and always seemed to be looking for the next thing. Josh sat on the sand and gazed at the ocean as if he never wanted to be anywhere else.

She shifted her body to be closer to him, but he stood up and stuffed the nachos in the bag.

"This has been great, but I've got to go. I have to put in a couple of hours at the Pullmans'." Josh folded the blanket and hiked to the car.

Rosie blushed, wondering if he knew what she had been thinking. She brushed the sand off her legs and ran to the car to keep warm.

"Does Josh have a crush on you?" Rachel asked now, sitting on the bench outside the store.

"Hardly." Rosie sat beside her, satisfied that the sign looked perfect. "He's never touched me; it's like hanging out with a brother."

"Do you want him to touch you?" Rachel inquired.

"Josh is anti-relationships," Rosie shook her head. "He's easy to be around because we're just friends."

"If you wanted a friend you'd buy a puppy." Rachel stood up. "I have to go wrap a chocolate log. I'm meeting Patrick's grandmother."

"It's getting serious?" Rosie smiled at her new friend.

"Patrick's started talking about children," Rachel said. "He wants four kids and a house with a goldfish pond."

"What do you want?" Rosie prompted.

"I can't think about the future, I'm too worried about tonight. The only thing scarier than a Jewish father is a Catholic grandmother." Rachel frowned. "I hope she likes chocolate nougat."

Rosie sat on the bench, watching couples stroll through the village. The street was almost empty. Tourists were in their hotel rooms changing for dinner. Soon the restaurants would open and men in sport shirts would escort their dates to candlelit tables.

Rosie thought about Rachel and Patrick, and Angelica and Dirk, and Ben and Mary Beth. The store occupied her during the day, but at night she was alone. She lay in the middle of the four-poster bed each night feeling like someone shipwrecked on a desert island.

"I called your cell phone but you didn't answer." Josh bounded towards her. "I sold a 1964 Bugatti today! We need to celebrate."

"That's fantastic." Rosie beamed. "Let's go to Gino's Pizza, I'll buy."

"I'm taking you somewhere special." Josh grinned. "I'll drive, but you have to close your eyes."

"Why do I have to close my eyes?" Rosie ran into the store and grabbed her purse. She locked the front door and followed Josh to his car.

"It's a secret destination." His blue eyes sparkled. "You're a local now, this is your initiation."

Rosie climbed into the passenger seat of Josh's hatchback. The car smelled of surfboard wax, and Josh's surfboard lay on towels in the back.

"Don't look in the backseat," he warned. "It's a surprise."

"Is it a dead body and we're driving to the graveyard?" she asked. "If anything happens to me, Estelle will send her Irish setters to find me."

"Don't you trust me?" Josh said mischievously, turning to Rosie. His cheeks were tan and his blond curls reached his collar.

"I trust you." Rosie squeezed her eyes shut. "But I feel like I'm in a Hitchcock movie. The heroine accepts a ride from a charming man she barely knows and disappears."

Josh drove out of the village towards the mountains. The breeze touched Rosie's cheeks, and she heard leaves rustling in the trees. They parked on the side of the road and Josh instructed her to open her eyes.

"Where are we?" Rosie wondered aloud. The car was parked on a wide lane with oak trees. There was a tall fence covered with ivy. Behind the fence there were bushes and in the distance the outline of a large house.

"Follow me," Josh instructed. He stepped out of the car and turned towards the fence. "But be quiet."

"Are we robbing a house?" Rosie asked in alarm.

"We're not stealing anything, and technically the house belongs to the public. We're just entering without authorization." Josh took a basket out of the backseat and inched along the fence. He walked till he found a break in the ivy. He felt for a latch, and swung open the gate.

Rosie entered behind him, jumping as the gate closed. They were in the middle of a garden with trees shaped as animals. There were gorillas and camels and lions. Rosie felt like she was in some strange storybook circus. Any minute the gorillas would start talking and the lions would charge towards her.

"What are we doing here?" Rosie's eyes were wide.

"Just follow me." Josh grinned.

Rosie followed him through a maze of gardens, each more elaborate than the last. There was a Japanese garden bursting with pink and white blossoms. They passed a water garden with floating lilies, and a tropical garden with birds of paradise and purple irises.

Finally they entered a small garden with low-lying plants. A butterfly rested on almost every leaf. Rosie had never seen so many butterflies. She stood still as a statue, afraid if she moved they'd fly away.

"This is my favorite," Josh said as if he created the garden. "It's called the butterfly garden. All the flowers contain food attractive to butterflies. The butterflies lay their eggs and feast for days before they fly away."

"They're like kaleidoscopes." Rosie peered at a butterfly with gold-and-turquoise wings. "I feel like I'm in *The Lion, the Witch and the Wardrobe*. When is the Ice Queen going to appear and cast a spell on us?"

"She can't, she's dead," Josh replied. "Let me arrange our picnic, and I'll explain."

Josh spread a checkered blanket on the ground and opened the basket. There was a loaf of bread and a jar of peanut butter and a container of jam. He unscrewed a jug of milk and handed a cup to Rosie.

"We're having peanut butter and jelly?" She laughed.

"I asked Morris to pack a picnic basket; he said peanut butter and jelly was your favorite," he confessed. "I'm a terrible cook. I can heat up cold pizza or cook rice and beans, but I thought you've had enough Mexican food."

"My fingers are turning green from guacamole," Rosie admitted and sipped her milk. "Now, tell me where we are. I don't want to be stopped by some security guard with a semiautomatic and a German shepherd."

"A Polish opera singer named Ganna Walska bought the house in the 1940s and spent four decades creating the gardens. She went through six husbands and every time she got divorced she poured more money into the grounds." Josh handed Rosie a sandwich. "When we were kids we used to sneak through a hole in the fence and play hide-and-go-seek. Ganna would come out with a broom, shrieking to get off her property."

"You were a little thug." Rosie grinned and pulled off a corner of the sandwich.

"Sometimes we'd come at night, and we'd see Ganna waltzing outside in a ball gown. She died thirty years ago and they opened the property to the public. It's called Lotusland now. I haven't been back in a long time."

"It's like an enchanted forest." Rosie lay on the blanket and looked up at the stars. "If we fall asleep the trees will wake up and talk."

"It's not every day I sell a Bugatti." Josh lay down next to her. "And you've been working hard, I figured you needed a break."

"I lie awake at night and think I'm crazy," Rosie admitted. "I don't know anything about owning a store."

Josh's arm brushed against hers, and she could see his muscles through his t-shirt.

"You're pretty brave to try something new." Josh raised himself on his elbow and turned towards her.

Rosie stopped staring at the stars and glanced at Josh. She didn't know if she lifted her face or if he lowered his, but suddenly they were kissing. His mouth fell on hers, and his hands traveled over her body.

"You're so beautiful, you taste like milk and peanut butter," Josh whispered into her hair.

"You say that to all the girls," Rosie joked, wanting him to keep touching her.

"There aren't any girls," he answered, pulling away and sitting up abruptly.

"I didn't mean that," she said hurriedly. "I'm not good at accepting compliments."

Rosie sat up and leaned against Josh's chest. She wanted him to kiss her again, but he picked up his sandwich and started eating.

"When I was a kid I liked to pretend I discovered a pirate's treasure," Josh said. "I spent hours deciding how I'd divvy it up. I'd give my mother a diamond tiara and my sister a gold charm bracelet. I'd hand out gold coins to all my friends and I'd give my dad a silver money clip."

Rosie sat silently, her knee resting against his. She could still taste his lips and feel the weight of his chest against her breasts.

"But I looked at the adults I knew and none of them seemed happy even though they lived in huge estates and wore fancy clothes. Ganna Walska wore a million-dollar sapphire-and-diamond pendant," Josh continued. "But she always seemed so sad."

"Jewelry can be beautiful, like butterflies or classic cars," Rosie offered.

"I guess you're right." Josh turned as if he just remembered she was there. "Let's finish our sandwiches and then we should go. We don't want someone to find us or disturb Ganna's ghost."

Josh packed up the picnic basket and led Rosie through the maze of gardens. Rosie held his hand tightly, afraid she'd trip in the dark. They climbed in the car and drove to the village. The wind had picked up and she closed the car window.

"I'm sorry if I rambled," Josh said as he pulled up behind Rosie's car. "Lotusland brought up a lot of old memories."

"I had a great evening." Rosie thanked him. "I've never had a picnic in a magic garden."

"I'll see you tomorrow." Josh leaned over and kissed her cheek.

Rosie got in her car and touched her fingers to her mouth. She turned on the ignition and watched Josh drive away.

Eight

Rosie stood in the Pullmans' kitchen the day before the Fourth of July, chopping onions. Every inch of counter space was piled with food: plates of chips, bowls of salsa, platters of sliced meat and cubed cheese. There were whole watermelons, crates of mangoes, bunches of purple grapes, and boxes of peaches and nectarines. Rosie could barely move without bumping into stacks of plates, rows of glasses, and gleaming piles of silverware.

"Hi, Rosie." Estelle swept in, carrying linen napkins. She wore khaki slacks, an orange sweater, and white sneakers. Her face was free of makeup except for a light powder and lipstick. "It is so good of you to help. The caterers are buzzing around, but they don't seem to be doing anything. I found two of them feeding bread to the ducks."

"Hopefully just stale crusts." Rosie put down the knife and brushed tears from her eyes.

"Are you crying, dear?" Estelle stepped closer.

"I've been chopping onions for hours." Rosie sniffed, wiping her hands on her jeans.

"Rosie, sit down." Estelle pointed to the kitchen table. "You've been so quiet the last few days. You've said almost nothing at dinner and Morris said you haven't been eating breakfast."

"I'm not hungry in the morning," Rosie answered.

"You used to wolf down Peg's blueberry pancakes. I hope you're not working too hard! You didn't have to help with the July Fourth party."

"I want to help," Rosie said, and pushed the hair from her eyes. "It gives me a chance to try my recipe before the store opens."

"Did you call Ben and tell him not to come to the party?" Estelle inquired.

"I don't care if he comes." Rosie shrugged.

"It doesn't look that way to me. Would you like me to call him, or Angelica could tell him not to come," Estelle offered. She folded napkins into neat squares and stacked them on the counter.

"Ben and I were together for ten years." Rosie looked at Estelle. "I should be able to be in the same house with him. Anyway, he probably won't come. He's probably attending some celebrity-filled bash in Malibu."

"It will be a fabulous party and I want you to have fun," Estelle replied. "We'll have a pancake breakfast in the morning, followed by games on the lawn. In the afternoon we'll move to the pool. I've hired a magician and a juggler to perform. In the evening there will be cocktails on the porch, followed by dinner on the lawn. I hired the most marvelous jazz band, and there will be a twelve-tier chocolate cake for dessert."

"A magician!" Rosie exclaimed.

"Thursday we'll have champagne brunch in the conservatory. Nobody gets up before noon, but I instructed Peg to leave coffee and muffins in the kitchen, just in case. After brunch, Oscar will lead a tour of the grounds. People from LA love to see his car collection and all his Grammys. I'm going to show off my new tea roses: my Elizabeth Taylor and Richard Burton are in bloom." Estelle paused. "The grand finale will be a magic show on the lawn! I know magicians are for children, but this guy is marvelous. If Ben shows up, you can ask him to saw Ben in half."

"I'll think about it." Rosie grinned.

"Really, Rosie, you are as pale as my tuberoses." Estelle inspected her closely. "If you're nervous about the fish taco shop, you can delay the opening."

"I can't wait for the opening!" Rosie insisted. She stood up and walked to the sink.

"It's going to be a huge success. I've told my garden club and my book club all about Rosie's Fish Tacos."

"I hope you're right. Sometimes I think I have no idea what I'm doing," Rosie said uncertainly. She rinsed a tomato and picked up the knife.

"I thought Josh was helping you at the store." Estelle folded the last napkin. "Morris said he prepared a picnic for you and Josh the other day."

"Josh was helping." Rosie's eyes filled with tears. "But I haven't seen him in a few days."

"Rosie! You are crying and there isn't an onion in sight," Estelle exclaimed.

"Josh and I were getting to know each other." Rosie put down the knife. "We'd go to the beach after work or just sit around and eat pizza. He was a great help getting the shop ready."

"What happened, dear?" Estelle put her hand on Rosie's.

"A few nights ago he took me to these incredible gardens called Lotusland. We had a picnic under the stars and he kissed me."

"Lotusland!" Estelle started. "I haven't heard that name in years."

"After he kissed me, he behaved oddly." Rosie grimaced. "I haven't seen him since. He hasn't been at the store and I haven't seen him on the grounds."

"Oh, I see," Estelle said slowly. She fiddled with her earrings as if she was thinking what to say. "Do you have feelings for him?"

"Josh is funny and sensitive and he has the most beautiful blue eyes." Rosie gulped. "But he doesn't believe in relationships or marriage."

"A kiss is hardly a proposal." Estelle tapped her fingernails on the table. "If you like him, you should tell him."

"Tell him?" Rosie repeated.

"Tell him you enjoy his company." Estelle nodded. "You can even say you love the color of his eyes, men like compliments. If you let him know you're not looking for a commitment he won't run away."

"It's nice to have a friend," Rosie said, remembering the way his eyes crinkled when he smiled. "He made me laugh."

"I saw him in the garage earlier." Estelle waved towards the French doors. "He's polishing Oscar's cars for the weekend."

"I'll go talk to him." Rosie wiped her eyes. She walked to the French doors and turned around. "How did his parents die?"

"What did you say?" Estelle looked up from the napkins.

"Josh mentioned his parents are dead," Rosie continued. "But he didn't say anything else."

"Goodness!" Estelle jumped and walked towards the entry. "I forgot they're delivering the ice sculpture! I better tell them where the walk-in freezer is or it'll melt all over my foyer."

Rosie watched Estelle cross the lawn and wondered why she was in such a hurry. Could there be something Estelle wasn't telling her? She gathered a stack of napkins and reminded herself to ask Estelle about it later.

Rosie opened the garage door and saw headlamps and gleaming bumpers. She smelled leather and wax and cherry air freshener. A radio blasted and there was a silver tray with half a turkey sandwich and a glass of lemonade.

"Hi!" she called out, suddenly wondering if she should turn around and leave.

"Hey." Josh poked his head out of an orange Fiat. He wore a faded t-shirt and khaki shorts and flip-flops on his feet.

Rosie remembered the touch of his lips on hers and the weight of his chest. She tried to smile, but her face froze and she glanced nervously at her hands.

"I was just passing by," she explained. "Estelle said you were polishing cars for the party."

"Oscar wants every car to shine." Josh nodded. "I've been working around the clock."

"Need any help?" She walked towards the Fiat. "I've been on onion-chopping duty, but I had to take a break. My eyes were watering and my feet were killing me."

"I'm almost done." He put down a jar of car wax. "Just the Aston Martin and the Bentley."

"Then I better go, there is still lots to do." She paused and looked at Josh. "You've been such a help with the taco shop, I wanted to return the favor."

"I owe you an apology." Josh touched her shoulder. "I asked you to a picnic and I kissed you."

"Didn't we apologize enough when we first met?" Rosie smiled.

"I kissed you and then I disappeared," he said firmly.

"You've been busy getting ready for the party." She ran her fingers over the Fiat's bumper.

"I was scared," Josh continued as if Rosie hadn't spoken. "I don't want to lose your friendship."

"How would you do that?" Rosie asked, sitting on a workbench against the wall.

Rosie studied a silver Porsche with chrome wheels and black

feather seats. She imagined sitting in the passenger seat, cruising along the Pacific Coast Highway. Josh would be driving, his surfboard sticking up in the back. He'd point out surf spots with one hand draped across her thigh.

"Some people can't sing or draw." Josh sat beside her. "I can't be with someone long-term—"

"Singing and drawing are talents," Rosie interrupted.

"So is being in a relationship," he said earnestly. "I can't argue like some couples, and act as if things are going well when I think they're about to fail."

"Not everyone is like Sally. Just because she broke up with you because you didn't want to be a lawyer doesn't mean it would happen again. Lots of couples want the same things."

"Like you and Ben? Or Angelica and Matthew?"

"Like Oscar and Estelle, or Rachel and Patrick," Rosie countered.

"Wait till Rachel and Patrick have to choose between having a rabbi or a priest at their wedding." He chuckled. "Or when they have to decide whether the Easter bunny will come to their house or if they will put up a Christmas tree."

"It was just one kiss," Rosie said quietly. "It didn't have to mean anything."

"You're smart and sensitive, but you're also beautiful." He touched her hand. "I don't want to have a fling and lose a friend."

"So you only have flings with enemies?" Rosie tried to laugh.

"I meet pretty women sometimes," Josh admitted. "But I don't often meet someone who's happy sharing peanut butter and jelly and a carton of milk. Or someone who's happy sitting on the sand and watching me surf."

"Should I have demanded caviar and champagne?" She punched his arm playfully. "Or expected you to take me to the opera?"

"I shouldn't have kissed you." He took her hand and held it in his palm.

"Kissing was nice." Rosie nodded and remembered what Estelle said. "But I could use a friend who makes a mean peanut butter sandwich."

"That's a relief. Thank god I learned how to spread jam on a slice of bread." Josh wiped his brow.

"At least you're not allergic to peanut butter," she answered, and thought of Ben. "When you're around I can eat peanut butter whenever I like."

Rosie sat in the back of the Bentley while Josh polished the dashboard. The steering wheel was maple and there was an ivory chessboard between the seats. They chatted about the Fourth of July party and the American flag Estelle had created in the flower bed.

"I usually stay in the garage the whole weekend and avoid the party." Josh shuddered. "There are too many fake tans strutting around the lawn."

"Estelle wants to introduce me to all the guests." Rosie rolled her eyes. "She wanted me to print business cards announcing the grand opening of Rosie's Fish Tacos."

"If you need to escape you can hide in the garage," he offered.

"I'll keep it in mind." She glanced at her watch. "I should go. I told Estelle I'd help with the place cards."

"Don't let her put you next to an aging movie executive with a hairpiece and false teeth," he grinned. "He'll promise you a job as long as you take a spin with him in his convertible."

"I'll make sure I sit next to Colby Young," she teased him.

"Colby Young is nineteen!" he exclaimed.

"Nothing wrong with a little eye candy." She smiled and turned towards the exit.

✳

Rosie walked outside and took a deep breath. She was relieved that she and Josh were friends. She hadn't realized how she missed his laugh, the way his eyes sparkled when he talked.

Workers strung colored lanterns over the grass and carried vases bursting with flowers. Round tables were draped with silk table-cloths and topped with silver candelabras. There was a dance floor painted with red roses and a stage full of gleaming brass instruments.

"What do you think?" Estelle had changed out of her khakis and sneakers. Her floppy hat covered her forehead, and she wore white slacks and an emerald-green blouse.

"It's a scene from *A Midsummer Night's Dream*," Rosie breathed.

"We're going to serve prime rib and oysters on the half shell and jumbo shrimp. I reminded the band I wanted them to play Cole Porter and Louis Armstrong."

"It's gorgeous." Rosie felt a pinprick of excitement. There would be twinkling lights and waiters passing around champagne flutes. Maybe Ben would apologize for everything that happened and she'd dance and eat oysters. The mist would settle over the lawn and the air would smell of cigars and perfume and the whole night would be unforgettable.

Rosie heard Ben's voice before she saw him. She was chatting with Angelica in the library when she heard a couple exclaim over the paintings in the hall.

"Is that a real David Hockney?" a female voice asked.

"I've been here before," the man responded. "The house is full of original artwork. There's a Manet in the living room and a Degas in the conservatory."

Rosie gripped her champagne glass so tightly she thought it would splinter in her hand.

"Breathe," Angelica instructed. Angelica wore a white flapper dress and double strands of pearls around her neck. Ruby earrings dangled from her ears, and she wore a sapphire ring on her right hand.

"We need to start a personal collection, sweet cakes," the woman continued. "Some modern pieces, a Schnabel or a de Kooning."

"I love Schnabel," the man agreed. "His plate paintings were extraordinary."

"Sweet cakes!" Rosie fumed when the couple had wandered off. "Mary Beth has known Ben for two months and she's already calling him sweet cakes. What's he going to be in a year: honey pie? Why is he here with her anyway! I'm the one who invited him; how dare he bring that viper in a skirt and heels."

"Ben didn't bring her," Angelica said slowly. "She's the plus one of Scott Hines. He's a film producer who is friends with my father."

"I don't understand." Rosie's heart beat faster.

"All the guests are allowed a plus one," Angelica explained. "My mother says people in Hollywood change partners so frequently it's impossible to keep track of who is dating whom. Mary Beth came with Scott; she must have found Ben as soon as she arrived."

"But Ben came to see me," Rosie said. "I'm the one who invited him. How dare she crash the party."

"She didn't technically crash it, she does have an invitation. You'll have to ask Ben why they're together," Angelica agreed. "I'm very sorry, I was about to tell you that Mary Beth is here. That's why I came to find you."

"I can't ask him now, he's busy planning his new collection. Ben doesn't even like art," Rosie continued, too angry to respond to Angelica. "Ben and I have only been in New York once and we didn't even go to the Met. We spent all our time in the East Village watching low-budget films by NYU students."

"I'd like a Schnabel in my apartment." Angelica sipped her champagne. "I love his use of form and color."

"Ben was making it up. He wouldn't know a Schnabel if it was standing in front of him," Rosie fumed. "He loves films by Truffaut and Godard and Francis Ford Coppola."

"It doesn't matter if Ben has taken up nude water polo," Angelica interjected. "You're not together anymore."

"What's he going to do next?" Rosie demanded, and spilled champagne on her dress. "Perhaps he'll host dinner parties with live sharks as centerpieces."

"We didn't have to invite him," Angelica reminded her. "Why don't I tell them that you're feeling a little under the weather and it would be better if they left?"

"You and Dirk are going to spend four months on location with Ben and Mary Beth." Rosie grabbed a stack of napkins from the sideboard and patted the stain on her dress. "Now that she's here, I'm going to have to deal with it. I need to be able to hear their names without falling apart."

"It's barely been a month." Angelica hesitated. "Maybe it's too early to see Ben's face."

"Are you worried I'm going to make a scene?" Rosie asked. "I promise I'll behave."

"You might want to start by not shredding the cocktail napkins." Angelica pointed to the wad of napkins at Rosie's feet.

"I'm working on it," Rosie answered anxiously, and tossed the napkins in the garbage.

Rosie moved to the kitchen to check on her fish tacos. She stood at the window and lanterns swayed in the breeze and guests nibbled hors d'oeuvres. The band was playing "What a Wonderful World," and couples glided across the dance floor. It wasn't even dusk but there was already an unreal feeling in the air as if nothing existed beyond the tall iron gates.

Rosie's day had started off perfectly. Estelle had convinced her to have a massage, and she lay under hot towels having her body pulled and pummeled. She ate blueberry pancakes for breakfast and chatted with a few early arrivals. Then she jogged ten laps around the lake, went back to the cottage, and climbed under the down comforter.

When Rosie woke it was late afternoon. Sleek sports cars pulled up the driveway. The band was rehearsing, and she heard Estelle directing the caterers. She sat in the bath for a long time and when she stepped out she felt sexy and excited.

She slipped on her red silk dress and stepped into her new Manolos. She marched across the lawn feeling like Scarlett O'Hara in *Gone With the Wind*. She would worry about Ben and Josh and the fish taco shop tomorrow. Tonight she was going to enjoy the party.

But now she stood at the sink in the kitchen and her eyes filled with tears. She was suddenly back in their bedroom in Santa Monica with the sheets twisted on the floor. Ben had denied that anything happened and then finally mumbled Mary Beth's name. The man she had loved for ten years became a stranger in a single afternoon.

"You look like Nero watching Rome burn." Morris appeared in the kitchen. He wore white tie and tails and black wingtip shoes.

"Wow!" Rosie turned from the window. "You look fantastic."

"Oscar likes everyone to dress the part." Morris fiddled with his bow tie. "I don't mind. It reminds me of my stage days. Let me guess, Ben made an appearance."

"He hasn't seen me yet, but I heard his voice," Rosie acknowledged. "With Mary Beth, discussing art. Ben doesn't have any interest in art, the only things on our walls were movie posters. Mary Beth came with another guest, but she's attached herself to Ben like a barnacle on a rock."

"A few years ago Oscar held a small dinner party; Neil was the guest of honor. His latest album had just gone platinum and he arrived in a chauffeur-driven Rolls-Royce. I watched him step out of the car, followed by Amber and a couple of blond groupies. Neil passed right by me and didn't even nod."

"What did you do?" Rosie asked.

"I marched up to him during cocktails and asked him how his mum was. She had a bad case of gout and I asked if it was any better. He almost spilled his drink, he was so desperate to get away from me."

"This is different. I invited Ben, but I didn't know Mary Beth would be at the party too. When he finds me it will be so embarrassing." Rosie wavered. "I'm better off if I go back to the cottage."

"You still have to talk to Ben. I followed Neil to the porch and we had a real conversation. I told him I loved being a butler and he admitted Amber was driving him crazy. She left her bras and panties all over the house and she ate cookies in bed." Morris chuckled. "Neil can't stand a mess."

"You think if I talk to Ben, he'll admit screwing Mary Beth was a mistake and beg me to take him back?" Rosie turned to Morris.

"Not necessarily." Morris shook his head. "You'll realize that you're both just people leading your lives: nothing's perfect and no one's got the lock on happiness."

"Ben sounds happy." Rosie grimaced. "He's starting a modern-art collection."

"Go on." Morris propelled her gently to the French doors. "You're going to be the fish taco queen."

Ben stood on the lawn with a tall blond woman and two men. He wore a black tuxedo and a white bow tie. His hair was slicked back and his cheeks were tan and smooth. He held a champagne flute in one hand and his arm curled around Mary Beth's back.

Rosie was transfixed. She couldn't move forward and she couldn't retreat. She closed her eyes, but when she opened them Ben was still there, whispering in Mary Beth's ear.

Mary Beth wore a flapper-style blue dress with a flared skirt. A strand of pearls hung around her neck and gold bangles dangled at her wrists. Her heels were so high they were almost stilts, and her dress was so sheer Rosie could see the outline of her thighs.

Rosie wanted to run to the cottage or turn back to the kitchen. But Morris guarded the door like a soldier, so she willed her legs to move forward.

"Rosie!" Ben said brightly as she approached the group. "There you are, I've been looking for you everywhere."

"Angelica and I were in the library and then I was talking to Morris in the kitchen," Rosie said, thinking that Ben had been too busy planning his new art collection to spend time looking for her. "It's nice to see you."

"It's great to see you too, you look lovely." Ben smiled. "This is Colby Young, and Colby's manager, Ryan Addams. And this is Mary Beth Chase. I didn't even know she was going to be here; we ran into each other when we arrived."

"Ben mentioned something about a Fourth of July party in Santa Barbara, but I've been so busy on the set, I didn't pay attention," Mary Beth said sweetly. "Then this morning an old friend said he was going to a holiday bash in Montecito and asked if I wanted to be his plus one." She fluttered her long eyelashes and chuckled. "It's such a small world, I should have known it was the same party. I called Ben but he was already on his way and I couldn't reach him."

"What a crazy coincidence," Rosie said through gritted teeth.

"I'm glad I came, it's a fabulous party." Mary Beth nodded at

Rosie and then turned her attention to Ryan. "Colby's new single is number one on iTunes!" She flashed a white smile. "How do you do it? You haven't let another artist get the number-one spot in months."

"It's all Colby," Ryan replied. He wore white tie and tails and white sneakers with purple laces. He was in his mid-thirties with short light brown hair and sharp cheekbones.

"It's never about the talent." Mary Beth leaned towards Ryan conspiratorially. "You have to tell me your secrets."

"Are you in movies or music?" Colby asked Rosie.

"I was in the movie business, but I'm sort of on sabbatical." Rosie blushed. "I'm staying with the Pullmans. I'm opening a fish taco shop in the village."

"I grew up in Pismo Beach!" Colby exclaimed. "I love fish tacos."

"Colby still eats like a teenager." Ryan chuckled. "We have to keep the tour bus stocked with Ho Hos and Twizzlers."

"He looks like a teenager," Mary Beth drawled. "Those blue eyes and baby cheeks."

"Colby turned twenty last month." Ryan smiled. "Broke the heart of every tween girl in America."

"How have you been?" Rosie turned to Ben.

"Shooting's almost wrapped, and I'm considering a few projects."

"Ben is so modest, that's what's refreshing about him," Mary Beth cut in. "All the major studios want him to direct; he gets new offers every day." She squeezed his arm. "Luckily he has me. I'll make sure he gets the deal that Ben Ford deserves."

"Rosie!" Angelica called from across the lawn. "I need you in the kitchen."

"Excuse me," Rosie mumbled, her tongue suddenly made of rubber.

"It was nice meeting you." Colby shook her hand. "Let us know when you open your taco shop; we'll come by and chow down!"

Rosie crossed the lawn and took deep breaths. She kept her eyes on Angelica, who stood at the top of the steps waving a white napkin.

"I wasn't going to cause a scene," Rosie insisted, climbing the steps to join her.

"You looked like you needed saving." Angelica followed Rosie into the kitchen and poured a shot of vodka.

"No, thank you." Rosie shook her head. "I've been drinking champagne."

"Champagne is sugar water; you need medicine. Drink it." She handed the glass to Rosie.

Rosie downed the shot and sank onto a chair. "It was humiliating. Mary Beth pretended she didn't know it was the same party that Ben was invited to, but I could tell she was lying. She only came because he was here; she practically glued herself to his side."

"Forget about it," Angelica instructed.

"She's a piranha!" Rosie took the bottle and poured a second shot. "No one is safe from her. She was ready to get into Ryan Addams' pants because he manages Colby Young."

"Does Colby really have that dimple on his chin or do they photoshop it in for his photos?" Angelica inquired.

"I don't know, I wasn't looking at Colby!" Rosie gasped. "I was being annihilated by a python in designer shoes. How can Ben stand next to her, let alone sleep with her?"

"Men have a fascination with snakes, it's something biblical," Angelica responded. "Ryan seemed kind of cute. I could get Dirk to fix you up with him."

"I don't want to be fixed up. I don't want to date. I don't even want to be at this party." Rosie's eyes filled with tears.

"Ben's the one who's missing out. He won't realize how good

he had it until you're gone for good," Angelica said firmly. "You're beautiful and smart and you're opening your own store. Morris said you've been spending a lot of time with Josh."

Tears fell down Rosie's cheeks. She remembered Josh's lips on her mouth. She thought about their conversation in the garage, how he just wanted to be friends.

"Josh and I are nothing," she whispered, and slipped outside. "I should leave before I embarrass myself and spoil your party."

"Rosie!" Angelica stood at the kitchen door.

Rosie took off her shoes and raced across the lawn. The band played "I've Got You Under My Skin" and she didn't stop until she reached the lake.

Rosie sat by the lake, throwing pebbles in the water. She couldn't face going back to the cottage. She had spent hours getting ready for the party, and she didn't want to see the bottle of perfume or her new lipstick sitting on the dressing table.

Her mind was blurry from vodka, but she saw Ben as clearly as if he was standing in front of her. His tux had fit so perfectly she knew it wasn't rented. He was a glossier, more sophisticated version of Ben, but when his eyes met hers there was a glimmer of the boy she knew.

Rosie thought about Mary Beth and had the urge to throw up. Mary Beth had looked at Rosie as if she was completely unimportant. She clutched Ben's arm like a gangster's moll in a blue dress and heels.

The grass was soft and Rosie lay back and closed her eyes. When she opened them again the lake was shrouded in fog and the music had stopped. It was midnight and the party must have ended an hour ago. Her legs were stiff and she was cold and damp.

She longed for a cup of hot chocolate and walked towards the house.

The lawn was almost deserted. Waiters loaded silver trays and band members packed up their instruments. The lights were on in the house, and voices drifted through the French doors. She looked closely and wondered if Ben and Mary Beth were still there.

The remains of the chocolate cake rested on a red silk tablecloth strewn with roses. Rosie grabbed a knife and cut herself a thin slice. She found a fork and sat at one of the round tables facing the dance floor.

"There you are!" a male voice exclaimed. "I've been looking for you everywhere."

Josh wore a white tuxedo jacket and a white silk shirt. His hair curled behind his ears and his blue eyes were luminous in the dark. He wore a black bow tie and he had a red handkerchief in his breast pocket.

Rosie wiped chocolate from her mouth. "I was feeding the ducks."

Josh sat down and picked up a fork. "This cake is amazing! Peg went all-out. Her prime rib was delicious and the oysters were perfect."

"I thought you hid in the garage all weekend," Rosie recalled.

"I came to find you," Josh offered. "I figured we could brave the party together."

"I didn't last very long," Rosie said, and smiled weakly. "You were right about the fake tans."

"It's like being at the circus, but the animals talk." Josh ate another bite of cake. "You look beautiful."

Rosie glanced at her wrinkled dress and looked at Josh. "You look pretty fancy."

"Estelle and Oscar take the party seriously." Josh smoothed his collar. "It's fun to dress up now and then. It's too bad we missed the band."

"Do you like to dance?" she asked, and ate a bite of frosting.

"I love jazz, I'm a huge Cole Porter fan." Josh nodded.

"I didn't feel like dancing," Rosie said, picturing Ben and Mary Beth standing so close they were almost one person.

"Let's dance now." Josh stood up. "There aren't any other guests to disturb us."

"We can't dance, the music stopped." Rosie waved at the empty stage.

"I'll hum." Josh took her hand. "I know all the tunes."

"I'm really cold. I fell asleep on the grass." Rosie felt the pressure of his palm on hers.

"I'll warm you up." Josh pulled her to her feet.

Josh led Rosie onto the dance floor and started humming "Begin the Beguine."

Rosie rested her cheek on his shoulder and his hand pressed the small of her back. She smelled Josh's aftershave and felt the stubble on his chin.

"Rosie," Josh whispered. "I'd like to kiss you."

Josh pushed Rosie's hair behind her ears and touched her lips. Then he stopped dancing and pulled her to him. He kissed her so urgently, Rosie couldn't catch her breath.

"Come with me," he urged.

"Where are we going?" she asked and wanted him to kiss her again.

Josh didn't answer. He walked quickly across the lawn, keeping her hand in his. He entered the garage and closed the door behind them.

"I can't see anything." Rosie peered into the darkness.

Josh reached the Bentley and opened the door. The interior light came on and bathed them in a yellow glow.

"Come here." He pulled Rosie into the car. He kissed her harder, sending an electric current down her spine.

She kissed him and tasted chocolate and champagne. "We shouldn't be in here," she said, rearranging her hair. "What if someone comes into the garage?"

"I just wanted to be with you somewhere warm and quiet." Josh took her hands and held them in his. "The caterers are still cleaning up in the kitchen."

"It reminds me of the party scene in *Sabrina*; it's one of my favorite movies." She leaned against the leather headrest. "Audrey Hepburn sees William Holden dancing with a woman on the tennis court. She's always been in love with him and hoped tonight they'd be together, so she's devastated. She sneaks into the garage and turns on all the car engines. Just when she's about to faint from carbon monoxide poisoning, Humphrey Bogart appears and saves her. She should be grateful, but she'd rather die than be without the man she loves."

Josh stiffened beside her and adjusted his bow tie.

"Is that how you feel? You're still in love with Ben and I'm the guy who's rescuing you?"

"No, of course not," Rosie said in surprise. "I was just remembering a scene from the movie."

"It doesn't sound similar to me at all," Josh responded and opened the car door. "Maybe this was a bad idea. We should go, it's late and someone might find us after all."

The mood was broken and Rosie didn't know how to get it back. Josh stepped onto the concrete floor and she followed him.

"I had a lovely time dancing." She peered at him in the dim light. "It was the best part of the party."

"So did I," he said, and his face softened. "I'm just tired, it's been a long day. I'll see you tomorrow."

*

Rosie entered the cottage and slipped off her sandals. Had she made a mistake with Josh by mentioning the movie? She didn't mean anything by it and she had enjoyed kissing him. His mouth was warm and when he held her she didn't think about anything else.

A car drove down the driveway and the last light on the lawn flickered off. She unzipped her dress and climbed onto the quilted bedspread. Her eyes closed from exhaustion and she fell asleep.

Nine

The late-morning sun filtered through the curtains and Rosie stretched her arms. It was the day after the Fourth of July party and people were lounging on the veranda, leafing through newspapers and sipping cups of coffee. Estelle had on a yellow hostess gown and a wide-brimmed hat, and Oscar wore white slacks and a V-neck vest.

The whole night had been too much: Mary Beth coming as another guest's plus one and seeing Ben and Mary Beth together for the first time. Mary Beth acting like some kind of viper and then Rosie falling asleep and waking up cold and damp beside the lake. And just when she and Josh were having a good time and she was finally enjoying herself, he got angry because he thought she was still pining over Ben.

Was she still in love with Ben? What did it matter anyway when Mary Beth was wrapped around him like Fourth of July streamers on a lamppost. Rosie had invited Ben to the party so they could talk and they hardly said a word to each other except to comment on the fish tacos and Colby Young's music.

Her phone lay on the table and she picked it up. Josh hadn't left any voicemails and she wondered if he was still upset. It had been lovely kissing him and she didn't want whatever they were starting to stop.

The phone buzzed and Ben's number appeared on the screen. She was tempted not to answer it, but then she'd spend all day wondering why he called.

"Hello," she said tentatively.

"Hi, Rosie. It's Ben. I hope I'm not calling too early."

"It's almost noon." Rosie glanced at the clock on the desk. "I was just getting ready to go to brunch."

"I called to apologize," he began. "I had no idea Mary Beth was coming; I was completely surprised when she appeared. I may have mentioned to her that you invited me to the Pullmans' Fourth of July party, but we've both been so busy. It was a last-minute thing for her. She and Scott have been friends for years and she thought it would be good for networking."

Rosie didn't know what upset her more. That Mary Beth pretended she didn't know it was the same party, or that Ben was so infatuated, he couldn't see that she was lying.

"I looked for you all night to talk to you in private," Ben cut into her thoughts. "But I couldn't find you. I wanted to know everything you've been up to."

"I'm very busy," she said, trying to keep her voice light. "You know, getting the taco shop off the ground and doing things around the estate."

"You certainly seem to have a lot going on," Ben agreed. "Are you too busy to meet me for brunch?"

Her palms sweated and she clutched the phone tightly. "Meet you for brunch today?"

"I'm staying at the Biltmore. Mary Beth had to go back to LA this morning, an emergency on her latest project. We could meet at the Coral Casino. They serve the best burgers in Santa Barbara."

The Coral Casino was part of the Four Seasons Biltmore and it was one of the most glamorous places on the coast. It was built in 1939 and all the big movie stars used to drive up the Pacific Coast Highway for its society events. She had seen pictures of Gary Cooper and Gregory Peck drinking martinis at the pool bar with the sun setting behind them and the palm trees lit by gold and silver lights.

"I suppose I could get away for a couple of hours," Rosie said, wondering if Estelle would mind. But the house was full of guests; Estelle wouldn't miss her at all.

"Great," Ben said enthusiastically. "I'll wait for you by the pool, see you soon."

Rosie pulled up in front of the Four Seasons and glanced up at the tall palm trees. The hotel resembled a Spanish hacienda and there was a fountain and lush foliage. Valets sprinted between convertibles, and men and women wore wraparound sunglasses and leather sandals.

"Are you staying with us or joining us for lunch?" The valet opened her car door.

"I'm meeting someone at the Coral Casino," she said, checking her reflection in the mirror and wishing she had worn brighter lipstick.

"It's to your left." The valet pointed towards the beach. "Just follow the path and you can't miss it."

The whole coastline lay before her and the Channel Islands were like sparkling emeralds. There was a long, low building with sliding glass doors and art deco furniture. The floor was blue and gold tile and there was an oak bar and a sitting area with potted plants. Waiters in white jackets carried silver trays and there were vases filled with tropical flowers.

She ventured out to the pool and shielded her eyes. Ben sat at a round table and she almost forgot how handsome he was. Sunglasses were perched on his forehead and he wore a sports shirt. He waved and she walked uncertainly towards him.

"Rosie, it's good to see you." He stood up and kissed her on the cheek. "You look beautiful. You're all tan and fit; being in Montecito agrees with you."

"Thank you," Rosie answered, wondering if she should be pleased. Was Ben giving her a compliment or was he implying she didn't belong in LA?

"Isn't it incredible." Ben waved at the Olympic-sized swimming pool and white cabanas. "Can you believe you and I are sitting by the pool at the Coral Casino? I've already seen Sean Penn and Channing Tatum. And I swear that was Damien Chazelle in the changing room. I didn't say anything in case I was wrong, but I wanted to shake his hand and say *La La Land* is one of the best movies I've seen."

Rosie sipped a glass of ice water and blinked into the sun. It would be so easy to slip into their old habits and talk about everything: who was the hottest director in Hollywood and which were the films to watch before next year's Academy Awards.

"It's lovely here," she agreed. "I'm glad I came."

"I ordered for both of us, I hope you don't mind," he said as the waiter set down two platters. "Most of the dishes are to share and you know how I get when I'm hungry, I start forgetting my own name."

"It all looks delicious." Rosie nodded and noticed Ben had ordered her favorite dishes: house-made quesadillas and burgers with Monterey Jack cheese and applewood bacon and avocado. There was a chicken salad and mahimahi tacos with tahini and cherry tomatoes.

"You really do look wonderful," Ben said approvingly, eating a bite of his quesadilla. "And you've been so productive. I thought you'd come up here and learn to play tennis and instead you're about to become a fish taco mogul."

"Hardly." Rosie laughed. "I'm opening a little store in town."

"Estelle said you had a secret recipe and I tried your tacos at the party. They were amazing," he complimented her. "Mary Beth and I drove by the shop; it's in a prime location in the village."

"You drove by my store?" Rosie felt flattered and strangely unsettled at the same time. As if Ben and Mary Beth had peeked in the cottage window when she was taking a bath.

"The shop looks terrific." He nodded, wiping salsa from his mouth. "In fact, I brought you this." He reached down and put a briefcase on the table.

Rosie glanced at the crocodile skin and gold clasp and wondered if it was a present from Mary Beth. They had seen that briefcase in the Asprey catalog and Ben laughed it was the price of his first car.

"What's this?" she asked when he handed her a neatly clipped stack of papers.

"I had a lawyer draw it up. Even though you started the fish taco shop with funds from our joint account, it says I don't receive any monies from the profits," he said and his smile was boyish. "It's all yours, Rosie. You deserve it."

"I don't know if it's going to earn anything yet," Rosie said. "But, thank you."

"And you can sign this at the same time." He dug into the briefcase and handed her a paper.

Rosie scanned it quickly and looked up. "What's this? I don't understand."

"It's standard industry language," he explained. "You release any claim to intellectual property that might be used by MB&B Productions. Not that you ever would, but say MB&B Productions develops a project that you think is similar to an idea we had together. It keeps it simple so there's no misunderstandings."

The date on the paper danced before her eyes and she gasped. The sun seemed too bright and the sound of people splashing in the pool was deafening.

"This is why you wanted to come up and see me." She waved the paper in front of him. "Not because you wanted to get back together, because you wanted to be sure I didn't interfere with your new venture."

"Relax, Rosie, it's not a big deal." He sipped his water. "When we started out we were so young we didn't put anything in writing. But we're grown-ups now and we're talking about big percentages. It makes sense to have a contract."

"You lied to me about having a woman in our bed and you lied about wanting to come up here to see me and you lied about looking for me at the party," she retorted. "You even lied to Mary Beth about liking Schnabel. Who knows how long you've been lying. Maybe you never loved me at all."

"You're being unreasonable. I have to think about Mary Beth too; she's putting all her resources into our new projects." He looked at Rosie pleadingly. "You and I have just outgrown each other, it's no one's fault. Of course I loved you, and I'm so grateful for our time together. I wouldn't be here without you."

"I don't want to hear about what I did for your career." Her cheeks flushed. "I want you to say you couldn't live without me. But I guess I was wrong."

"I'm sorry, Rosie." His voice softened. "You didn't just make me a good director, you made me a good person. But I can't pretend to have feelings if they aren't there anymore. I hope we can still be friends."

Rosie looked at Ben's designer sunglasses and leather watch-band and wondered how she could have imagined they still had a future together.

"I have plenty of friends." She scribbled her name on the paper. "Good luck with Mary Beth, you belong together. I don't want to see you again."

She stumbled past a woman in a floppy hat who she was positive was Cameron Diaz, and made a beeline for the entrance of the Four Seasons. It wasn't until the valet had delivered her car and she drove out of the circular driveway that her legs stopped trembling. Then she headed inland towards the Pullmans' estate and the air finally left her lungs.

It was midafternoon by the time Rosie got back to the house, and all the guests had left. Rosie jumped out of the car when she reached the house and found Estelle in the rose garden, kneeling in the dirt. She had changed into yellow capris and a broad straw hat. She was patting seeds into the ground and talking in a calm, coaxing voice.

"Am I interrupting?" Rosie asked.

"I always talk to my new roses when I plant them." Estelle squinted up at Rosie. "I want them to feel loved."

"I can come back another time." Rosie hesitated.

"Morris left me a pitcher of iced tea." Estelle pointed to a tray sitting on the lawn. "Come join me. We missed you at brunch today. Everyone was raving about your fish tacos at the party."

"I had somewhere to go." Rosie poured a glass of iced tea. "Ben called and invited me to brunch at the Four Seasons."

"Ben? At the Biltmore?" Estelle repeated.

"Mary Beth went back to Los Angeles this morning but Ben

said he wasn't leaving until tonight," she continued. "I thought I should go and see what he wanted to talk about."

"You mean find out if he wanted to get back together?" Estelle prompted.

"Not exactly." Rosie shielded her eyes from the sun. "Mary Beth was rude to me last night and Ben practically ignored me. I don't know what I wanted, I just thought I should see him."

"What happened?" Estelle took off her gardening gloves.

"We ate at the Coral Casino. I've always wanted to go there and at first it seemed so easy. Ben ordered my favorite foods and we talked about actors and directors. Then he handed me a signed paper that he doesn't get any profits from the fish taco company even though I started it with money from our joint account."

"That's thoughtful of him." Estelle nodded approvingly.

"It was to appease me!" The anger welled up inside her. "He wanted me to sign a paper that said I give up rights to any intellectual property that might be developed by his new production company. The paper was dated three weeks ago. The only reason he came to the Fourth of July party is so I would sign it. He was afraid I'd sue him for the profits of any upcoming movie!"

"Oh, Rosie," Estelle breathed. "I'm sure he didn't mean it like that."

"He told me he was coming to the party to listen to what I had to say." She gulped. "But the only thing he wanted to hear was me saying he and Mary Beth could do whatever they liked. I told him I never want to see him again."

"That is dramatic." Estelle nodded. "How do you feel?"

"At first I couldn't get air in my lungs but the closer I got to the cottage, the better I felt. I love Montecito and the fish taco store, but there's something else. Something I need your advice with."

"I'm listening." Estelle leaned forward.

"Josh kissed me at the party last night and it was lovely," Rosie began. "But then I said something and he thought I was still miss-ing Ben. I don't know what to do now."

"Tell him the truth, that you had brunch with Ben and it's over."

"What if he thinks he's just a rebound," she wondered. "I enjoy being with him and I don't want it to stop."

"Hmmm, men can be sensitive, just like my roses." She stroked a yellow rose. "I know, invite him to dinner."

"You want me to ask Josh on a date?" Rosie asked.

"It's the twenty-first century, it happens all the time." Estelle chuckled. "Tell him he can pick the restaurant, that will appease his male ego."

"I suppose I could." Rosie ran her fingers over her glass.

"Do it today while the kiss is still fresh in his mind," she coun-seled. "After all, what do you have to lose?"

Rosie hurried across the lawn and noticed a male figure standing in front of the garage. She walked closer and realized it was Josh.

"I was looking for you earlier," Josh said. "You weren't at brunch."

"Ben called and asked me to meet him at the Biltmore." Rosie gulped. She had to be completely honest with Josh or they didn't have any chance at all.

"And you went?" Josh stuffed his hands in his pockets.

"I had to." Rosie looked at Josh. "He wanted me to sign some legal documents relinquishing any claim to his new production company. It's over. I told him I don't want to see him again."

"I see," Josh said, and his shoulders relaxed.

"I was wondering if you'd like to go to dinner," Rosie contin-ued before she lost her nerve. "I'm sure you're busy clearing up after the party but maybe tomorrow night."

"You're asking me on a date?" Josh's eyes widened.

"It's the twenty-first century, I hear it's done all the time," Rosie bantered.

"I'm free tomorrow night." Josh nodded. "On one condition, I pick the restaurant."

"It's a deal." Rosie grinned and thought Estelle should start a dating service. "Why don't you pick me up at the taco shop after work?"

Rosie stood behind the counter of the fish taco store and waited for Josh. The last few hours she had spent glancing at her watch, checking her hair in the mirror, applying another layer of lip gloss.

She couldn't remember feeling this nervous about a date since she went to the movies with Peter Harper in the eighth grade. Then she devoured *Seventeen* magazine, reading what to do if he put his arm around her, or worse, what to do if he didn't. She didn't feel much different now. What if they ran out of things to talk about or what if Josh didn't kiss her again?

The bell tinkled and Josh appeared at the door wearing navy pleated slacks and a striped blazer. His shoes were black and shiny and his hair was neatly combed. Rosie wanted to giggle and tell him he looked like he was going to church, but he seemed so serious she kept silent.

"Hi." He pecked her on the lips. "You look lovely."

"Thanks." Rosie had tried on every cotton dress she owned, but none of them seemed right for an intimate dinner. She finally chose a purple dress she used to wear to cocktail parties and hoped it didn't scream "Hollywood."

"I thought we'd take my car." Josh ran his hands through his hair. "We'll drop off my surfboard at my place first.

"My boss recommended the restaurant," Josh said, opening the door of his hatchback. "I hope you like French cuisine."

"As long as we don't eat escargots." Rosie slid into the passenger seat. "I can't swallow them without picturing the snails in our garden."

"Why don't you come inside for a minute." Josh pulled up in front of a ranch-style house a few blocks from the beach. "I'll put the surfboard in the garage."

Josh had never talked about his house and she didn't know what to expect. It was a low ranch-style house painted yellow and surrounded by a picket fence. The front door had a brass knocker and the windows were covered in shutters.

The entry was narrow, with a low table covered with envelopes. Rosie walked farther into the living room. The floors were dark wood and the walls were painted yellow. There were leather sofas and a brown rug that stretched across the room. Rosie walked to the back door and found a small patch of lawn and a fountain.

"Your house is so . . . nice," Rosie murmured.

"You thought I lived in one room that smelled of pizza and stale beer?" Josh came in the garage door.

"I didn't really think," Rosie admitted.

"It was my grandmother's," Josh said. "I've added a few things: the leather sofas, the flat-screen TV. I installed the fountain; it sounds like the surf at night."

"How long have you lived here?" Rosie asked.

"Five years," Josh said. "It's perfect for me. It's close to the beach and there's enough space for my baby."

"Your baby!" Rosie repeated.

"C'mon." Josh took her hand. "I'll show you."

Rosie followed Josh to the garage. His hand felt warm and familiar. She felt the prickle of excitement of their skin touching and remembered kissing in the Bentley.

"Isn't she beautiful?" Josh flicked on the overhead light.

There was a fire engine–red convertible with a maple dashboard and bucket seats. The hood was open, revealing a gleaming silver engine. The steering wheel was polished maple and there was an old-fashioned glove box.

"It's a 1952 MG roadster." Josh ran his hands over the paint. "Many collectors consider it the perfect British sports car. I rebuilt it from scratch."

"It's gorgeous," Rosie breathed, noticing the spoke wheels and the silver MG emblem on the hood.

"I'm going to sell it at the Pebble Beach Concours d'Elegance in August." Josh got into the driver's seat. "If I get a good price, I'll have enough to buy the Classic Car Showroom. Hop in, the seats fit like a glove."

Rosie sat in the passenger seat and admired the rounded gearshift. Josh pointed out the analog clock and the antique pedometer. Rosie looked at his face: open, animated, and suddenly she wanted him more than anything. She reached over and kissed him hard on the mouth.

Josh kissed her back and whispered, "We could stay here for a while. I'll show you the kitchen and the bedroom. The reservation isn't until eight p.m.; French restaurants always serve late."

Josh led Rosie through the house into the bedroom. There was a potted plant and a chipped dresser. He turned to her and pulled her gently towards him.

"Come here," Josh breathed. "You're so beautiful, I can't stop thinking about you."

"I can't stop thinking about you either," she said and ran her fingers over his shirt.

He unbuckled his belt and unbuttoned his shirt. His shoulders were broad and his chest had a deep tan.

"Are you sure this isn't too soon?" he asked. "We can wait."

"Perfectly sure." She unzipped her dress and it fell to the floor. He scooped her up and lowered her onto the bed.

"I'm falling for you, Rosie," he breathed, kissing her neck and her breasts.

"I'm falling for you too," she gulped, her body twisting under his.

He lowered himself into her, and Rosie clung to his back, her body opening and blooming. His chest was smooth against her breasts and he moved faster, burying his mouth in her hair. She came first, the liquid warmth enveloping her. Josh moaned and rolled onto the mattress.

"We're going to miss our dinner reservation after all," he said finally, glancing at the clock on the dresser.

"Confession time: I secretly hate French food," she admitted guiltily. "One of the producers, Adam Stein, adores French food. Every time we went to dinner it was fondue or soufflé or duck l'orange." Rosie tucked her body against his. "French restaurants are always the same. The waiters are pretentious and the chefs use too much butter."

"Why didn't you say so?" he asked. "I wanted to take you somewhere special, the kind of dinner you're used to."

"I didn't want to spoil it," she said and smiled. "It was so sweet of you to make the reservation. And you looked as nervous as if you were on a job interview."

"You looked like you were going to a movie premiere." Josh pointed to the purple mini tossed on the floor.

"I didn't have anything else to wear," Rosie countered. "I haven't been on a date in a long time."

"We can go to Sam's Shake Shack," he suggested. "And have burgers and milk shakes."

"Why don't we stay here." Rosie reached forward and kissed him.

"I could rustle up a peanut butter and jelly sandwich." He kissed her back.

"I'm not in the mood for peanut butter," she gulped.

"What are you in the mood for?" he whispered, his fingers stroking her nipples.

"All of a sudden I can't think of a thing." Rosie groaned as Josh spread her legs and rolled on top of her.

"I'm starving." Rosie sighed. They had both dozed off, pressed against each other like kittens. It was dark outside, and a light fog trickled in through the window.

"Let's see what we have in the kitchen." Josh stood up and reached for his shirt.

"Isn't that a little formal for eating out of the fridge?" Rosie waved at the striped blazer and pleated slacks.

"You're right." He walked to the dresser and took out a pair of shorts and a t-shirt. "But what about you, I don't want you to get anything on that dress."

"I can stay naked or you can lend me a t-shirt and sweats," Rosie suggested.

"Naked is tempting," Josh flirted. "But a little distracting in the kitchen."

He tossed her a t-shirt and sweatpants. "Let's go, before I eat a whole box of Cocoa Puffs."

Rosie slipped on the sweatpants and followed him to the hallway. "Cocoa Puffs sounds a lot better than French onion soup and spinach soufflé."

They assembled turkey and Swiss cheese and avocado. Josh chopped onions and sliced tomatoes. Rosie spread mayonnaise on bread and found a packet of chips and some salsa.

"I can't believe you eat white bread!" she exclaimed when they sat across from each other at the kitchen table.

"When I was I kid I'd bike over after school." Josh bit into the sandwich. "My grandmother made me the same sandwich every day: white bread, processed turkey, and American cheese."

"At least she didn't feed you SPAM." Rosie grimaced. "My brother lived on SPAM when we were teenagers."

"I'd wolf down the sandwich and head to the beach." Josh wiped his mouth. "I kept a surfboard hidden in her garage."

"Your mother didn't know you surfed?" she asked.

"She thought it was dangerous." He shrugged. "She'd show me articles about shark attacks and guys getting concussions from their surfboards."

"I knew you were a rebel." Rosie grinned.

"I was in love with the ocean." Josh put down his sandwich. "It's like believing in God; I couldn't fight it."

"Your place is so homey." Rosie glanced at the bread box on the counter. The counter was orange Formica and there was a welcome mat at the back door.

"You mean it's different from the places in LA. Everyone has a penthouse with floor-to-ceiling windows or a mansion with miles of Italian marble," Josh commented.

"I didn't mean that," Rosie said hurriedly. "I like your house, it's warm and friendly."

"It may not be a four-acre estate with a tennis court and a swimming pool like the Pullmans' but it has everything I need: a garage to restore cars and a hose in the garden to wash off sand from the beach and a closet for my wet suits," Josh replied.

"You forgot what else it has," Rosie said, eating turkey and cheese and mayonnaise.

"What's that?" he asked, wiping mayo from his mouth.

"A bed with a very firm mattress."

"I hadn't really appreciated it before, but you're right." He leaned forward and kissed her. "Maybe we should try it again, just to make sure it's still firm."

"That's a great idea." She kissed him back. "But first I need a glass of milk to go with this sandwich."

Rosie and Josh sat at a booth in Sam's Shake Shack, sharing a banana split. It was late and the shop was almost empty; a couple of teenagers held hands in the booth next to them. Rosie nibbled walnuts and watched Josh's face as he talked. She loved the way his eyes crinkled when he laughed.

After they finished eating their sandwiches and made love again, they walked along the beach, bundled up in Josh's fisherman sweaters. They talked about the grand opening of Rosie's Fish Tacos that was in five days and Estelle's Irish setters.

"I love big dogs," Rosie said and dug her toes in the sand. "I've always wanted an Old English sheepdog or a collie. Some breed that you have to spend your whole life grooming."

"We had two Afghan hounds when I was a kid." Josh twined his fingers around Rosie's. "They had more hair than most of my mother's friends. When they stood on their hind legs they looked like women in fur coats."

"I've never seen an Afghan hound." Rosie wanted to ask Josh more about his parents, but she was afraid the smile on his face would disappear.

"I like dogs but I'm not very fond of cats," Josh admitted. "They look at you as if they know everything."

"I completely agree," Rosie murmured. She tucked her arm in his and the future seemed as bright as the stars in the night sky.

*

"The Concours d'Elegance is the most important car event in the world," Josh said now, sitting across from her at the Shake Shack. He ate a spoonful of vanilla ice cream with chocolate sauce. "People come from everywhere: princes from Europe, lords from England, bankers from New York. The cars drive up 17-Mile Drive—it's one of the most dramatic spots on the coast. It's always foggy and the waves crash right below you; it feels like you are on an ocean liner.

"Then they have this crazy, formal reception in Pebble Beach. It makes a Hollywood premiere look like burgers at Johnny Rockets. There are sautéed prawns and beluga caviar and whole tents of prime rib and salads and desserts. I try not to eat for a week beforehand." Josh grinned. "I want to sample everything.

"After cocktails people make the rounds of the other tents, looking at the classic cars. Lamborghinis and vintage Jaguars and Bugattis. It's like walking into the pyramids and discovering the tomb of some ancient pharaoh." Josh paused and ate a bite of banana and whipped cream.

"The dinner is served by waiters in white jackets: seven courses paired with the finest wines. The organizers want everyone to get a little drunk so when the auction starts they bid high." Josh's eyes sparkled. "This year my MG is going to be there. She's going to be the belle of the ball."

"It sounds amazing." Rosie licked chocolate syrup from her spoon.

"Maybe you can come with me," he suggested. "As long as you don't wear that purple mini."

"Jennifer Lawrence has that dress!" she exclaimed, scooping up nuts and ice cream and bananas.

Josh reached over and kissed Rosie's lips. "I bet Jennifer Lawrence doesn't look as good in a t-shirt and sweats."

Ten

I wish we could be there for the opening of Rosie's Fish Tacos," Angelica's voice came over the phone. "Dirk and I are having dinner with an executive from Bravo. They're making a reality show about a British movie star falling in love with an American actress; maybe they'll choose us!"

"As long as they don't check Dirk's passport to see if he's really British," Rosie said out loud, pressing the mute button.

"I ran into Colby Young at Whole Foods," Angelica continued. "He is so sweet: he wrote my parents a thank-you card for the party. He asked when your fish taco store is opening."

"He remembered?" Rosie balanced the phone on her shoulder while she wiped the counter for the tenth time.

"He's crazy about fish tacos," Angelica replied. "I told him the grand opening is Saturday, and he said he'd try to drive up the coast. He was with his manager, Ryan Addams. I think Ryan is sweet on you. When Colby mentioned your name, Ryan nudged Colby in the ribs."

"I met Ryan at the Fourth of July party," Rosie recalled. "They were talking to Ben and Mary Beth. Ben and Mary Beth probably told him terrible things about me, like I was an axe murderer or just spent a month in rehab."

"You're being paranoid. Ryan had a starry look in his eyes," Angelica insisted. "I think he's sexy in an earnest Hollywood-exec way. He reminds me of those other cute Ryans: Ryan Seacrest and Ryan Gosling. It must be something in the name."

"I have to prepare a hundred tortillas, sauté ten pounds of cod, and make twenty pounds of guacamole." Rosie glanced at her watch.

"You're going to sell out in the first hour." Angelica blew kisses into the phone.

Rosie hung up, feeling guilty she hadn't told Angelica about Josh. But Angelica would have told everyone she met at the Coffee Company and Whole Foods. Their romance was too young to be turned into instant Hollywood gossip.

In two hours the store would open and Rosie's first customers would walk through the door. The past five days she had worked feverishly: timing herself until she could prepare a taco in three minutes, passing out "buy one get one free" flyers, and stopping by every store on East Village Road to invite shopkeepers to a post-opening party at the Pullman estate.

"It's not a movie premiere or a book launch." Rosie frowned when Estelle suggested holding a grand-opening party. They were in the Pullmans' kitchen and Estelle wore her gardening slacks and a wide straw hat.

"What better way to build local support than to host a soirée!" Estelle sipped a cup of Earl Grey tea and nibbled a macaron.

"Mrs. Pullman is having her annual post Fourth of July letdown," Morris groaned, polishing silverware at the kitchen table.

"If I am, there couldn't be a better cure than holding a party."
Estelle finished her tea and placed the cup in the sink. "We'll serve
sangria and Peg's Mexican chocolate cream pie. I'll buy chocolate
fruit cupcakes from your friend Rachel, and we'll have centerpieces
of my peach-colored roses."

"It is a good idea," Josh agreed when Rosie told him about Estelle's
plan to have a party. She brought him a plate of macarons and sat
in the garage while he tuned Oscar's 1969 BMW. "If you get the
support of other business owners, you'll have a terrific start."

Rosie watched Josh work and felt the familiar sexual tug. Since
their dinner date, they had been inseparable. Rosie rose early so
she could meet Josh at Butterfly Beach. She ran the length of the
beach while he surfed. Then they ate scrambled eggs at the Village Diner or grabbed smoothies and bagels from the Orange
Juice.

In the evening they shared deli sandwiches and Josh worked on
Oscar's cars while Rosie checked her to-do list. Late at night, they
crept to Rosie's cottage and sank under the down comforter. After
they made love Josh kissed her forehead and quietly got dressed.
In the morning, she found his imprint on the pillow.

Now Rosie tied her apron around her waist and glanced around the
fish taco shop. Estelle had stopped by early in the morning with
a vase of roses. Morris presented Rosie with a painting of a girl
perched on a surfboard, drinking a bottle of Coca-Cola. Josh brought
her a cup of milky coffee and promised he'd return in the afternoon
with a pack of hungry surfers.

Rosie turned on the stove and her eyes suddenly filled with
tears. What if she had invested all her money in the shop and it sank

like an albatross. She was surrounded by people who believed in her: Estelle, Morris, Rachel, Josh. What if she had been coasting on Ben's genius for ten years and alone she was a failure?

She remembered when she and Ben took their movie to Sundance. The day they arrived in Park City they strolled down Main Street and ate truffle mac and cheese at Robert Redford's restaurant, Zoom, and even attended an after-party at O.P. Rockwell, where they drank craft whiskies and tried not to gape at James Franco and Keira Knightley.

But on the night of their movie's screening, Ben was suddenly too nervous to leave the hotel room. He sat hunched on the bed, flipping through the program and drinking cups of stale coffee.

"You haven't showered yet." Rosie opened the door.

She had gone out to buy a pair of stockings, and when she returned Ben was still sitting on the bed. They had spent almost their entire savings on the trip and their room was the cheapest in Park City. The bed filled the entire space and there was a space heater and a chipped mini fridge.

"I didn't realize so many films were scheduled at the same time." Ben waved the program. "What if no one comes to the screening?"

"Of course people will come." Rosie sat cross-legged next to him. "It's the best film you've done."

"I know that and you know that, but it's being shown at the same time as films by Sofia Coppola and Paul Rudd." He sighed. "We'll go back to LA without a buyer and never afford to make another film."

The vintage Pucci dress she had saved up for was hanging over the shower. She slipped it on and hurried out of the room.

Rosie sat in the lobby bar of the Waldorf Astoria and fiddled with a glass of water. It was where all the A-list actors and producers stayed, and there was that incredible buzz of money and power and fame. Ron Howard and Brian Grazer of Imagine Entertainment sat in one corner, and she was sure she had seen Matthew McConaughey and Kate Hudson.

Her hands were clammy and she wondered if this was going to work. But then she pictured Ben sitting on the bed like a boy who was afraid to ride the school bus because no one would talk to him and picked up her phone.

"Please tell Mr. Cameron that's a very generous offer, but Mr. Ford can't make any decisions until after the screening," she said loudly into the receiver. "I did see how many zeros were in the offer but that doesn't change his mind. And no, I can't reveal the identities of the other potential buyers," she said with a little laugh. "Surely Mr. Cameron knows how important discretion is in Hollywood." Rosie glanced around to make sure people were listening. "Mr. Ford will make his decision after the screening tonight. He'll be at Ben Affleck's party at the Riverhorse on Main. Please thank Mr. Cameron for the champagne and caviar he sent over, it was very thoughtful."

Rosie pressed end and wondered if she had gone overboard with the champagne. Would James Cameron send champagne to an unknown director because he wanted to buy his film? It was too late now. All she had to do was get Ben to put on his suit and go to the screening of his own film.

"Did you hear the audience when the final credits came up?" Ben asked. It was almost two a.m. and they were finally walking back to their room. It had been an incredible night. The screening was packed and Rosie had recognized Barry Levinson and Javier Bardem. When the lights came on, Ben got a standing ovation and people flocked around him for his autograph.

"It felt like doing an endless loop on Space Mountain at Disneyland. And the after-party was insane." He turned to Rosie. "That was us, Rosie, talking to George Clooney. And I'm pretty sure Imagine Entertainment is making an offer. Brian Grazer said we would hear from them in the morning." He paused. "Brian did say something strange. He asked if James Cameron really sent over champagne; he only does that with the hottest new directors. I didn't know what he was talking about."

"I may have let it drop that James Cameron was making an offer," Rosie said casually.

"You did what?" he asked.

"You were afraid that no one would come," she answered. "I ran down to the Waldorf Astoria and pretended I was taking a call from James Cameron's assistant."

Ben wrapped his arms around her and kissed her.

"You're amazing, Rosie," he said when they parted. "I'm nothing without you."

"It's the film that is amazing," she said, and her smile was as wide as the mountains. "I just made sure everyone would come and see for themselves."

But now she was selling her own fish tacos and what if no one liked them? Rosie dribbled olive oil onto a skillet and inhaled the pungent fish smell. She sliced tomatoes and shredded heads of lettuce. She added more cottage cheese to the guacamole, the tension rolling off her shoulders. The next time she glanced at the clock an hour had passed and she felt excited and ready. She washed her hands and stood at the front door.

"Are you sure you don't want to throw up a 'gone fishing' sign and quit before it's too late?" Rachel appeared at the door holding a paper bag. "This is for you."

Rosie took out a golden horseshoe and turned it over. She looked at Rachel and was puzzled. "What's this?"

"It's an old Jewish tradition," Rachel explained. "You put it over the door and it brings good luck to all who enter."

"Aren't you talking about a mezuzah?" Rosie asked.

"I'm trying to make my traditions more universal." Rachel sighed and walked into the store. "There's no reason why Catholics and Jews shouldn't share the same ideals."

"Is this about the meeting with Patrick's grandmother?" Rosie asked. "Did she grill you about whether you eat kosher and celebrate Hanukkah?"

"Not quite, but she did ask what I thought of the names Christian and Mary," Rachel groaned. "Then she made me promise if Patrick and I got married I would not have our son circumcised."

"You just started dating." Rosie smiled.

"I felt like I was making a pact with the devil." Rachel sat on a stool at the window. "She was about to make Patrick pull his pants down so I could see the lovely foreskin on his penis."

"I'm trying not to picture that," Rosie giggled and closed her eyes.

"He does have a lovely penis," Rachel mused. "But not displayed over tea and scones with his grandmother."

"Is it bad to feel sick to your stomach at the opening of your own store?" Rosie sat on the stool next to Rachel. Her eyes scanned the counter and she admired the old-fashioned napkin holders and the bottles of salsa.

"When I opened Gold's Chocolates my hands were so sweaty, the chocolate melted before I could ring it up," Rachel recalled. "The store looks great. I love the roses and the advertisement for Coca-Cola."

"Morris said it was 'retro-chic,'" Rosie said. "I don't even sell Coke or 7Up, but it was sweet of him to bring a gift."

"You've got a great team behind you." Rachel nodded. "How are things with Josh?"

"We've been together every day this week," Rosie said slowly. "But I'm still afraid he's going to wake up and realize he can't do this."

"Sometimes it just takes the right woman," Rachel replied. "Look at Matthew McConaughey or George Clooney. They were Hollywood's most eligible bachelors and now they're married with children."

"What if the shop is a failure and I have to move back to LA and work at a movie studio?" Rosie asked.

"I don't worry as much as you and I'm Jewish." Rachel hopped down from the stool. "I have to go. You're going to do great. Break a leg!"

Rosie watched Rachel walk down the street to Gold's Chocolates. Tourists wandered in and out of art galleries. A young mother pulled a toddler in a red wagon. Rosie took a deep breath and flipped the sign to OPEN.

Rosie stared glumly at the cash register. She had imagined this day for so long: sunburned tourists clutching cold sodas, children dragging in buckets of sand. They would leave with sizzling fish tacos, and a new line of customers would take their place. It was almost one o'clock; the lunchtime "rush" was over. She hadn't sold a single taco.

"Excuse me, what can I buy with ten dollars?"

Rosie looked up and there was a girl with straight hair and brown eyes. She was about ten years old and wore a pair of denim shorts and a halter top.

"You could get our lunchtime special: two fish tacos and an Italian soda," Rosie offered.

"Does the soda have bubbles? I only like drinks with bubbles." The girl walked to the counter and swung herself onto a stool.

"The sodas are in the fridge." Rosie waved behind her. "Pick any flavor."

"My mother always gives me money when she and my father get in a fight." The girl waited while Rosie filled her order. "She digs in her purse, hands me a bill, and says 'get yourself something, honey, while your dad and I work this out.'"

"Tell her you had a delicious lunch." Rosie handed her a white paper bag with the words 'Rosie's Fish Tacos' in red letters.

The girl unwrapped the taco and took a large bite. "This is really good!"

"I just opened today." Rosie grinned. "You're my first customer."

"I want to own a jewelry store when I grow up." The girl sipped her soda. "My mom said I should learn to support myself so I don't have to rely on some guy to buy me stuff."

"Luckily you don't have to worry about that for a while." Rosie chuckled.

"I'll bring my parents here." The girl finished her meal and hopped down. "They both love fish tacos; it's one of the few things they have in common."

"They have you in common," Rosie said.

The girl stood at the door, smiling. "I'm going to tell my mom you have a cool shop, and you're really nice."

"Thank goodness we missed the lunch rush." Estelle walked in as the girl left. "Dear, these are my friends from the garden club. I told them they have to try your fish tacos."

Estelle was accompanied by four women who looked like they usually lunched at the Four Seasons. They wore floral dresses of different lengths, and broad hats with silk ribbons. Their shoes were Ferragamo and their purses were Chanel.

"We'll have one of everything." Estelle waved at the menu board behind the counter. "Marjorie's daughter is head of the Boys and Girls Club in Montecito. She's going to bring the children here for a field trip."

"That's wonderful!" Rosie beamed, assembling tortillas.

"And Portia is having a Mexican-themed engagement party for her son. It would be marvelous if you catered it."

"Estelle always gives the best recommendations," Portia said, taking Rosie's business card. "I'll be in touch."

"We're going to eat them in Marjorie's garden. Her hyacinths are in bloom." Estelle stood at the cash register. "Morris and Peg are scurrying around preparing for tonight's party."

"You didn't have to throw a party." Rosie handed Estelle warm tacos wrapped in wax paper.

"Peg is making tortilla soup and Morris is going to serve Mexican beer with lime wedges." Estelle beamed. "Has Josh been in yet?"

"He's coming after work," Rosie answered. "He's going to bring in a bunch of surfers."

"If you have any tacos left," Estelle said gaily. "Tell Josh we expect him tonight too."

Estelle and the other women strolled down the sidewalk. Estelle moved like a benevolent queen imparting favors on her subjects. Rosie was so grateful for her support, she wanted to run into the street and hug her.

The rest of the day passed slowly. A group of teenagers ordered a dozen tacos and paid with quarters. A couple from Iowa told Rosie all about their vacation while she prepared their meal. A family with two screaming children left taco baskets piled on top of each other like Legos.

Rosie's head throbbed and her feet ached and she hoped Josh would arrive soon. She wanted to go to Estelle's party and drink chilled champagne.

"Still open for business?" A head poked in the door.

"Colby!" Rosie put down the empty taco baskets.

"I told Angelica we'd drive up." Colby wore checkered board shorts and a black t-shirt. Sunglasses covered his eyes and a baseball cap hid his blond curls.

"You drove to Montecito for fish tacos?"

"This boy drove to the Oregon coast for fish tacos." Ryan Addams walked in behind him. Ryan's short brown hair was slicked back and he wore a chrome watch and leather loafers.

"Only once." Colby grinned. "And they were awesome."

"I'm honored." Rosie walked behind the counter, trying not to blush. One of the biggest pop stars in the world was in her store to buy fish tacos!

"I'll take any excuse to get out of town." Colby leaned on the counter. "I've been in the recording studio for weeks."

"How many tacos would you like?" Rosie asked, laying out tortillas.

"Four for me," Colby said. "Two for Ryan; he's a wimp."

"I can't eat too much or I'd have to spend all day on the treadmill like regular people." Ryan punched Colby's arm. "Colby has the metabolism of a whippet."

"Ryan works me like a dog," Colby bantered back. "I drive him crazy eating Milk Duds and guzzling Cokes."

"Soda is terrible for the vocal cords." Ryan shuddered. "It coats them with sugar."

"Recording twelve hours a day is bad for your vocal cords," Colby countered. "Mind if we eat here?"

"You have the counter to yourselves." Rosie handed him two red plates. "You just missed a couple of kids who were on a search-and-destroy mission. This place looked like a two-year-old's birthday party when they left."

"Children are worse than puppies." Ryan opened his fish tacos. "My mastiff puppy chewed up three pairs of Gucci loafers."

"Get a regular-sized dog and he'll stay away from your Guccis," Colby said, eating his taco. He looked at Rosie and smiled. "Hey, these are great."

"I've never owned a store before," Rosie admitted. "I feel like I'm jumping off a high dive."

"Did you know Colby owns restaurants in six states?" Ryan asked.

"I've always liked food," Colby said. "When I was little, my mom let me play in the kitchen. I learned to play the drums on her pots and pans, but I also learned how to make polenta and curry."

"What kind of restaurants do you own?" Rosie asked curiously.

"I was in Chicago on tour, and I couldn't find a restaurant with a panini press. So I opened my own." Colby shrugged. "I have a rice pudding store in New York, and burger joints in Texas and Florida."

"I keep telling Colby to collect Matchbox cars or Star Wars figures," Ryan groaned. "Do you know how much work goes into opening a successful restaurant?"

"Ryan is just chaffed because I'm not under his thumb twenty-four seven," Colby said good-naturedly. "Once I snuck on a plane to New York to buy some of my rice pudding."

"And caused a riot!" Ryan interjected. "Colby got stampeded at Fifth Avenue in Manhattan. The police had to arrive on horseback to pry the girls off him."

"The police let me ride a horse!" Colby exclaimed. "It was cool."

"I read what was happening on Twitter," Ryan said. "And then I tried calling Colby but he was in the hospital 'under observation.' I sweated off three pounds before I could get through to him."

"Ryan thinks I'm still fifteen years old," Colby ate his second taco. "I love performing but I'm trying to grow as a businessman. I want to open a deep-dish pizza restaurant in Manhattan Beach.

Have you ever tried to order deep-dish pizza in LA? It's impossible. Makes me want to get on a plane to Chicago."

"You're not getting on a plane to Chicago without telling me," Ryan protested. "Your insurance is going to double if you keep cavorting around the country."

Rosie started to clean up and glanced at the clock. In fifteen minutes she'd flick the sign to CLOSED and Josh still hadn't shown up.

The door opened as she put away tortillas. Josh stood at the counter with three guys wearing board shorts and Rainbow sandals.

"Sorry we're late." Josh's damp hair stuck to his neck. "The swells were huge and I couldn't drag these guys out of the water."

"You almost missed out pal." Colby turned around. "We were about to order everything she's got."

"You were?" Rosie asked.

"I told you they're awesome," Colby said to Rosie. "I love cold fish tacos for breakfast with ketchup and a glass of orange juice."

"Josh, this is Colby Young and his manager, Ryan Addams," Rosie introduced them.

"The singer?" Josh raised his eyebrows.

"Angelica's a friend of mine. She told Colby about Rosie's fish tacos, so we made a road trip up the coast from LA," Ryan explained.

"You drove to Montecito for fish tacos?" Josh asked.

"We're staying at the Four Seasons Biltmore," Ryan continued. "It's right on the beach and they have wonderful service. They even allow you to bring dogs."

"There must be good fish tacos in LA." Josh's voice was tight.

"It's great that they came, I'm so grateful." Rosie stood next to Josh, squeezing his hand.

"We'd like to order." Josh crossed his arms over his chest. "These guys are starving."

"Are you local?" Colby inquired, leaning his elbows on the counter.

"Josh works at the Classic Car Showroom, and he takes care of Oscar's cars," Rosie said, laying out tortillas.

"Sweet!" Colby smiled his big, white smile. "I'm a huge car fan. I've got my eye on a silver Lamborghini."

"You are not buying a Lamborghini," Ryan piped in. "With the way you take curves, you'd drive straight into the Pacific Ocean."

"Ryan drives like an old woman." Colby rolled his eyes. "He thinks I should buy a Bentley."

"Tough choices," Josh said curtly. He grabbed the fish tacos and passed them to his friends.

"We better go." Ryan glanced at his Rolex. "We promised Oscar we'd stop by and play him the new tracks."

"Keep up the good work." Colby gave two thumbs-up. He pushed his baseball cap lower on his forehead and hopped off the stool.

"Angelica said you're staying in the guest cottage." Ryan turned to Rosie. "Maybe we'll see you later."

Rosie turned back to the counter and finished cleaning up. She wrapped lettuce and tomato in plastic wrap, covered tortillas in aluminum foil, and wiped down the counter. She opened the cash register and counted crisp new bills. She exhaled slowly; the day had not been a disaster.

"How long were they here?" Josh asked tightly.

"I'm not sure." Rosie smiled. "But they bought a lot of tacos."

"They could buy tacos anywhere." Josh's eyes narrowed.

"It was nice of Angelica to tell them." Rosie took off her apron. "Maybe they'll spread the word."

"I'm sure Angelica had her reasons," Josh continued, sounding like a stubborn child who was trying to get his point across.

"What does that mean?" Rosie asked, surprised at Josh's tone.

"Angelica thinks anyone who doesn't live in LA is dead," Josh answered.

"You think Angelica sent them to lure me back to LA?" Rosie demanded.

"Colby's a sweet kid with about a hundred million dollars in the bank. His manager is pretty slick," Josh said slowly. "They didn't drive ninety miles for tacos."

"I don't know what you're implying but I need as many customers as I can get," Rosie answered. She ran a cloth over the counter and grabbed her purse. "Let's go to the party, I'm exhausted."

"I have to give these guys a ride back to the beach." Josh nodded at his friends, who sat at the counter eating their tacos. "Maybe I'll see you later."

Rosie stood on the Pullmans' porch, her eyes glued to the driveway. She wore her red dress and her gold Manolo sandals. Her hair fell softly to her shoulders and her skin had a golden glow. She had been so excited to step out of the cottage and see guests beginning to arrive. But now the party was in full swing and she had the sinking feeling Josh wasn't coming.

Estelle had transformed the lawn into a Mexican fiesta. There were stations of tortillas, refried beans, steak, shrimp, fresh baked chips, and salsa. Round tables were set with red and white tablecloths and vases held red and white roses. A piñata hung between two oak trees and a dessert table held the ingredients for ice cream sundaes.

"Dear, what are you doing?" Estelle approached her. She wore a long white hostess gown and gold sandals. "Everyone wants to meet the guest of honor."

"I'm waiting for Josh," Rosie mumbled.

"This is your night and you can't let anything spoil it." Estelle squeezed her hand. "Let's pop into the kitchen and have a cup of tea."

Estelle led Rosie into the kitchen and made her sit at the table. She put on the kettle and passed Rosie a plate of melba toast.

"Eat this," she instructed. "And tell me what's wrong."

Rosie nibbled the toast and told Estelle how Josh showed up while Colby Young and Ryan Addams were in the taco shop.

"He acted jealous!" Rosie exclaimed. "Colby is barely twenty and I couldn't be less interested in Ryan."

"As I recall Ryan is quite handsome, and Colby is cute in that overgrown puppy way," Estelle murmured.

"I've met them both once," Rosie protested. "They came to try my fish tacos. It was sweet of Angelica to tell them, since she and Dirk couldn't make it to Montecito."

"One would think Angelica could attend her best friend's grand opening." Estelle pursed her lips.

"She had a meeting with a producer," Rosie defended her friend. "Josh was so cold, I hardly recognized him."

"Men have giant egos, even the sweet ones like Josh." Estelle pulled out a chair. "He may have felt threatened."

"Threatened?" Rosie asked.

"When Angelica comes home she throws around the names of her Hollywood connections. 'I saw Mila Kunis at yoga this morning,' 'I ran into David Spade at Whole Foods, he's much taller in person,'" Estelle explained.

"She does." Rosie laughed.

"You lived in that world," Estelle continued. "But Josh has

always been in Montecito. Maybe he just didn't want to listen to Colby and Ryan run on about the music industry. It's all I hear when Oscar's clients come to dinner."

"But they just came to try my fish tacos," Rosie said. "All they talked about was how delicious they were."

"Josh will come around." Estelle patted Rosie's hand and stood up. "In the meantime, a couple dozen people want to meet you. Let's not keep them waiting."

Rosie followed Estelle onto the lawn and was immediately surrounded by guests congratulating her. She sipped a glass of sangria and picked at a side of refried beans. But the sangria made her head throb and the beans tasted like glue.

"You didn't tell me Colby Young was going to be here." Rachel approached her. Her dark hair framed her face and she wore a silver necklace with a heart-shaped locket.

"I didn't know he had arrived," Rosie replied.

"I just saw him near the pool," Rachel gushed. "You have to introduce me. I have his poster above my bed."

"You can't be interested in Colby. He's practically a teenager!" Rosie admonished.

"I used to have a mad crush on Justin Timberlake and the Jonas brothers. But they grew up." Rachel sighed. "Colby has those puppy dog eyes and that clear voice. I get goose bumps when I listen to his music."

"I barely know him." Rosie wavered. "He's here to see Oscar."

"I gave you peanut brittle when you were depressed. I need his autograph."

"What would Patrick say?" Rosie smiled. "He wouldn't approve of you cavorting with a pop star."

"Patrick is at the town meeting discussing zoning ordinances," Rachel grumbled. "I want to have fun."

"You win." Rosie walked towards the pool. "But you can't attack him and no French kissing."

"Just one peck on the cheek," Rachel promised, hugging her arms around her chest.

"Rosie!" Colby jumped up. "We didn't know tonight was your party. I hope you don't mind if we gate-crash."

"I'm happy you are here," Rosie replied. "This is my friend Rachel, she owns Gold's Chocolates."

"I'll give you a lifetime supply of chocolate truffles if you write your name across my chest," Rachel breathed, her eyes glued to Colby.

"What do you think, Ryan?" Colby's eyes twinkled. "You know how I love truffles."

"I'm Ryan Addams, Colby's manager." Ryan shook Rachel's hand. "He'd love to give you an autograph, but he's not allowed to write on skin."

"There goes my career as a tattoo artist." Colby winked. "We were about to go swimming. Would you ladies like to join us?"

Rosie shot Rachel a look, but Rachel was already nodding enthusiastically. "We'd love to, but I didn't bring a bathing suit."

"We got ours from the cabana." Colby pointed to the tent beside the pool. "There's a boys' cabana and a girls' cabana. The Pullmans stock everything: swimsuits, robes, slippers."

"Really?" Rachel turned to Rosie for confirmation. "Let's go, I'm dying to get wet."

Rachel dragged Rosie into the cabana and threw open a chest of drawers.

"I don't want to go swimming," Rosie whispered.

Rachel held up a pink-and-green two-piece. "Oh my god, Colby is gorgeous. He's my *Seventeen* fantasies come true."

"You're practically engaged to Patrick," Rosie reminded her. "Remember Patrick's lovely foreskin."

"I don't want to see Colby's penis." Rachel slipped out of her dress. "I just want to see him without a shirt. If I faint will you promise not to resuscitate me? I only want Colby's lips touching mine."

"I have to get back to my party," Rosie protested.

"Please, Rosie. You're talking to a girl from New Jersey," Rachel pleaded. "I've never met anyone really famous. I'll remember this night forever."

"All right, I'll go swimming," Rosie gave in. "But only till Morris rings the dinner bell. I'm not missing Peg's tortilla soup."

Rosie found a black-and-white-striped two-piece with crocheted straps. She tied her hair in a ponytail and slipped on a pair of flip-flops.

"You look great in a bathing suit," Rachel whistled. "Josh is a lucky man."

"Josh isn't here." Rosie grimaced, remembering how curt he was at the fish taco shop.

"He wouldn't miss your party." Rachel tied the straps of her bikini. "He worked as hard on Rosie's Fish Tacos as you did."

"Josh and I got in a fight." Rosie wavered. "I don't know if he's coming."

"If he doesn't come he's going to miss a lot of great food and wine." Rachel dragged Rosie out of the cabana. "Tell me honestly, should I suck in my stomach?"

"You're beautiful. Your curves make you look like Venus de Milo."

"You walk in front of me," Rachel instructed. "So Colby sees your gorgeous legs."

Colby lay on a chaise lounge by the pool. He wore blue board shorts and no shirt. Rachel gasped and Rosie tried not to giggle.

Colby's stomach was completely flat and his chest belonged in an Abercrombie & Fitch ad. Ryan lay next to him, dressed in patterned shorts and a yellow polo. His sunglasses were perched on his forehead and he wore loafers without socks.

"Ryan doesn't like to get his hair wet." Colby grinned. "I'm trying to convince him to go swimming."

"The water is cold," Ryan protested, and combed his hand through his hair.

"It's perfect!" Colby jumped in, splashing water outside the pool.

"I'll sit out too," Rosie said. "My head throbs and I drank too much sangria."

"I'm coming in." Rachel jumped in the water. "The water is divine."

Rosie sat next to Ryan and watched Colby and Rachel duck in and out of the water like sea lions.

"Sometimes I feel like I'm Colby's keeper," Ryan said. "Last night he jumped off the Santa Monica pier at midnight."

"He's very sweet." Rosie smiled.

"He's a fireball," Ryan answered. "I'm only thirty-three, but when I'm around Colby I feel like an old man."

"Do you mind that he gets all the attention?" Rosie wondered aloud.

"It's my job to make sure he gets attention." Ryan shook his head. "I'm not big on the spotlight. I like to work behind the scenes."

"I was like that with Ben. I enjoyed being the silent partner while he got all the acclaim. It worked well," Rosie mused. "Until Mary Beth offered him a bigger spotlight."

"In my opinion Ben traded down," Ryan replied gallantly. "Mary Beth Chase is an overinflated Barbie doll. Her breasts look like defense weapons."

"Thanks," Rosie giggled. "I'm not very good with men. I think I scared the guy I'm dating away."

"Then he's crazy." Ryan turned to Rosie. "Colby whistled like a schoolboy when you appeared in that bikini."

"Hey, you two!" Colby called from the pool. "Come join us. We want to play Marco Polo."

"I better go in." Ryan took off his shirt. "Colby will crack his head open and I'll have to cancel his tour."

"I'll come too," Rosie said. Suddenly the cool blue water looked inviting. Estelle was right. Tonight was her party and she wasn't going to let Josh spoil it.

"Oh my god!" Rachel rested on the pool steps and clutched her neck. "I lost my necklace. Patrick gave me the locket. He'll kill me."

"I'll find it." Rosie pushed her wet hair behind her ears. "I'm good at holding my breath underwater."

They had been swimming for almost an hour, giggling and splashing like children. They swam relay races and played a heated game of Marco Polo. Rachel refused to be "it" because she didn't want to close her eyes and miss a second of Colby's dreamy body.

Rosie dove underwater and found the necklace stuck in the drain. She tried carefully to dislodge it, conserving the air in her lungs. It wiggled free and she shot to the surface, bumping her head on the diving board. The pain hit her like a hammer. She gasped for air and struggled to the side of the pool.

"Are you all right?" Ryan crouched next to her. "You hit your head pretty hard."

"I think so." Rosie touched her head. Her vision was blurry and there was a bump swelling under her hair.

"Let me look at it." Ryan guided her to a chaise lounge and

helped her lie down. He leaned close and rubbed her head. "Does that hurt?"

"A little." Rosie nodded, closing her eyes.

"Colby got a concussion once." Ryan felt the bump. "Open your eyes and tell me how you feel."

Rosie slowly opened her eyes. There was a man standing by the cabana. He wore navy slacks and his blond hair curled behind his ears. He was frowning and his mouth was set in a firm line. Rosie closed her eyes and when she opened them again he was gone.

Rosie jumped up unsteadily and stumbled to the lawn. She maneuvered through the tables, bumping into guests who were sitting down to dinner. She chased Josh to the driveway but he was walking too fast, and she slipped on the gravel. Her vision blurred and blood pooled on her knee. There was the sound of a car door closing and Josh's car roared down the driveway. She tried to get up, but her knees gave out and she sank onto the pavement. Then she closed her eyes and fell back on the pebbles.

Eleven

Steam drifted up from the bath and Rosie stepped gingerly onto the marble floor. She wrapped herself in a fluffy yellow towel and studied herself in the mirror. Five days ago her injuries looked more gruesome, but she still had bruises on her knees and an egg-shaped bump on her head.

She patted herself with the towel and reached for a yellow terry-cloth robe. It hurt when she bent down and it hurt when she got up too fast. But she barely noticed the pain; all she could think about was that she hadn't heard from Josh since the party.

"You look like you bought your Halloween costume early," Morris said to Rosie after Josh drove away the night of the party.

Morris had carried Rosie to the master bathroom and run a hot bath. He washed her cuts and put an ice pack on her head. The bathtub filled with bubbles, and he brushed the gravel and dirt from her knees. Rosie submerged herself in the hot water and never wanted to get out.

"I opened my eyes and Josh was staring at me as if I was Hester Prynne in *The Scarlet Letter*," Rosie moaned. "Then he turned around and left."

"You hit your head on the diving board." Morris bathed her elbow in disinfectant. "Ryan was making sure you were breathing."

"I only went swimming because Rachel wanted to see Colby's abs." Rosie's eyes filled with tears. "I shouldn't have come to the party without Josh. I should have driven straight to his place after the store closed."

"This was your night," Morris insisted. "Josh should have brought a bouquet of roses and a box of chocolates."

"Maybe he did." Rosie flinched. "And he threw them in the trash when he saw me with Ryan."

"Soak in the bath for a while," Morris instructed. "When you're cleaned up, we're going to go down to the lawn and celebrate your opening. There's a Mexican chocolate cream pie with your name in red frosting."

Morris powdered Rosie's face and selected a silver hostess gown that covered her ankles. He arranged her hair in an updo and applied green eye shadow and dark red lipstick.

"I can't face anyone." Rosie stared at herself in Estelle's full-length mirror. The heavy makeup made her look like Cleopatra.

"I learned one thing being in the band." Morris studied his handiwork. "Even when my heart was breaking, the show must go on. If you disappear all the goodwill you built up will dissolve like fairy dust."

Rosie leaned on Morris' arm, her head spinning like a Ferris wheel. Lights twinkled in the trees and the band played soft dinner music. Ryan and Colby were sitting with Oscar, and Estelle glided from table to table.

"Are you okay?" Ryan appeared at her side. "I thought you were going to faint and then you bolted."

"Burst of adrenaline." Rosie smiled. "Morris gave me a couple of Advils; I'm fine."

"We were worried," Ryan said. "Your friend Rachel keeps wringing her hands and moaning."

"I'll tell her I'm all right," Rosie answered. "First I need something to eat."

Morris put together two plates of tortillas and refried beans and steak. He went to the bar and poured two glasses of brandy. He placed the brandy under Rosie's nose and ordered her to drink it.

"I'd like to make a toast." Estelle stood up, tapping her fork on her glass. "It's not often a new shop opens in Montecito, and it's not often a bright young person leaves LA to settle in our town. Tonight we have both: Rosie's Fish Tacos celebrates its grand opening and I hope with its success, Rosie Keller will call Montecito home. I have grown to love this young lady and I'm sure you will adore her fish tacos. She uses top-secret ingredients I'm not at liberty to divulge." Estelle stopped and smiled. "Now I think Rosie would like to say something."

Rosie shot a frantic look at Morris. She squinted under the bright light and took a deep breath.

"I want to thank everyone for coming," she began. "And I especially want to thank Estelle and Oscar for their hospitality. When I came here this summer, I didn't have a plan. Estelle showed me that you have to love what you do and throw the rule book out the window. I love Rosie's Fish Tacos, and I love being in a place with such kind and generous people."

"Tell us your secret ingredients," a tall white-haired man, called out.

"I can't do that." Rosie grinned. "You'll have to come by and figure it out yourself."

Rosie cut the first slice of cream pie and everyone clapped.

Waiters passed around dessert plates and refilled sangria glasses. Rosie felt suddenly exhausted and dropped into her seat.

"You can stop smiling now," Morris whispered.

"My face is frozen." Rosie grimaced. "And the lights keep twinkling even when I shut my eyes."

"Lean on me," Morris instructed.

Rosie closed her eyes and leaned on Morris' shoulder. Glasses clinked and the band played a lively tune. She wished Josh were here so they could dance and feed each other chocolate cream pie. Tears fell silently down her cheeks and she brushed them away, hoping no one else could see them.

Her phone was on the bedside table and she picked it up. She had punched in Josh's number a dozen times, but each time she clicked end before he could answer. Josh had to trust her. She shouldn't have to explain what happened at the pool.

On her desk was the basket of chocolate Rachel had dropped off with a sweet card. Morris came every evening for five nights and took away the chocolate wrappers and brought Rosie a bowl of soup and crackers. Rosie nibbled a saltine and gave the tray back to Morris, protesting she was too tired to eat.

She put in long hours at the store each day. She rang up sales, collected empty tortilla baskets, and handed customers sizzling bags of fish tacos. But her eyes were glued to the door. She hadn't seen Josh at the beach in the early mornings; he wasn't at the Pullmans' garage. He seemed to have disappeared without a word.

At the end of each day, Rosie turned the sign to CLOSED and counted the money in the cash register. She surveyed the shiny counter and the gleaming stove and experienced a momentary rush of pleasure. The store had a steady stream of customers and her fish tacos were getting rave reviews. But when she drove back to the cottage, her excitement evaporated. All she wanted was for Josh to appear and wrap his arms around her.

"Rosie." Morris opened the French doors of the cottage. "Here you are."

"I don't want any dinner." Rosie sat against the headboard. "I had a fish taco at the store."

"I didn't bring dinner," Morris answered. "Estelle would like you to eat with her and Oscar in the dining room."

"I can't go out, I've been on my feet all day," Rosie groaned.

"You haven't been in the main house since the party." Morris straightened magazines and threw chocolate wrappers in the garbage. "Mrs. Pullman is worried about you."

"Tell her I'm busy selling fish tacos," Rosie urged.

"You tell her at dinner," Morris said. "Peg made summer nut squash soup and roasted potatoes."

"You're not going to leave until I say yes." Rosie sighed.

"I'll help you get dressed." Morris smiled and opened her closet.

Rosie entered the dining room and noticed the candles flickering on the table. The table was set with white-and-gold china, and there was a vase of irises on the sideboard. There was fresh baked bread and pots of whipped butter with chives. It all smelled so good, her stomach flipped over.

Morris had insisted she dress formally, so she wore a long cotton dress. Her hair was pulled back and she wore mascara and lipstick.

Rosie picked up a warm roll, breathing in chives and oregano. Suddenly she was starving, but she didn't want to start without

Estelle and Oscar. She put the roll on her plate and watched the door expectantly.

"Hi," a male voice said behind her.

Rosie turned and Josh stood in the doorway. His eyes were a pale, watery blue and he clutched a bunch of roses.

"I'm having dinner with Estelle and Oscar," Rosie said.

"Estelle and Oscar are at a gallery opening in Santa Barbara." Josh entered the dining room.

"Morris said Estelle wanted me to join them for dinner." Rosie frowned.

"I asked Morris to say that," Josh confessed. "So you'd have dinner with me."

"Oh," Rosie gasped, and tried to think of something to say.

"These are for you." He handed her the flowers. "They're Estelle's hybrid tea roses. This one is a Humphrey Bogart, and this is a Lauren Bacall."

"They're beautiful." She inhaled the sweet scent.

"I may not know a lot about films, but I have seen *Casablanca* and Humphrey Bogart ended up without the girl." Josh sat opposite Rosie. "I don't want to lose you before we even got started."

"I wasn't going anywhere." Rosie gulped.

"I behaved badly. I let jealousy eat me up." He took her hand. "Instead of talking to you, I hibernated."

"I told you there was nothing going on." She remembered the pain of watching Josh walk away, of slipping and falling on the gravel.

"Guys like Ryan and Colby have everything." Josh toyed with the linen napkin. "They reminded me how little I have to offer you."

"Colby is a kid," Rosie said. "And Ryan is just a friend."

"I don't mean to interrupt." Morris stood at the kitchen door. "But Peg insists I serve the soup."

Josh looked at Rosie, his eyes sparkling. "Will you have dinner with me?"

Rosie nodded and picked up a warm roll. "I'm starving!"

They ate summer nut squash soup with chunks of homemade bread. There were petit filets mignons and seasoned roasted potatoes. They both cleaned their plates, laughing at how hungry they were, fighting over the last roll.

"I haven't eaten much this week," Rosie admitted after Morris cleared away their plates. "I love making fish tacos. But if I eat another piece of cod, I'll grow gills."

"I've been working on the MG night and day." He wiped his mouth with his napkin. "I barely ate two pieces of pizza yesterday."

"I'm glad you came tonight," she said softly. The chandelier lights twinkled on the wineglasses, and she felt warm and happy.

"I should have come sooner." Josh picked up Rosie's hand and turned it over. "I had a bad feeling when I saw Colby and Ryan at the store. Their lives are concerts and parties and being friends with people like Beyoncé. I was afraid you'd talk to them and miss Hollywood."

"I love owning my own store, and I love Montecito," Rosie reminded him.

Josh ran his fingers over Rosie's palm. "Then when I saw you and Ryan at the pool, I thought you and he were together."

"I would never do that," she insisted.

"Ryan is so slick: the shades, the fancy clothes, the leather shoes. He's the kind of guy who gets whatever he wants," Josh said tightly. "Every day I was going to call you, but I just couldn't do it. I was afraid you'd already moved on."

Rosie studied Josh in the flickering candlelight. He looked like Rodin's sculpture *The Thinker:* tortured and brooding.

"I keep wondering if you're going to run away. You think that I miss the bright lights of Hollywood," Rosie said tentatively. "What if we're both wrong, what if we need to trust each other?"

Josh walked around the table and pulled Rosie out of her chair. He kissed her and she tasted butter and wine. She flattened herself against his chest, listening to the beat of his heart.

"Let's go to the cottage," she whispered.

"What about dessert? Peg made a chocolate flambé," he replied. "Morris was going to light it at the table."

"He'll forgive us." Rosie took Josh's hand and walked to the door.

Josh picked her up and ran to the cottage over the wet lawn. Her bruises throbbed and the scrapes on her knees burned and there was still a slight ringing in her ears. He opened the cottage door and set her down gently on the floor.

"Hold on, let me find the Advil." She grimaced, holding her sides. "I still ache all over."

"I shouldn't have carried you, I might have made it worse," Josh said, suddenly serious. "What about if I give you a massage."

"All I need is a glass of water and some aspirin." Rosie shook her head. "I don't want to put you to work."

"I am partially responsible," Josh reminded her. "I don't mind at all."

Rosie lay on her stomach on the bed and Josh sat beside her. He started at her shoulders and kneaded her back. His hands were warm and her whole body relaxed.

"You are good at this," she mumbled into the pillow. "You must have had a lot of experience."

"You can't surf and not know how to give a massage," Josh replied. "All surfers have come out of the ocean with gnarly cuts and bruises."

She turned on her back and looked up at Josh. His cheeks were smooth and his blond hair curled behind his ears. "I hope you didn't massage surfers in quite the same way."

He leaned down and kissed her. "Maybe not quite the same way."

"How was it different?" she asked.

His mouth traveled to her neck. "I never did this." He gently removed the strap of her dress and kissed the top of her breasts. "Or this."

"Then I'm the lucky one," she said, when he paused. "You get a five star review."

Rosie sat up and unbuckled his belt. He shrugged off his shirt and looked at her.

"Maybe we should wait," he said. "I don't want you to have a relapse."

"I'm perfectly fine," she murmured. "Let me show you."

She kissed him and pulled him on top of her. Josh pushed her arms over her head and looked in her eyes.

"You're all I think about, Rosie Keller," he whispered.

"You're all I think about too," Rosie said and shivered.

Josh pushed inside her and she moaned. His eyes held hers and they rocked faster, clinging to each other. Her body arched and the warmth exploded inside her. Josh gasped and dropped, spent and exhausted on the bed.

There was a knock at the cottage door. Rosie got up and pulled on her robe. She glanced at Josh sprawled naked on the bed, the sheet pulled over his chest.

She tiptoed to the door and found a tray with a peach rose in a crystal vase. There was a plate covered with a silver dome, and a note in Morris' handwriting.

Rosie carried the tray to the bed and uncovered a German chocolate cake. She unfolded the note and read aloud: "Didn't want to send the chocolate flambé, as burning down the cottage would not be advisable. XOX Morris."

"I smell chocolate." Josh turned onto his stomach, his eyes still closed.

"It's the chocolate cake Morris sent," Rosie giggled. "Help me, before I eat the whole thing."

Josh sat up, rubbing his eyes. He looked so handsome bare-chested, his blond hair curling behind his ears. A nervous lump rose in her throat. She cut two slices of cake and handed Josh a silver fork.

"I could get used to this." Josh ate a small bite. "Fancy sheets, gourmet dessert, fine china and silverware."

"You forgot the important part," Rosie teased. "Fantastic sex."

"I didn't forget." Josh kissed her. "But you may have to refresh my memory."

"First I want to finish the cake." Rosie grinned. "It was nice of Morris to leave it for us."

"He really cares about you," Josh said earnestly.

"What do you mean?" She looked up.

"He came to see me last night." He hesitated. "He said you weren't eating or sleeping."

"That's why you're here?" She stopped mid-bite. "Because Morris told you to come?"

"Estelle told him where I lived," Josh continued. "I was in my garage working on the MG. He laid into me: said either I should have the guts to tell you I didn't want to be with you, or be a man and show you I wanted you."

"He never said anything to me," Rosie mused.

"I said I was afraid you had something going with Ryan. He called me a chickenshit and a few other choice names." Josh paused. "And then he told me I was dead wrong."

Josh turned to Rosie and traced the shape of her mouth. "He said Ryan was here to see him."

Rosie blinked and then she began to laugh. She laughed so hard Josh had to hold her so she didn't tumble off the bed. She laughed until she fell against Josh and they collapsed on the pillows.

"Ryan Addams is gay!" she choked. "Why didn't he say so?"

"Ryan's family is very traditional. His father is in politics and his mother is big in her charity circle. It was hard enough that he moved away to Hollywood, and became a manager. If they knew he was gay, they would have made him come home. Besides, Morris didn't want to advertise it. Album-buying girls swooned over them wherever they went," Josh explained. "Even after he left the band, he didn't want to do anything to hurt Neil Friend. Morris is incredibly loyal even though Neil broke his heart."

"I thought Morris was still mooning over Neil," Rosie offered. "How long have they kept it a secret?"

"Ryan and Morris have been together two years," Josh said. "Nobody knows, not even Colby."

"Morris has a boyfriend! Morris has a boyfriend!" Rosie chanted.

"It was pretty brave of him to tell me," Josh said seriously. "And he's right; I was a chickenshit. I'm crazy about you, Rosie."

Rosie stopped giggling. She turned and looked at Josh's pale blue eyes and the creases on his forehead. The lump in her throat dissolved and she leaned close and whispered in his ear, "I'm ready to refresh your memory."

Josh pulled her against him. "Chocolate makes me sleepy," he murmured. "Can I have a rain check for the morning?"

Twelve

Rosie sat at her desk in the cottage with a pencil between her teeth. Her laptop was open and invoices and order forms were piled next to her. She punched numbers into a calculator, entering the results on a spreadsheet.

She hadn't realized the amount of paperwork owning a store entailed. Numbers danced before her eyes when she tried to go to sleep. But her sales were growing, and in the evenings she and Josh celebrated with a glass of Cabernet or a stroll around the lake. Rosie kept her fingers crossed that the store would continue to thrive.

Josh was supposed to meet her for a run before dinner, but he had been delayed at the Classic Car Showroom. He had been working around the clock: mornings on the MG, days at the showroom, and nights in Oscar's garage. They both were living on sex and adrenaline and barely found time to sleep.

When they did climb into bed, they wanted to tell each other stories, rub each other's back, find new ways to make love. It was late July and Josh was so close to completing the MG, his eyes shone with an inner light. Rosie was amazed that people waited in line for her fish tacos, and that they thanked her when they gave her money.

It felt like the days after Ben and Rosie got their first big production deal. Suddenly they both had assigned parking spaces on the studio lot and name tags that allowed them to eat at the cafeteria. Studio executives waved when they walked by, and the guy in the parking garage made sure her windshield was clean.

Now it was even better because she was doing it by herself. Rosie's Fish Tacos might not be a blockbuster movie that was going to play in fifty states or an indie that would be reviewed in *Variety*, but she made every taco and customers wanted to buy them.

The best part was waking up next to Josh in the morning, finding his running shoes in her closet, seeing his work shirts folded neatly in her drawers. She felt like she could jog twenty times around the lake, prepare one hundred fish tacos, and have energy to spare. Estelle commented on her glow, and Morris laughed she was like a hot-air balloon. She needed lead in her shoes to bring her back to earth.

Rosie's phone vibrated and she answered, expecting to hear Josh's voice.

"I've been staring at numbers for hours. If I don't go for a run, my eyes are going to cross," she said, pressing the phone against her ear.

"I'd love to go for a run but I'm in New York." A male voice chuckled. "It's pouring rain, so I'd get pretty wet."

"Who is this?" Rosie stared at the unfamiliar number displayed on the screen.

"Ryan Addams," he answered. "The guy who healed your concussion."

"What a pleasant surprise to hear from you." Rosie smiled and walked to the cottage's window. "Though it wasn't a concussion."

"It was a pretty big bump," Ryan said. "How are things at the fish taco shop?"

"Great, exhausting, exhilarating," Rosie replied in a rush. "Having your own store is like having homework for the rest of your life. There's always something to do."

"You better get used to it," Ryan offered. "It's about to get worse."

"What do you mean? Why are you in New York?" Rosie asked.

"Colby is promoting his new album. He's done all the late-night shows: Jimmy Fallon, Stephen Colbert, and *Saturday Night Live*. He even popped into *The Today Show* this morning. We needed a police escort to get to the studio."

"That's fantastic." Rosie beamed. "But why are you calling me?"

"Well . . ." Ryan hesitated. "Colby sort of dedicated a song to you."

"To me?" Rosie dropped into her chair.

"It's called 'Rosie.' He wrote it after our weekend in Montecito. You know how impetuous he is; he came home and wrote it in one night."

"Why would he write a song about me?" she inquired.

"It's about breaking free of the fast track and doing what you love," Ryan continued. "And it's on its way to number one on the charts."

"Wow!" Rosie picked up her pencil and doodled "Rosie and Josh" on her spreadsheets.

"You might want to catch the *Today Show* segment on YouTube," Ryan said slowly.

"Why?" Rosie wondered aloud.

"Let's just say Rosie's Fish Tacos is about to get a lot more popular."

"What did Colby say about me?" Rosie turned on her computer and waited for the site to load.

"All good things, I promise. Watch the clip. I have to go, Colby is on Anderson Cooper. God, I hope he's nice to Colby." Ryan sighed. "Anderson has a wicked sense of humor."

"What did Colby say?" Rosie repeated frantically.

"I'm getting the guillotine motion; I've got to turn off my cell," Ryan whispered. "Colby sends his love."

Rosie found the *Today* segment and clicked play. Colby wore checkered shorts and a white t-shirt. His hair was long and curly and he wore orange sneakers.

"Tell us about 'Rosie,'" Savannah Guthrie was saying into the camera. "The album was done, ready to go, and suddenly you wrote one more song. It's busting out on the charts. What was the inspiration?"

"My fans know I'm a foodie." Colby grinned like a kid admitting a gummy bear addiction. "Earlier this summer I heard about a new fish taco shop in Montecito. It is owned by a young woman named Rosie Keller. She quit her job as an executive at a movie studio and headed up the coast. The fish tacos are amazing; she won't tell me her secret." Colby smiled as if he was talking directly to Rosie. "She got off the Hollywood treadmill and did what she loved. Now she's making herself and a lot of taco lovers happy."

"Are you saying you want to get off the music treadmill?" Savannah asked earnestly.

"I have the greatest job in the world." Colby opened his arms as if he was hugging the audience. "But you don't have to dream big. Small dreams can be just as cool. That's what the song is about: do what you love and throw the rule book out the window."

"Great advice." Savannah nodded and folded her arms. "Anything you want to add?"

Colby's boyish face filled the screen. "Save me a fish taco, Rosie!"

"How about singing 'Rosie' for our studio audience." Savannah sat back in her chair.

"My pleasure." Colby grabbed a microphone. The camera panned to pigtailed girls throwing roses at the stage. They screamed so loud, Rosie couldn't hear the song. The camera zoomed in on four girls holding a banner proclaiming WE LOVE YOU, COLBY and faded to black.

Rosie stared at the blank computer screen. She wanted to call Ryan, but he was on the set of the Anderson Cooper show. She thought about calling Angelica, but she would just jump up and down with glee about the free publicity.

She and Josh were so happy, like puppies maturing together. What would he say when her name was number one on the Billboard charts? She threw on her running shoes and grabbed her iPhone. She found Colby Young on iTunes, and played "Rosie" as she ran laps around the lake.

"Peg made a roast and Yorkshire pudding," Morris said, walking into the kitchen with a basket of lemons.

"I feel like peanut butter," Rosie replied. She was hot and sweaty from her run and suddenly craved a peanut butter sandwich. She kept her back to Morris, intent on spreading peanut butter and jelly on whole wheat bread.

"You love Peg's Yorkshire pudding, you never eat without Josh, and you haven't had peanut butter since Ben came to the Fourth of July party." Morris grabbed the jar. "Tell me what's wrong, or I'm confiscating the peanut butter."

Rosie put down the knife and collapsed into the kitchen chair. She told Morris about Ryan's phone call and Colby's appearance on *The Today Show*.

"Is it a love song?" Morris wanted to know.

"No!" Rosie flushed. "It's about following your dreams."

"Is it badly written, does Colby sing off-key?"

"No, it's wonderful." Rosie shook her head. "Colby has a terrific voice."

"I don't see the problem." Morris rinsed the lemons in the sink.

"Josh hates Hollywood and all that glitz. Things have been going so well, I don't want to rock the boat."

"Josh walks around like a kid on Christmas morning. As long as Colby isn't declaring undying love, he won't mind. He might even be pleased."

"What if he's not pleased?" Rosie grabbed the peanut butter from the counter. "What if he gets scared and runs?"

"Give him a little credit for growing up." Morris put the lemons in a bowl. "Being with the right person will do that."

"Colby has eighteen million Facebook fans and thirteen million Twitter fans," Rosie said nervously. "I know what star power can do. What if Rosie's Fish Tacos turns into a three-ring circus?"

"Just be prepared and you'll be fine," Morris counseled. "Triple your avocado order and get some help baking tortillas."

"It's not the supplies I'm worried about," Rosie said, calculating how many extra tortillas she should buy and where to find the best discounts on Italian soda.

"Then what are you worried about?" Morris asked.

Rosie crossed her arms and said bleakly, "That a camera crew will arrive to see what Colby is singing about, and Josh will see them and run in the other direction."

"You overthink things." Morris picked up the basket. "So what if you're on television? Just avoid wearing black and white; it dances in front of the camera. And get some of that product that makes your hair flat. You're gorgeous, but it's going to frizz if you make tacos under bright lights."

Rosie took her sandwich onto the porch and sat on the swing.

"Here you are!" Josh appeared outside, carrying a plate heaped with pot roast and Yorkshire pudding.

"I needed to get away from my desk." Rosie rocked back and forth. "I was beginning to feel like Jack Nicholson in *The Shining*."

"All work and no play is not good." Josh sat beside her. "I talked to my boss, Al, today. He plans on retiring in December."

"Really?" Rosie breathed in Josh's scent. He smelled of lemon air freshener and car wax.

"I told him I was confident I could get a good price for the MG," Josh continued. "We started hammering out terms."

"That's fantastic!" Rosie beamed. Josh had talked about buying the Classic Car Showroom for so long sometimes she thought it was like dreaming about a perfect wave.

"I can't believe the Concours d'Elegance is in less than a month," Josh finished. "I need one more part and then she's ready. She's beautiful, Rosie."

"I'm almost jealous." Rosie tried to smile.

She debated whether she should mention Colby's song. Josh didn't listen to the radio and he barely glanced at Facebook. They didn't watch television at night; they were too busy exploring each other. He may never hear "Rosie" and the whole thing would blow over. But she looked at his sparkling eyes, his open, honest expression, and took a deep breath.

"Colby Young was on *The Today Show* today."

"Good for him." Josh chewed his steak. "He's a cool kid."

"He has a new album out. The single is at the top of the charts." Rosie paused. "It's called 'Rosie.'"

"'Rosie'?" Josh put down his fork. "Is it about you?"

"He wrote it after he came to the opening." Rosie kept talking without looking at Josh. "It's about leaving the rat race and following your dream."

"Is it good?" he asked.

Rosie handed him her headphones. "Here, listen."

"He's got a great voice." He passed the headphones back to Rosie.

"You like it?" She looked up.

"I'm more of a classic rock fan." Josh grinned. "But he sings from the heart. No wonder the girls love him."

"You don't care that the song is called 'Rosie'?" she inquired.

"It's not a love song, he's a bit young for that." Josh put a large helping of Yorkshire pudding on his fork.

"Are you implying I'm a cougar?" Rosie pouted as she swatted him playfully.

"Not to me." He stroked her hair. "To me you're a hot young chick."

"You really don't mind?" she asked seriously.

"It's incredible! It will be good free publicity for the store," he replied. "When I buy the showroom and your shop is doing well, we can start talking about stuff."

"What kind of stuff?"

"The things couples talk about." He curled his fingers around Rosie's.

"Sex, laundry, baseball?" Rosie swung back and forth on the swing.

"I know it's early." Josh stroked her knee. "But we could think about moving in together."

"Oh." Rosie gulped. She put the glass of milk down and wiped her mouth. "That's a huge step. Are you certain you really mean it?"

"Of course I mean it." He nodded. "Not just moving in, but a future. The station wagon, the dog, a couple of kids."

"I don't think anyone drives station wagons anymore." Rosie grinned.

"Yvette hasn't made me an uncle yet, and I always wanted to teach a kid to surf," Josh offered.

"You could probably find a kid if you went down to the beach," Rosie joked.

"I'm serious, Rosie." Josh held her hand tightly. "I'm not quite ready financially, but it feels right. We love each other, we want the same things."

"What if I want an Irish setter and you want a Dalmatian?" She grinned.

"I couldn't want a Dalmatian. They remind me of Cruella de Vil," Josh replied.

"What if I want to go sailing and you want to go skiing?" she asked.

"We'll go to Switzerland. We can sail on Lake Lugano and ski in St. Moritz on the same day," he offered, and ate the last bite of Yorkshire pudding.

"How do you know about Lake Lugano and St. Moritz?" Rosie asked.

"I was a history major, I know a lot of useless facts," he said. "Let's go to the Shake Shack. I'm craving a banana split."

"And we'll ask the waitress to put sprinkles on it to celebrate." She followed him to the driveway.

"To Rosie's Fish Tacos and the Classic Car Showroom and everything that comes next." He opened the car door and kissed her.

"We're going to have everything we dreamed of," she said, and kissed him back.

Rosie stood at the store window and watched the pouring rain. It almost never rained in California in August. But this morning, gray clouds formed over the mountains and drenched the village. A few tourists sat in cafes and stared accusingly at the sky. It was as if they had been promised a sunny vacation, and they wanted their money back.

It had been two days since Colby's television appearance and it hadn't stopped raining. Every day she waited for the sun to appear and new customers to line up at the door, but the streets were deserted and the cash register barely rang.

She picked up the phone and called Rachel's number.

"I'm so bored, I'm making faces at my reflection in the fridge," Rosie said into the phone. "I want to tell you something, come and keep me company."

"Why not?" Rachel's voice came over the line. "If I sit in this store any longer by myself, I'll be tempted to eat the whole display of chocolate-covered pineapple."

Rosie hung up and waited for Rachel to appear. The door opened and Rachel darted inside, shaking off her umbrella. "It's like a river out there. Ducks wouldn't go out in this weather."

"I haven't sold a fish taco all day," Rosie agreed. "Maybe I should advertise a rainy-day special."

"At least it gives me time to catch up on the gossip sites." Rachel clicked through her iPhone. "Did you know Colby has a new album out? I haven't had a chance to listen to it. Yesterday I was swamped making chocolate My Little Ponies. A customer ordered thirty chocolate My Little Ponies for her daughter's birthday party. These mothers keep trying to outdo each other. What happened to cupcakes?"

"That's what I wanted to talk to you about." Rosie nodded. "He wrote a song for me and sang it on all the late-night talk shows."

"What did you say?" Rachel looked up. "Don't tell me you're having a secret affair. Really Rosie, even I know he's too young. And what about Josh? You two have something special."

"Of course we're not having an affair. Colby wrote it after he came up to Montecito." Rosie arranged the folded napkins on the counter. "The song is about leaving the rat race and following your dream."

"Are you sure? What about the night of the party." Rachel eyed her suspiciously. "You looked fantastic in that bikini, and then you disappeared."

"I bumped my head in the pool," Rosie reminded her. "Then I fell down chasing Josh and scraped my elbows and knees. I was in no condition to sleep with anyone."

"I'm glad to hear it, I can't stand a cheater." Rachel nodded. "Though he is gorgeous. His dimples are the size of nickels."

"Even Josh wasn't worried about the song." Rosie laughed. "He thinks I'm too old for Colby to be interested. Colby went on *The Today Show* and Anderson Cooper."

"Anderson Cooper is hot. It's too bad he's gay," Rachel murmured. "What did Colby say?"

"He raved about my fish tacos. Ryan called to tell me. He thinks I'm going to get a lot more customers." Rosie stared at the rain drenching the window boxes. "I thought so too but I guess I'm wrong."

"His fans are pretty vigilant," Rachel responded. "Once they surrounded his house because there was a rumor that he buzzed his hair. It was a false alarm, but they weren't satisfied until he appeared on the balcony. Colby even cut off a few locks of hair to reward the fans who spent all night waiting to see him. He's so thoughtful."

The bell above the door tinkled and three girls ran in. Their hair was wet corkscrews and their socks and sneakers were soaked. They squealed like baby pigs and collapsed into a fit of giggles.

"I can't believe we did it," said a dark-haired girl. "I ruined my new shoes. My mother is going to kill me."

"Is this the fish taco store Colby Young talked about on *The*

Today Show?" a blond girl demanded. She wore striped socks and sneakers with pink laces.

"This is Rosie's Fish Tacos." Rachel got up from the stool. "And that's Rosie."

"You're Rosie?" a red-haired girl with a face full of freckles breathed. "Do you know Colby Young?"

"We've met a few times and he's a friend of mine," Rosie acknowledged.

"Stop being coy." Rachel shot Rosie a look. "Rosie hit her head at a pool party and Colby and his manager saved her. The experience bonded them, they'll never forget it."

"He's such a hero," the dark-haired girl gushed. "What happened?"

"We were all playing Marco Polo and my locket got wedged in the drain," Rachel replied. "Rosie tried to retrieve it, but it wouldn't budge and she almost ran out of air. She shot to the surface and hit her head on the diving board. Colby and Ryan rushed to her rescue and gave her mouth-to-mouth resuscitation."

"Colby did that?" a girl gasped.

"It was one of them." Rachel shrugged. "I can't remember who. There was blood and Rosie was moaning with pain."

"Wow, that's incredible," the blonde gushed and turned to Rosie. "You must have been so brave."

"She couldn't let down her customers," Rachel enthused. "After she got all cleaned up she came right to the store and made Colby's favorite fish tacos."

"Oh my god! The fish tacos," the redhead squealed. "Colby tweeted that they're the best. We made our mothers drive from Bakersfield. We'll have two each, and I'll take a couple for my mom, and one for my little sister. She's only five, but she already has a Colby Young lunch box."

"I have to text Melissa and Morgan." The dark-haired girl took out her phone. "They're never going to believe we met a girl who bled all over Colby Young!"

The redhead agreed. "I feel like I'm going to pass out. I need something to eat!"

Rosie bundled their tacos and handed them napkins and plastic forks. She added three bottles of orange soda and a side of chips and salsa. "Thank you for coming all the way from Bakersfield. Maybe you can tag us on Facebook and Instagram."

"Can I get a picture with you?" the blonde asked. "I'll post it on Snapchat."

"Sure." Rosie walked from behind the counter and the redhead snapped their photo with her phone.

"Maybe one day I'll get a photo with Colby Young." The blonde sighed. "That would be the best day of my life."

The girls ran down the street, shrieking and laughing. Rosie turned to Rachel and placed her hands on her hips.

"What was that all about?" Rosie asked, closing the cash register. "You made it sound like a scene in an afternoon soap opera. It was a little bump."

"Call it creative marketing; it's in my genes." Rachel grinned. "How many tacos did they buy?"

Rosie opened the cash register and counted receipts. "Sixteen."

Rachel nibbled a tortilla and stared at the wet pavement. "You better get ready for the deluge. It's time to build an ark."

The rain cleared the next morning and left the cobblestones bright as new pennies. Rosie went to work early, cradling a cup of coffee. She turned onto East Village Road and there was a crowd snaking down the street. Women flipped through magazines and mothers balanced toddlers on their hips. And there were girls of all ages. They chewed gum and scrolled through their iPhones, squealing and trading screens.

Rosie walked closer, wondering if they could all be waiting for her to open the store. She searched for her key and spotted Rachel standing by the door.

"At least you got here early." Rachel was waiting on the sidewalk.

"These people can't all be wanting fish tacos?" Rosie gulped, wondering if she had ordered enough avocado.

"It's called 'Colby Young tweeted to thirteen million fans that Rosie serves the best fish tacos.'" Rachel pushed inside and dragged Rosie with her. "My father owned the biggest department store in New Jersey. Once the Jonas Brothers made a surprise appearance and the fans practically ripped the carpet from the floors. The place was gutted. And insurance refused to pay. His policy didn't say anything about a stampede of teenage girls."

"But Colby isn't here, it's just me," Rosie insisted.

"He sprinkled you with Colby Young fairy dust." Rachel propelled Rosie to the front door. "You're going to be a star."

"I thought I was prepared, but I can't serve all these people." Rosie panicked, turning around and seeing the mass lunge towards the entrance.

"That's why you're lucky to have me as a friend. I brought some of Patrick's cousins; they're going to cook. Patrick will drive to the store if you need extra supplies, and I'm going to help run the counter."

"What about Gold's Chocolates?" Rosie peeked out the window at the crowd.

"Patrick's grandmother is taking over for the day," Rachel answered. "Her eyesight isn't very sharp and I'm not sure she listened to my directions. I hope she doesn't poison anyone."

"How can I thank you?" Rosie asked, turning on the stove.

"Don't call your firstborn Colby. I want to name my baby after him, and then we couldn't be friends." Rachel grinned.

"Deal." Rosie tied an apron over her shorts.

Rachel flipped the sign to OPEN. "Let the games begin."

Thirteen

Rosie opened the door of the library, looking for Estelle. In the last few days she had only seen her in passing. Rosie hadn't joined the Pullmans for dinner; she hadn't jogged around the lake. She barely had time to throw her clothes on in the morning, grab a croissant from the kitchen, and dash into the store.

From morning to night, the customers kept coming. Rosie hired three of Patrick's cousins to cook full-time, and the phone rang off the hook. People wanted to know whether she had a "Colby" special, and how often he visited the store. Rosie had more than ten thousand likes on her Facebook page and her Twitter following was growing faster than Selena Gomez's.

Santa Barbara Magazine did a cover story on the girl who discarded her Birkin bag for an apron. Rosie complained to Rachel that she never owned a Birkin and Rachel insisted it was good journalism. Martha Stewart featured Rosie on her blog, and Ryan Seacrest's television crew appeared one morning to do an interview. Rosie stared into the camera that she used to stand behind and couldn't string two words together.

Josh was wonderfully supportive. He brought sandwiches to the store so she ate something besides beans and tortillas. At night he massaged her back and listened to her stories about teenage girls camping out in the shop, certain Colby would make a surprise visit. When Rosie insisted he hadn't been there in weeks, they looked at her coyly and ordered another round of tacos.

"Rosie!" Estelle stood next to the fireplace in the library. "I was going to send out a search party; I haven't seen you in days."

"You know where to find me." Rosie grinned. "Chained to the counter of Rosie's Fish Tacos."

"Still very busy?" Estelle sorted long-stemmed roses. She snipped their thorns and arranged them in a crystal vase on the side table.

"It's the most wonderful thing I can imagine, but at the same time it's exhausting," Rosie conceded. "I don't know whether to buy myself a new pair of shoes to celebrate or get a pillow and blanket and sleep in the back of the store."

"Celebrity is a terrible and wonderful gift." Estelle admired her handiwork. "But people wouldn't keep coming if the tacos weren't good. You should be proud, you've achieved great success in a short time."

"I've been meaning to talk to you." Rosie hesitated. "Colby wrote his song about 'doing what you love and throwing out the rule book.' You're the one who gave me that advice. I stole your line."

"I'm flattered my little words of wisdom caused a fuss." Estelle beamed. "My children don't listen to me often, I'm glad someone does."

"How is Angelica?" Rosie asked. "I've been so busy, I feel a little guilty. I haven't talked to her in ages."

"She and Dirk are actually arriving any minute. She called and asked if they could stay for the weekend." Estelle glanced at her watch. "She has some news. I hope it's not an engagement ring.

Dirk has excellent manners but there is something . . . insincere about him," Estelle mused. "You must join us for dinner and bring Josh. I've been meaning to ask, how is Josh handling your success?"

"He's been amazing," Rosie assured her. "I thought he wouldn't approve of Colby's endorsement, but he seems pleased."

"Josh is falling for you." Estelle gathered rose petals. "I can tell by the way he looks at you. And he's more confident. He walks taller and his shoulders seem broader. You've made him into a man and he's ready to accept that responsibility."

"We talked about the future," Rosie confessed. "Josh is hoping to buy the Classic Car Showroom, then he wants to move in together. He even mentioned buying a station wagon and having children."

"That's wonderful if that's what you want." Estelle looked at Rosie. "You don't seem that pleased."

"I want to be with Josh." Rosie hesitated. "He's funny and sweet and sexy. When I'm with him I feel safe and secure."

"Then what's the problem?" Estelle asked.

"I don't want to live together," Rosie explained. "I lived with Ben for eight years and it didn't work. You plan a future together, but either of you can walk out at any time."

"Married people leave their spouses all the time," Estelle countered.

"But it's different when you're married. There are mortgages and joint bank accounts and IRAs. Anyway, I believe in marriage: exchanging vows, making a home, building a family."

"Nothing can make two people happier than a good marriage." Estelle nodded. "Tell Josh you don't want to move in with him."

"What if he takes it the wrong way?" Rosie wondered.

"Knowing what you want is half the battle, saying it is the other half," Estelle counseled. "Not wanting to move in with Josh is part of maturing. You're learning to make the right decisions."

"Mom!" Angelica burst through the door. She wore a form-fitting two-piece suit that made her look like Wonder Woman. Her newly colored auburn hair cascaded down her back and she wore red stilettos.

"Darling." Estelle kissed her cheek. "I'm so glad you're here. Where's Dirk?"

"He made a beeline to the garage. Dirk is pining for Daddy's Alfa Romeo. If he didn't worship me, I'd worry that he only wanted me to get Daddy's cars." Angelica laughed. "Rosie, I haven't talked to you in ages! I can tell you both my news."

"News?" Estelle glanced at Angelica's left hand. Estelle's cheeks paled and she twisted her tennis bracelet.

"It's too exciting, we just came back from London." Angelica perched on a velvet ottoman.

"Wow! London," Rosie exclaimed. "What were you doing there?"

"It was a very quick trip," Angelica replied. "We went to meet Ridley Scott!"

"Ridley Scott?" Rosie's eyes were wide. Ever since film school, Ridley Scott had been one of her and Ben's idols. Ben was crazy about *Gladiator* and *Black Hawk Down*, and Rosie had watched *Thelma and Louise* a dozen times.

"Ridley spends a lot of time in London," Angelica smoothed her skintight skirt. "He saw some rushes from *The Philadelphia Story* and invited Dirk and me to meet him. It was the most exciting thing in the world. We stayed at Claridge's and dined at The Connaught."

"I love Ridley Scott, I'm so jealous. Give us all the details," Rosie said, her voice filled with awe. "What did he want to talk about?"

"He's shooting a movie in Vienna about a doctor and the monster he creates. It's sort of a modern-day Frankenstein," Angelica gushed. "He wants me to play the doctor's love interest, except I fall in love with the monster: like Fay Wray in *King Kong*."

"You're going to be in a Ridley Scott movie." Rosie smiled, genuinely pleased for her friend.

"I'm channeling the part," Angelica stood up and did a slow turn. "Ridley sees her as a redhead with tight skirts and lots of cleavage. Dirk thought I should have implants, but I might just wear a padded bra."

"That is wonderful news, darling." Estelle beamed. "I'm tremendously proud."

"The best part is shooting starts a few weeks after *To Catch a Thief* wraps. We'll be in Europe for almost a year."

"You're going to love Vienna." Estelle smiled. "The opera house is spectacular and the symphony is world class. I may have to come and visit."

"You and Daddy should come, and you too, Rosie." Angelica turned to Rosie. "We can see the fashion shows in Milan and go skiing in St. Moritz."

"I'd love to come. Ridley Scott is the only director I know who understands the importance of location, casting, and a great script." Rosie nodded.

"Owen Wilson is going to be in the new movie too," Angelica squealed. "Dirk is just going to hang out in Vienna; you can eat schnitzel with him."

"I don't think I'll be able to leave the fish taco shop." Rosie shook her head.

"Have you heard about Rosie's amazing success?" Estelle asked.

"Of course I have. 'Rosie' is at the top of the charts, I even heard it on the radio in London. That's my other exciting news." Angelica smiled. "We ran into Colby and Ryan in Beverly Hills. Colby said he wants to talk to Rosie about something. He wouldn't tell me what it was. He just kept throwing secret glances at Ryan."

"He hasn't called me." Rosie frowned.

"Are you having an affair with him?" Angelica asked. "He's cute, but he's barely twenty."

"Of course I'm not having an affair," Rosie protested.

"Then I don't know what all the hush-hush was about." Angelica smoothed her hair. "But I invited Colby and Ryan to stay here this weekend."

"How lovely," Estelle chimed in. "I'll tell Peg and we'll have a proper dinner party. I'll ask her to make Cornish hens and scalloped potatoes. And we'll dress up; I haven't dressed properly since Rosie's opening."

"I'll leave you two to catch up. I'm so happy for you, Angelica." Rosie gave her a hug and walked to the door. "I'm going to soak in a hot bath."

Rosie strolled back to the cottage picturing Angelica on the set of a Ridley Scott movie in Vienna. Ben and Mary Beth were going to film *To Catch a Thief* in the South of France. For a moment there was a twinge like a deep muscle pain. She remembered the nights with Ben in the edit suite, the thrill of seeing the day's rushes on the screen.

But she passed Estelle's rose garden: pink and yellow and orange in its summer splendor. Morris carried a tray of cold drinks and Oscar barked into his cell phone. The lawn was emerald green and swans glided on the lake. No harbor in Monaco or square in Vienna could be as beautiful as the Pullman estate in Montecito.

Rosie stood in the Pullmans' living room, waiting for Josh to bring her a cocktail. She wore a midnight-blue dress with a shirred bodice. Her hair was piled in a bun and she wore bright red lipstick.

She had been nervous telling Josh about the dinner. He grimaced whenever she mentioned Angelica, and he thought Dirk was pretentious and a bore. But he had been happy to accompany her. He even wore a blazer and twill slacks and he smelled of mint aftershave.

"Rosie! It's great to see you," Colby greeted her. He wore a sports jacket over a black t-shirt and held a bottle of wine wrapped in cellophane.

"I haven't thanked you for everything you've done for the taco shop." Rosie blushed and nibbled sausage in puff pastry.

"I get tweets all the time saying how much people love your fish tacos." Colby grinned. "One woman offered me twenty thousand dollars if I told her your secret recipe."

"Twenty thousand dollars!" Rosie gasped. "I could never share my recipe."

"Don't worry, I wouldn't sell you out even if I knew it," Colby assured her. "I want to talk to you about something. Are you free tomorrow afternoon?"

"Sure." Rosie nodded, wondering what Colby could possibly want to talk about.

"We'll pick you up." Colby smiled and held up the wine bottle. "Where is Estelle? I brought her a little gift to thank her for having us this weekend."

Colby moved away and Angelica entered on Dirk's arm. Her eyes were painted like a cat's, and she wore a silver gown with a plunging neckline. An oval diamond sparkled at her neck and large diamonds dangled from her ears.

"Rosie!" Dirk kissed Rosie on the cheek. "Angelica keeps me up to date; what an inspiring story. Whoever thought you could do so well selling tacos."

Rosie imagined Angelica and Dirk talking about Rosie's Fish Tacos and flinched. She suddenly felt naked standing next to Angelica in her couture gown and glittering jewelry. She put down her plate and searched the room for Josh.

"Rosie, I need you in the kitchen," Morris interrupted, standing in the hallway. "Culinary emergency."

"What's wrong?" Rosie asked when she followed Morris into the kitchen.

"I was trying to save you," Morris said. "You looked like Cinderella when the clock strikes midnight and she's afraid her carriage will turn into a pumpkin."

"Was it that obvious?" Rosie sank into a chair.

"I know how you feel. When I first became Mr. Pullman's butler, Neil and the band would come for the weekend. They lolled around the pool while I served them oysters and caviar." Morris arranged canapés on a tray. "Angelica and Dirk aren't better than you because they prance around a movie set."

"Angelica is a wonderful actress," Rosie defended her. "I'm happy for her and Dirk."

"You have everything: a successful store, a great relationship." Morris looked at Rosie. "Unless you want your old life back?"

"Of course I don't," Rosie said nervously. "I'm grateful to the Pullmans for having me and everything that they've done. It's just that Dirk makes me feel like Alice in Wonderland when she became very, very small. And Angelica is more breathtakingly beautiful every time I see her."

"Take your hair down; a bun doesn't suit you." Morris waved at her hair. "And get rid of some of that lipstick. Just be yourself, you have a lot to be proud of."

"Okay." Rosie took the bobby pins out of her hair and rubbed her mouth.

"That's much better." He propelled her towards the door. "Now go stand next to Josh and you'll feel six feet tall."

✳

Josh was standing at the bar talking to Ryan. Josh's eyes lit up when he saw Rosie, and he draped an arm around her shoulder. "Ryan and I have been talking about cars. He has a 1976 E-Type Jag. I'm envious, that's one of my favorite cars on the road."

"I bought it after Colby's first album went platinum," Ryan explained. "I was still living in a studio apartment, but the purr of her engine made me melt."

"I'd love to see her," Josh said enthusiastically. "You'll have to drive up the coast to Montecito."

"Colby won't drive in it with me, he says it doesn't go fast enough." Ryan chuckled and fiddled with the olive in his martini. "Driving isn't only about speed, it's also about enjoying the ride."

"That's what I tell customers at the showroom." Josh nodded. "Buyers should purchase cars that match their personalities. Some people were made to drive Maseratis, and others are suited to Rolls-Royces or Peugeots. Personally I love British cars: Jaguars and Rovers and MGs."

"Rosie!" Angelica approached the group. She held a cocktail plate and smelled of French perfume. "You didn't tell me that you and Josh were an item. How could you keep it a secret?"

"I didn't want to tell you over the phone," Rosie explained and felt Josh tense beside her.

"I know now," Angelica said brightly. "Morris told me. Are you still living in your grandmother's house?" She turned to Josh.

"It's been my house for five years," Josh said tightly.

"Such a cute house, and so close to the beach." Angelica nibbled puff pastry. "I remember the summer I went away to college. You'd always show up to work in board shorts and flip-flops."

"That was more than ten years ago." Josh glared at Angelica. "I've learned how to put on a pair of slacks and a shirt."

"You and Rosie look wonderful together," Angelica gushed. "Who would have guessed I'd send Rosie here for the summer and she'd put down roots: her own store and a cute surfer boyfriend. I'm quite jealous. I'm going to spend the next year living out of a suitcase."

"Angelica got a part in a Ridley Scott movie." Rosie turned to Josh. She was desperate to ease the tension in the air. "It shoots in Vienna."

"I'm going to have to pick Rosie's brain; she knows more about film than anyone," Angelica purred. "She has seen every Ridley Scott movie."

"I always forget Rosie was in the movie business." Ryan turned to Rosie. "Which is your favorite Ridley Scott film? I'm a sucker for *The Martian* with Matt Damon."

"*Thelma & Louise* is a classic; Susan Sarandon and Geena Davis practically defined the female buddy movie." Rosie reflected. "But *A Good Year* is a personal favorite. The setting was Provence, and Russell Crowe and Abbie Cornish were amazing."

"See? Rosie is an encyclopedia," Angelica said proudly. "Don't you miss the movies just a teensy bit? I'd die if I had to live in the real world all the time. A movie set is so much fun."

"Josh and I watch tons of movies." Rosie squeezed Josh's hand. "Last night we saw *La La Land* on Netflix. Ryan Gosling and Emma Stone were brilliant."

"I'm so happy to see my loved ones together." Estelle beamed, walking over to the group. She wore a gold hostess gown and an opal pendant.

"Mother." Angelica kissed her on the cheek. "You look beautiful. What are you wearing around your neck?"

"A gift from your father." Estelle touched the opal. "He just signed a new Swedish band. He shouldn't have bought me such expensive jewelry, but it's very pretty."

"It's lovely," Rosie offered.

"What's lovely is having my favorite people under one roof."

Estelle looked around the group. "Peg made a scrumptious dinner. Shall we go into the dining room?"

Rosie hung back, wanting to talk to Josh alone. But Josh was already striding towards the table. Rosie trailed behind him. Maybe he wasn't put off by Angelica. Maybe he was enjoying himself and couldn't wait to try Peg's Cornish hen.

Estelle sat at the head of the table, flanked by Angelica and Dirk. Rosie never realized how much Estelle and Angelica resembled each other. In their silver and gold gowns they looked like royalty. Angelica regaled the table with stories of the set, giving a perfect Katharine Hepburn impression.

"I would like to make a toast." Estelle stood up. "To all you marvelous young people for filling up this house. It gets a little quiet around here during the week; I haven't taught my roses to talk. And I'm so excited for everyone's success: Colby's album, Rosie's store, Josh close to buying the dealership, and Dirk and Angelica's new movie roles. I can't think of anything that would make this night more perfect." She touched her neck. "And to my darling husband for spoiling me with pretty trinkets and so many years of love."

"I'd like to make a toast too," Angelica announced. "I'd like to thank my parents for creating a safe harbor and letting me venture out on my own. I've found my own harbor now. I'm excited about my career, but I'm even more excited to announce Dirk and I are getting married."

The room went completely silent. Dirk smiled like the Cheshire cat. Estelle froze and Oscar reached for his wineglass.

"Dirk presented me with this beautiful ring when we were in London." Angelica opened her evening bag and took out an emerald-cut diamond ring. "It was so romantic; it was pouring rain and we were sitting in the drawing room at Claridge's. Dirk got down on one knee and said his grandfather proposed to his grandmother in the same spot sixty years ago. The ring belonged to his great-grandfather. He won it from the Duke of Marlborough in a duel."

Rosie glanced at Morris, who was standing at the kitchen door and holding a plate of rolls. Morris rolled his eyes and Rosie stifled a laugh.

Dirk stood up and smoothed his hair. "The day I met Angelica is the day my life began. She is my greatest treasure and I will devote my life to making her happy."

Morris clutched his sides and Rosie shot him a stern look.

"This is a surprise." Oscar rose from his chair. "But everyone was surprised when Estelle married me and things have worked out very well. Estelle, shall we toast our new son-in-law?"

Rosie's eyes filled with tears. Suddenly Dirk didn't seem like an imposter; he looked like a man in love. Angelica wasn't playing a part; she was a young woman ready to walk down the aisle. Rosie glanced at her own naked ring finger and tucked her hands in her lap.

"We're going to have the wedding in Monte Carlo, when shooting wraps on *To Catch a Thief*. I found a tiny stone church overlooking the harbor. And we'll hold the reception on the studio's yacht. Of course, you'll all come. And Rosie." Angelica looked at Rosie. "I'd like you to be my maid of honor."

Everyone was looking at Rosie, expecting her to jump up and hug Angelica. She pictured Angelica wearing a satin gown and carrying a bouquet of roses. The first dance would be on the deck of a yacht, the lights of Monte Carlo twinkling on the water.

"Rosie?" Angelica prompted her.

"Congratulations, I'm so happy for you," Rosie said effusively.

"The store just opened and I'm not sure I can leave it for that long—"

"Of course we'll come," Josh cut in. "Rosie would never miss her best friend's wedding."

"We'll make it a big party," Colby enthused. "We'll rent hot-air balloons and go parasailing."

"It does sound divine, darling," Estelle agreed, her face finally breaking into a smile. "I'll come over in the fall and we can shop for gowns in Paris. Rosie, you can make a quick trip too so we find you the perfect dress."

Rosie stared at her soup and mechanically moved the spoon to her mouth. Everyone else was animatedly making plans. Ryan told Josh about a classic car dealership in Nice. Colby and Oscar discussed the size of yachts, and Angelica and Dirk held hands across the table. Rosie didn't dare look at Josh. She didn't want him to see her fighting back tears.

"Rosie, are you all right?" Estelle asked. "You're quite pale."

"It's nothing, the soup is a little spicy. I just need some air." Rosie stood up and ran out of the room. She kept running until she reached the lawn and stepped right in the path of the sprinklers. The spray drenched her dress and her hair and she slid and landed on the grass.

Rosie sat on the lawn and hugged her chest. She was too embarrassed to return to the dinner party and too chilled to walk to the cottage. She took deep breaths and tried to stop her teeth from chattering.

She was appalled by her own behavior. Over the years, Rosie bought dozens of espresso machines and waffle irons as gifts from the bridal registry at Williams-Sonoma. She played silly party games at friends' bridal showers. She and Ben sat in stuffy churches watching the bride and groom exchange their vows.

They would drive home from a wedding reception and critique

the band and the cake and sometimes the choice of bride or groom. They would murmur things like, "We should have a cupcake tree at our wedding" or "We should take salsa classes for our first dance." Then Ben would go back to editing the day's rushes and Rosie would tackle her to-do list, and their wedding plans would simmer on the back burner.

But tonight Angelica's emerald-cut diamond glinted in the candlelight and Rosie felt a physical pain. She imagined the church—light streaming in through stained-glass windows, stone floor strewn with rose petals—and she was swept up with longing.

Suddenly she knew why she was so upset. It wasn't that Angelica was having a wedding in Monaco and would sail around the Mediterranean on her honeymoon. It was that Rosie knew that she had found the man she wanted to marry, but what if he didn't feel the same?

She sat up and stared into the mist. She pictured walking down the aisle towards Josh. He'd be wearing a black tux and she'd be dressed in a simple ivory sheath. She imagined Josh saying his vows, repeating each word in a loud, clear voice. Then his mouth would find hers in a kiss that seemed to last forever, and the minister would pronounce them husband and wife.

Rosie sighed and picked wet grass from her legs. She could tell Josh she didn't want to move in with him, but she couldn't ask him to marry her. He would have to get down on one knee, or take her hand at dinner and propose.

She watched plenty of talk shows where the woman said she proposed and now the couple was celebrating their tenth anniversary with two children and a rescue Labradoodle mix. But if she asked Josh and he said he needed more time, she couldn't handle the rejection. Ben had broken her heart and she wasn't ready for more pain.

"What went on in there?" Josh demanded, striding towards her.

Rosie jumped. Josh's arms swung at his sides and his eyes glinted in the dark.

"I felt sick," Rosie said. "I'm a little better."

"Why didn't you want to go to Angelica's wedding?" Josh loomed over her. "Are you ashamed of me? You don't think I can mingle with film stars and movie producers. I know all the capitals of Europe; I speak a little French. I've even been on a plane." Josh glowered. "Not a private jet, but I can buckle a seat belt without spilling my drink."

"That has nothing to do with it." Rosie had never seen Josh so angry.

"You didn't tell your best friend we were together! Were you afraid she wouldn't approve?" he demanded. "I'm not good enough because I don't drive an Aston Martin or live in a beach house on the sand."

"You don't like Angelica," Rosie reminded him. "You've said that a dozen times."

"We've had our differences," Josh conceded. "But she's your best friend. I would never miss her wedding."

"That's not why I didn't want to go," she said quietly.

"Ryan wasn't embarrassed to hang out with me. We even found we had things in common. Are you afraid to run into Ben and Mary Beth?" he prodded. "Are you still in love with him? Do you miss going to movie premieres and seeing your name on the screen?"

"I never think about Ben or Hollywood." Rosie flushed. "I love our lives. I love the fish taco store and Butterfly Beach and Montecito village."

"Then what is it, Rosie?" Josh demanded, his eyes glinting in the dark. "Why didn't you want to be Angelica's maid of honor?"

"I thought you wouldn't want to go," Rosie said lamely.

She couldn't tell Josh the truth. She couldn't tell him she didn't want to just share a bed and matching cereal bowls. She wanted to stand up in a church and exchange vows that would tie them together forever. He'd think she was jealous of Angelica's large diamond, of the storybook wedding in Monte Carlo.

"Couples make sacrifices for each other," Josh persisted. "You didn't even ask me if I wanted to go. You hurt Angelica's feelings and offended Estelle and Oscar."

"I said I was happy for her." Rosie gulped and her eyes filled with tears. "It was just all so sudden. Angelica put me on the spot and I didn't know how to answer."

"Maybe you don't know how you feel about us," Josh said quietly. "Maybe we're moving too fast."

"What does that mean?" She looked up. "Our relationship has nothing to do with Angelica's wedding."

"It does if you don't want to be seen with me." He jammed his hands in his pockets.

"You don't know what you're talking about. I only want to be with you." Rosie looked at Josh and her stomach tightened. She wanted him to put his arms around her and cover her lips with his own.

"You don't know what you want." Josh turned and strode towards the driveway. "If owning a couple of local stores and living in a ranch-style house isn't enough, you better tell me now. I'm never going to be more than I am."

"That's not what I meant at all!" Rosie ran after him.

"I'm going home, I'll see you tomorrow."

Rosie looked up at the house and noticed Angelica and Dirk standing at an upstairs window. Dirk had his arms around Angelica and she threw her head back and laughed. Oscar and Estelle sat on the swing on the porch. Oscar smoked a cigar and Estelle hummed a song.

Rosie walked dejectedly back to the cottage. Josh's shirts hung neatly in the closet and there was an empty space in the bed where he usually slept. Her eyes hurt and she was suddenly freezing. She unzipped her dress and pulled the comforter over her head.

Fourteen

Rosie heard someone knocking on the cottage door and opened her eyes. It was early afternoon and the sun streamed through the French doors. The sprinklers made gurgling noises and voices carried across the lawn.

If only she could do dinner last night all over again. If she had agreed to be Angelica's maid of honor, Josh would be lying beside her in bed. They'd be planning their trip and looking up quaint bed-and-breakfasts and cafes on the French Riviera.

There was another short knock. Rosie slipped on her robe and opened the door.

"I saw Josh peel down the driveway last night." Morris held a silver tray. "I figured if you weren't up by noon, I'd bring breakfast."

"I appreciate it but I'm not hungry." Rosie walked back inside and perched on the bed.

"Orange juice to bolster your immune system." Morris set a glass on the table. "A poached egg for protein and grapefruit to make your skin glow."

"No, thank you. It's Sunday, and Patrick's sister is minding the store. I'm going back to sleep."

"What happened?" Morris demanded.

Rosie sat against the headboard and hugged her knees to her chest. She told Morris how angry Josh became because he thought she was ashamed of him. Josh asked her to move in with him and she realized she didn't want to live together; she wanted to get married.

"I can understand why Josh was upset." Morris nodded. "I can't imagine anything more fabulous than a wedding in Monte Carlo. It's the sexiest place on earth. The men and women dress in the most divine fashions and the ocean is the color of topaz."

"You're not helping," Rosie said miserably.

"You're behaving like a throwback to the 1950s," Morris scoffed. "If you want to get married, tell him."

"I can't do that, I guess I'm too traditional." Rosie shook her head. "Josh has to be the one to propose."

"Men aren't magicians, they can't read minds," Morris said. "You have to be honest with Josh and tell him how you feel."

"I don't even know what came over me." Rosie stood up and paced around the room. "Ben and I lived together for eight years and I didn't think about marriage. We used to talk about it like we discussed traveling to Spain or Peru. It sounded wonderful but we could do it in the future, when we didn't have so much work."

"It's called being in love," Morris said soberly. "It's like a head cold. It clogs your brain and makes your eyes water."

"I thought being in love releases endorphins, like chocolate." Rosie sighed.

"That's the version you read in *Cosmopolitan*," Morris corrected. "The real thing is messy and exhausting. That's why you need a proper breakfast." He pointed to the tray.

"Why aren't I happy running the store and being with Josh?"

Rosie admonished herself. "Why do I want a poufy white dress and a piece of paper and the same last name for our children?"

"Because you're human." Morris stood at the door.

"In my next life, I want to come back as a dog." Rosie stabbed the egg with a fork and looked at Morris. "Thank you for always propping me up when I'm down. You're a great friend and I really appreciate it."

"That's what friends are for." Morris nodded. "Finish your egg, you need the protein for strength."

Rosie's phone buzzed as she scraped the remains of the egg. She glanced at the screen, hoping it was Josh. She'd tell him to come over and they'd both apologize. Then they'd go into the village and read French guidebooks over croissants and cups of milky coffee.

"Hey," Colby's voice came over the line. "I hope you haven't forgotten our date. Can you be ready in thirty minutes?"

Rosie jumped up and looked at herself in the mirror. She still wore last night's makeup, and her hair frizzed in a halo around her head.

"I forgot all about it!" Rosie exclaimed. "I'm not feeling well."

"You're going to love it," Colby said cheerfully. "We'll pick you up, wear comfortable clothes."

"Where are we going?" Rosie asked.

"It's a surprise," Colby answered as if he was used to women following him anywhere.

"If I was you, I'd change into a long-sleeved shirt and sneakers," Colby said when she answered the door. "And a hat with a broad brim."

"Are you kidnapping me?" Rosie pulled a cotton shirt over her halter top. She took off her sandals and found a pair of sneakers under the bed.

"We're taking you somewhere you've never been." Ryan appeared behind Colby. His hair was slicked back and his sunglasses were perched on his forehead.

"I'm taking my phone." Rosie grabbed it from the side table. "If you drive across the border, people will come find me."

Rosie followed them to Colby's silver convertible and slid into the backseat. She had forgotten the pleasure of driving along the coast. The ocean was pale blue and the sand glistened like a string of pearls. A few sailboats sat on the horizon, their white sails billowing in the breeze.

Colby turned the car inland and they climbed towards the mountains. The palm trees became olive trees and the road wound between rolling vineyards and farmland. The clear air filled Rosie's lungs, pushing away the black cloud that enveloped her.

They drove through woods and past waterfalls. Rosie turned around and the village below was like pieces on a board game. The ocean became a blue blot and the boats were tiny white specks. They kept climbing and Rosie's ears rang and she tied her hat on her head.

"Where are we going?" She leaned forward and asked Colby, who maneuvered the stick shift like a race-car driver.

"We're almost there," he yelled, taking a turn and stopping in front of tall iron gates. They were in a clearing: The mountains loomed above, the ocean a clear piece of glass far below. Behind the gate was a cluster of buildings painted in different colors. There was a paddock with a white fence and a long house with wide porches.

"Where are we?" Rosie got out of the car. The air was hot and stale, and bugs slapped at her skin.

"Welcome to the Circle Bar B Ranch." Colby jumped out of the car. "It has been the favorite destination of countless celebrities such as Clark Gable and Rita Hayworth and more recently the Kardashians and Kanye West."

"And Colby Young," Ryan broke in.

"I may have increased its popularity." Colby grinned. "But that's because it's awesome. They have a guesthouse, a dinner theater, and shops that resemble a western town."

Rosie walked towards painted buildings with signs that said GENERAL STORE and BLACKSMITH. She peeked in the window and there were bags of feed and rows of saddles and cowboy boots.

"What are we doing here?" Rosie asked.

Colby's eyes twinkled as if he was about to let Rosie in on a big secret.

"We're going riding." Colby walked towards the paddock and pointed at a dappled horse. "That's Drummer, your horse."

"My what?" Rosie ran behind him. "I haven't been on a horse since my seventh birthday party. I got so scared, I couldn't eat the cake."

"There's nothing to be afraid of, Drummer is as docile as a lamb. And the trails are amazing." Colby waved his hand. "You can see the whole coast from Point Conception to Point Dume."

"Why are we going riding?" Rosie suddenly wished she were back in the cottage, sipping orange juice and eating Peg's poached egg.

"A change of scenery is energizing," Colby continued. "Plus, these are the most spectacular views in Southern California. Enrico is going to be our private guide and carry our picnic basket. All you have to do is hop on Drummer and follow him."

"Why is it so important that we go riding?" Rosie eyed the horse. The horse's nose was damp and he swung his tail lazily in the air. "What do you guys have planned that you're not telling me."

"Trust me, you'll enjoy it. Besides, you don't want to miss out on prosciutto on rolls, and strawberries and fresh whipped cream. Enrico," Colby called. "Did you pack the Kenwood Chardonnay?"

"Sí señor." Enrico nodded.

"And you're going to miss a fine Chardonnay," Colby coaxed. "C'mon, riding Drummer is easier than riding a tricycle."

Rosie looked helplessly at Ryan, but he laughed and shrugged his shoulders. "I was terrified the first time I rode Mickey." Ryan pointed to a large black horse. "It'll be worth it when you see the view."

Rosie took a deep breath and climbed on Drummer. The horse bucked gently, and Rosie was certain she'd end up sprawled on the dirt. But he quieted down and waited for Rosie's command.

"See, there's nothing to it." Colby jumped on his horse. "Enrico, let's ride. I'm getting hungry."

Enrico led the group and Rosie followed. Ryan trotted behind her and Colby brought up the rear, singing songs from his new album. The sky was cloudless and the sun was a yellow ball. She was glad she wore her hat and wished she had a wet cloth to wipe her forehead.

They rode on steep paths shaded by oak trees. The ground was like a velvet carpet and the air smelled of ferns and moss. They stopped at a waterfall and let the horses drink in the stream. The higher they climbed, the more Rosie thought the whole thing was a dream.

As they reached the summit, even Colby grew quiet. The only sound was the occasional squirrel darting through the trees. The trail ended and there was a wide clearing. Rosie was afraid if she looked down, she might faint.

"Are you afraid of heights?" Ryan asked.

"I don't think so." Rosie gulped. "But I've only been this high up on an airplane."

"Hop off and follow me." Ryan pulled his horse to a stop.

Rosie dismounted and followed Ryan up a narrow path. There was a clump of trees, and on the other side a rock that jutted out over the valley.

"There," Ryan said, as if he created the valley himself. "Look."

Rosie looked up and saw deep forests and rushing streams. There was every color of the rainbow: purple flowers and green grass and blue waterfalls. Far below was the Pacific Ocean. It wasn't the ocean Rosie knew, with seagulls skimming the waves and swimmers rolling in the surf. It was an ocean painted by an impressionist painter, caught at the magic hour.

"Oh, it's gorgeous." Rosie put her hand over her mouth.

"You can see the Channel Islands, and all the way to San Diego." Colby bounded behind her.

"I feel like God," Rosie murmured. "Looking down on creation."

"We'll come back after lunch." Colby waved at the view. "Riding for two hours makes me starving."

Enrico had spread out a blanket, and there were plates of sandwiches and fresh fruit. There was a jug of lemonade, a bottle of wine in a silver bucket, bowls of strawberries, and a tub of whipped cream.

Rosie nibbled green grapes and watched Colby devour a sandwich like a schoolboy. She felt suddenly strange. She barely knew Colby and Ryan, and now she was sitting on top of a mountain, removed from everything by a long, winding trail.

"We didn't just bring you up here to admire the view," Colby said when he finished his second sandwich. "We have a proposition for you."

Rosie choked on a grape. "I appreciate everything you did for the store, but I'm not that kind of girl."

Colby and Ryan looked at each other and Colby burst out laughing. "You're beautiful, but I have a steady girlfriend."

"You do?" Rosie asked. Rachel would be devastated. All the gossip magazines claimed Colby was single.

"We keep it secret because she got a few death threats from my fans," Colby said. "It's a business proposition. Did you know you can't get a fish taco in North Dakota or Missouri? I want to expand Rosie's Fish Tacos; not just to states like Hawaii and Oregon that love Mexican food. I want to bring it to states that have never seen a tortilla and don't have an ocean. And I want to introduce Rosie's Fish Tacos to high-end grocery stores: frozen entrées, Rosie's guacamole in hip packaging."

"I don't want to sell Rosie's Fish Tacos," Rosie said hesitantly. "I like running the store."

"We'd be partners," Colby explained. "We'll provide the capital; you supply the recipes. Our lawyers will figure out the percentages. If we get a response like the one you're getting at the shop, it's going to be huge."

"Why tacos?" Rosie frowned. "You've got your panini places and your burger joints."

"Colby makes more money with his restaurants than album sales and tours combined," Ryan chimed in. "Americans are always hungry."

"No one thinks a kid my age knows what he's doing." Colby was suddenly serious. "Someday there's going to be a new face on the cover of *Rolling Stone*, and I want to keep creating. Opening restaurants is like writing songs."

Rosie pictured walking into Vons and seeing Rosie's Fish Tacos in the frozen food section. She imagined visiting Rosie's Fish Tacos stores in Virginia and Wyoming.

"I've never done anything like that." She ate a bite of her sandwich.

"You never opened a fish taco store before," Ryan reminded her. "You've got a golden touch."

"I don't know if I'm ready," she said lamely. Suddenly she remembered Josh saying he wasn't good enough and flinched. Would Josh be thrilled that they'd be financially stable, or appalled that she was teaming up with a celebrity? Maybe Josh wouldn't care at all. Maybe he had left for good.

"You know the Pullman estate? If this takes off like we think it will, you can buy an estate just like it. Do you know how much the Kardashians make on their line of clothing? One hundred million a year," Ryan offered.

"I'm not the Kardashians," Rosie said and dipped a strawberry into whipped cream.

"But Colby is," Ryan insisted. "With Colby's name and your product, Rosie's Fish Tacos could be a very lucrative venture."

Rosie glanced from Ryan to Colby. They were like two puppies, bursting with enthusiasm. "Can I think about it?" she asked.

"I've never had someone say they had to think about making millions for doing the same thing they're doing now." Ryan chuckled.

"Just for a few days," Rosie responded.

"I remember when Ryan discovered me singing at the baseball field and told me he was going to make me a star," Colby recalled. "I thought he was wacko and almost hit him with the bat."

"Luckily I'm a smooth talker, and a fast runner," Ryan added.

"It'll be fun, Rosie," Colby urged. "It's like riding Drummer, you just have to hop on and enjoy the ride."

They arrived at the Pullman estate when it was already dark. Rosie stepped gingerly out of the car. Her legs were stiff from clinging to Drummer as they descended the mountain. When she closed her eyes she still saw the sweeping view, the miles of uninterrupted green and blue.

Rosie hurried to the cottage, thankful for the cool fog after the blinding sun of the ranch. She didn't want to bump into Morris or Estelle. She needed to think about Colby's offer before they gave her advice.

She opened the cottage door and walked inside. The dress she wore to the dinner party was still crumpled on the floor. She was tempted to call Josh, but he was the one who had walked away. She wasn't ready to be the one who made the first move.

Her phone rang and her parents' number appeared on the screen.

"Hi, Rosie," her mother's voice came over the line. "Your father and I have been so busy preparing for the space launch, we haven't talked to you all summer. I called the home line and Ben said you were staying in Montecito."

Rosie smiled. Her parents used cutting-edge technology to design rockets, but her mother still preferred using a landline.

"I'm just taking a little break from Hollywood," Rosie said. "Angelica's parents offered me their guest cottage for the summer."

"The funniest thing happened today. My friend Lucille said her daughter heard a song on the radio by some young pop star. His name was Colby." Her mother paused. "The song was about a girl who leaves Hollywood to follow her dreams and opens a fish taco store in Montecito. It's called 'Rosie.' Apparently it's number one on the music charts and it's all about you."

"I was going to tell you," Rosie admitted, embarrassed. She never hid things from her parents, but she hadn't known how to tell them about Ben.

"What does Ben say about all this?" her mother asked. "He didn't say a thing when I called."

"We're taking a little time to figure things out," Rosie said evasively. "Ben and I have been together for so long, I just needed a summer to myself."

"Are you sure you're all right? You don't have to stay with Angelica's parents. You can come to Florida," her mother suggested. "The guest room is always here for you."

"Florida summers and I don't get along," Rosie said, recalling how the sky turned black in the afternoon and there were violent thunderstorms. "Every afternoon at two o'clock our dog, Baxter, and I hid under the bed."

"There was nothing to be afraid of." Her mother laughed. "As long as you didn't go swimming in the ocean."

"I'm fine here and the fish taco store is really taking off. I'll see you when I come visit in October," Rosie said and curled up on the sofa. "I'll bring you and dad a box of Sprinkles Cupcakes."

"That sounds delicious," her mother enthused. "Have a good summer, Rosie. We love you very much."

Rosie hung up and the good feelings of being loved receded. She remembered the way Josh stormed down the driveway without looking back. First she had to think about Colby's offer. Then she had to figure out how to get Josh to talk to her again.

Fifteen

Sunlight streamed through the window the next morning and Rosie stepped into the bath. She added a bottle of lavender bubble bath and inhaled the refreshing scent. She had gotten up early, thrown on her running shoes, and driven to Butterfly Beach before she was fully awake. Rosie ran the length of the beach, thinking about Colby's offer. She knew she was crazy to hesitate. Colby was handing her a golden future.

Was this how Ben felt when the studio hired Mary Beth? His years of wrestling with unruly scripts and inexperienced actors would give way to being offered the hottest projects. A-list actors like Ryan Reynolds and Scarlett Johansson would line up to work with him. People would murmur, "It's a Ben Ford film," when the lights went down and the credits rolled on the screen.

Rosie didn't have a dream of running a corporation, spending her days worrying about quality control and product placement. She loved the smell of fish sizzling on the stove at the taco store. She enjoyed chatting with Rachel on the sidewalk at the end of the day.

The feeling of satisfaction when she opened the cash register and counted the piles of new bills.

But Oscar and Estelle led wonderful lives. Their house was filled with antique furniture and fine china, and the parties on the lawn were from another era. And there was such a sense of peace when you entered the gate. It would be heavenly to have the kind of money to surround yourself with people you loved and beautiful things.

Rosie stopped running and did long stretches, watching the surfers paddle past the break. If Ben had only talked to her about how he felt, things might have been different. They could have debated attaching Mary Beth as executive producer. Rosie could have stepped back and focused her energy on their home.

She squinted and looked for Josh in the line of surfers. If they had any chance as a couple, they had to make this decision together. But what if Josh didn't want to see her? He was the one who said he wasn't good at arguing. He was better at walking away.

There was a knock at the cottage door and Rosie groaned. She wasn't prepared for a visit from Morris. She didn't want to be force-fed peanut butter sandwiches or told she deserved this because she didn't tell Josh how she felt about living together.

She waited for another knock, but there was silence. Maybe Morris thought she was asleep. She closed her eyes and submerged her body under the bubbles.

"Is there room for me in that bath?" a male voice asked.

Rosie flung her arms over her chest and opened her eyes. Josh sat on the edge of the bath. He was pale and he had a day's stubble on his chin.

"You don't have to cover yourself." He smiled. "Unless you were expecting someone else."

"I wasn't expecting anyone." Rosie pushed the bubbles from her cheeks.

"I owe you an apology." Josh dipped his hand in the water. "My sister called me last night. I told her what happened and she said I overreacted. Once she was asked to be a bridesmaid six times in five months. She loved every minute of it, but when her best friend asked her to be maid of honor, she walked into her closet and tossed all six bridesmaids dresses in the garbage. She said weddings make women do crazy things: not just the bride, but the bridesmaids, the mother of the bride, even the wedding planner."

"I like your sister." Rosie laughed.

"She's pretty smart." Josh nodded. "I'd still like to know why you don't want to go to Angelica's wedding, but I'm not going to take it personally."

"I can't explain," Rosie replied.

"You can tell me anything," Josh said. "We have to be honest with each other, Rosie."

"I'll always be honest," Rosie promised. She wanted to just keep looking at him. She felt as if she had conjured up his presence like a magician.

"I shouldn't have stormed off," Josh said seriously. "I don't want you to think I'm going to run every time we have an argument."

"I believe you." Rosie nodded and suddenly wanted him so badly. She could taste his mouth, feel his chest on top of hers.

"Is there anything you want to talk about?" he asked.

Rosie thought about Colby's offer. She remembered Estelle's advice to tell Josh she didn't want to move in with him. Morris had insisted that she tell Josh she wanted to get married because he couldn't read her mind. But right now all she wanted was him to wrap his arms around her.

"There is something." Rosie reached out of the water and kissed him. "It's a little complicated."

"Then why don't we talk about it later." Josh grinned and pulled her out of the bath. He put a towel around her and kissed her neck. "There's something important I want to do first."

"I guess it can wait," she whispered, every nerve in her body tingling.

They moved to the bed and Josh tore off his clothes. His breath was sweet and his shoulders were broad and Rosie swelled with happiness. He entered her and she dug her fingernails into his back, the waves building inside her. She gasped and held him until his body slackened and he rolled onto his side.

They slept with Rosie tucked against Josh's chest. When they woke they were starving and Rosie made a picnic of items she found in the cottage's fridge: a slab of Brie cheese, a bar of chocolate, a bowl of cherries.

"I feel like I'm raiding a hotel minibar," Rosie sat cross-legged on the bed and ate cheese on a sourdough roll.

"Will you come to the Concours d'Elegance?" he asked. "I'll have to work, but we can stroll through Carmel and drive along 17-Mile Drive. You've never seen views like it. The waves crash right on the rocks."

"I'd love to." Rosie nodded, thinking she should tell Josh about Colby's offer. But she wasn't quite ready to break the spell.

"I'll book a bed-and-breakfast," Josh said excitedly. "Carmel is a little like Montecito, except it's always foggy."

"Sounds romantic." Rosie nibbled dark chocolate.

"We'll get a room overlooking the ocean." Josh popped a cherry in Rosie's mouth. "It'll have a king-sized bed and one of those funky TVs that only work if you hold the antenna. We'll keep the window open so the fog blows in and I'll have to keep you warm."

They finished the picnic and Josh drifted off to sleep. Rosie watched his chest rise and fall and promised herself when he woke up she'd tell him everything.

Rosie opened her eyes and Josh's side of the bed was empty. The sheets were pushed back and there was a note on his pillow. He had to work on Oscar's cars, but he'd be back for dinner and dessert. He signed it with three x's and a P.S. to keep the bed warm.

She wrapped a robe around her and stood by the window. She could lounge around until Josh came back and then share more food and sex. But tomorrow she'd have to return to work and Colby expected an answer by Wednesday. She had to talk about the offer with Josh now, without the distraction of bubble baths and down comforters and dark chocolate.

Rosie entered the garage and her eyes adjusted to the dim light. She wore her red dress and gold Manolos. Her hair was glossy and her wrists were spritzed with perfume.

"This is a surprise." Josh looked up from the engine of a yellow Ferrari.

"I couldn't wait till you came back." Rosie smiled. "And I felt like dressing up."

"What's the occasion?" he asked, leaning against the car's bumper.

"Being together," Rosie replied. "Delicious food, great sex."

"I'm in favor of all three things." Josh kissed her. "I just have to fix this engine, and we can go back to being naked."

"I do want to talk about something." Rosie took a deep breath. "Colby and Ryan took me riding yesterday."

"Riding?" Josh's body tensed and the muscles on his neck twitched.

"At Circle Bar B Ranch. We rode to the top. The view was amazing, I could see all the way to San Diego." She paused. "Colby had a business proposition. He wants to expand Rosie's Fish Tacos to more states. He suggested a frozen food line and a line of guacamole sold at supermarkets and gourmet food stores."

"You want to sell the taco shop?" he asked stiffly.

"We'd be partners," she continued. "Colby and Ryan would provide the backing and I'd supply the recipes. He had some really good ideas: opening stores in states that don't have many Mexican restaurants. He thinks we could make a lot of money."

"We don't need a lot of money." Josh's brow furrowed.

"We don't need it," Rosie agreed. "But wouldn't it be lovely to own an estate like this. Our children could have a swimming pool, room to play, a couple of big dogs."

"Children don't need a big house. They just need parents who love them," Josh countered. "What if it wasn't a success? Celebrity restaurants are like hot-air balloons. If it fails, all that hard work would be for nothing."

"Colby is only twenty and he has a fantastic track record. Ryan said he makes more money from his restaurants than recording and touring combined," Rosie said defensively.

"I knew you'd get suckered back to Hollywood." Josh paced around the car.

"Nothing would change," Rosie answered. "I'd still run the taco shop."

"Everything would change," Josh cut in. "You'd have endless meetings with Colby and Ryan. You'd stay in LA during the week and come up to Montecito on the weekends."

"I thought you wanted us to be financially stable." Rosie was suddenly angry. "Why can't you be happy that I have this opportunity?"

"Why do you want more, when we're happy now?" Josh glared. "I want you and a couple of kids and a house near the beach. I don't want to eat TV dinners because you're at a store opening in Wisconsin. I don't want to watch you and Colby chatting with Jimmy Fallon on late-night television."

"Money isn't a bad thing," Rosie protested. "Oscar and Estelle are the happiest couple I know. Money can buy things for people you love; it means you can give your children everything they need."

"I want my children to have two parents who want the same thing," Josh said. "It's impossible when one parent is a celebrity."

"I wouldn't be a celebrity," Rosie fumed. "I'd just be partners with Colby, no one would know who I am."

"Stop trying to hold Rosie back!" a woman's voice interjected.

Rosie turned around and Angelica stepped out of the Aston Martin Spider. She wore a silk robe tied with a yellow belt. Her hair cascaded down her back and her diamond ring glinted on her finger.

"What are you doing here?" Rosie gasped.

"If you must know, Dirk and I had sex in the Spider." Angelica flushed. "I used to bring boyfriends here when I was in high school. Making love in the backseat of a car is so sexy. I lost an earring and I came to find it."

"You were eavesdropping?" Rosie asked, horrified.

"I couldn't just jump up and leave once you two started fighting," Angelica explained.

"Please leave now," Josh said. He clutched a cloth and his mouth was set in a firm line.

"Just because you live your whole life in a ten-mile radius, doesn't mean that Rosie wants to," Angelica said to Josh. "Colby is a huge star, he could make Rosie a millionaire."

"This has nothing to do with you." Josh gritted his teeth.

"You're just afraid that Rosie will realize she can do better," Angelica countered. "She's already discovered that. She told my mother she didn't want to move in with you."

Rosie froze. She inhaled sharply but the air wouldn't go into her lungs. Her knees buckled and she turned from Angelica to Josh.

"What did you say?" Josh's mouth quivered.

"Dirk and I had just arrived. I was standing outside and I overheard Rosie asking my mother for advice." Angelica patted her hair. "You asked Rosie to move in with you, and she didn't know how to tell you she didn't want to."

"Did you say that?" Josh turned to Rosie. His eyes were flat. His body was tense, ready for flight.

"It's not what I meant," Rosie pleaded. "That's what I wanted to discuss in the bath."

"Angelica heard you say it to Estelle," Josh repeated.

"I didn't mean it like that," Rosie said desperately.

"But you said it," Josh said slowly. "And you said you'd always be honest. I've got things to do. I'll see you later."

"It's not how it sounds." Rosie's eyes filled with tears. "I can explain."

Josh reached the door and turned the handle. "That's not necessary. Angelica made it perfectly clear."

"Josh, wait." She followed him onto the driveway. "I was going to talk about it, we just haven't had time. It's more complicated than that."

"We've had time to make love and eat chocolate." His eyes were dark. "There was plenty of time to talk about not wanting to live together."

"You don't understand," she begged. "Angelica twisted my words."

"Angelica would never intentionally hurt her best friend." Josh glared at her. "You're the one who is twisting things. You told Estelle you didn't want to live with me and now you can't think of any easy way to let me down. I've got to go, I'm late for work."

*

Rosie trudged across the lawn to the cottage and opened the door. Angelica sat on the sofa, leafing through a magazine.

"I hope you don't mind me coming in." She looked up. "The door was unlocked and I wanted to apologize."

"It's a little late for that," Rosie said tightly. "Josh doesn't want to talk to me."

"I'm sorry it came out that way," Angelica offered. "But I did you a favor. Josh would just hold you back."

"Hold me back!" Rosie retorted. "Is that what Ben's friends said about me? 'You should dump Rosie, she's holding you back.' If you love someone, they're not holding you back, they're part of the journey."

"But I heard you say you didn't want to move in with Josh," Angelica persisted.

"I didn't want to move in with him because I don't believe in living together. Either person can leave whenever they want to: just pack a suitcase and go." Rosie crumpled onto the floor. "I wanted to marry Josh, but I didn't know how to tell him."

"Oh." Angelica sat next to Rosie. "I didn't know."

"That's why I got flustered when you asked me to be your maid of honor. It's not that I didn't want to be at your wedding. It was because I saw Dirk's face when he looked at you and I wanted Josh to look at me like that." Rosie gulped and tears streamed down her cheeks. "I know it's silly. Plenty of couples live together forever, but I wanted a ring and a poufy white dress."

Rosie cried harder, rocking back and forth. Angelica let her rest her head on her shoulder. She waited till the sobs became hiccups and Rosie was finally still.

"You'd look terrible in a poufy dress," Angelica suggested. "You should wear something sleek, like an Alexander McQueen sheath."

"If you make me wear a satin bow as your maid of honor, I'll cut it off." Rosie hiccupped.

"I already designed your dress: lime green with white polka dots."

"Like Katherine Heigl in *27 Dresses*," Rosie giggled.

"You'd look wonderful in green." Angelica smiled. "It matches your eyes."

Rosie started sobbing again, tears falling on her gold Manolos. "I'm sorry I didn't agree to be your maid of honor right away."

"I'm sorry I chased Josh away," Angelica offered. "I had no idea you wanted to marry him."

"You and Josh might not get along, but he's everything I want," Rosie said. "He's handsome and funny and sweet. He's completely honest; I would never doubt him."

"He'll come back," Angelica insisted.

"He said he doesn't know how to fight, he just walks away," Rosie moaned. "What am I going to do?"

"I just played that scene in *The Philadelphia Story*. Katharine Hepburn jumps in the car and drives after Cary Grant. She tells him she loves him and they make up and live happily ever after."

Rosie stood up and smoothed her dress. "Josh is proud and he was so hurt. I doubt anything I say will make it better."

"There's nothing a beautiful girl in a red dress can't fix," Angelica said confidently. "It works every time in the movies."

The minute Angelica left the cottage, Rosie doubted Angelica's advice. Angelica was drop-dead gorgeous like Angelina Jolie or Jessica Biel. No man could resist her. But Ben had walked away from Rosie, and Josh could do the same. Rosie needed to talk to someone who didn't live on a movie set. She walked up to the house and looked for Estelle.

Estelle was perched on an armchair in the living room. An Irish setter nestled at her feet, and she flipped through *Town & Country*.

"Hi, Rosie." Estelle put the magazine down. "I was reading about Vita Sackville-West's garden at Sissinghurst. When we're in Monaco we must take a quick trip across the Channel to England. I would love to see Sissinghurst in person."

"It sounds lovely," Rosie replied glumly.

"Are you all right? You have been going through a lot and I can understand if Angelica's announcement upset you." Estelle took off her reading glasses. "You look like you've been crying."

"It's not that exactly. I'm thrilled for Angelica and Dirk." Rosie dropped into a floral armchair. "It's Josh."

"Did you tell him you didn't want to move in with him?"

"Angelica did." Rosie sighed. "And she left out the part that I wanted to marry him."

"Angelica!" Estelle exclaimed. "I thought she and Dirk left this afternoon."

"They had some business to finish up." Rosie waved her hand. "Josh and I got in a fight and Angelica decided she would fix it."

"You're not making sense," Estelle responded. "Start at the beginning."

Rosie told Estelle about Colby's offer and Josh's insistence that she turn it down. She told her about Angelica stepping out of the Aston Martin and accusing Josh of holding her back.

"Then Angelica told Josh she overheard me telling you I don't want to move in with him," Rosie finished miserably. "He didn't give me a chance to explain; he just walked out."

"Oh dear," Estelle murmured. "We both need a brandy." She walked over to the bar and filled two shot glasses.

"I haven't eaten anything," Rosie protested.

"It's medicine." Estelle downed her shot. "I love my daughter, but she can be quite heartless. Sometimes I wonder if I spoiled her as a child."

"Angelica thought she was doing the right thing," Rosie defended her friend. "She didn't know I wanted to marry Josh."

"What are you going to do?" Estelle inquired.

"I was hoping you'd tell me what to do," Rosie said. "You and Oscar are the happiest couple I know."

"We are happy," Estelle agreed. "But we give each other lots of room to be quarrelsome. It's the benefit of having a big house; you can walk away without leaving the grounds."

"Angelica thinks I should find Josh and tell him I want to marry him," Rosie replied.

"You can't do that until you decide what to do about Rosie's Fish Tacos." Estelle rubbed the rim of her shot glass.

"But we need to decide that together, as a couple," Rosie insisted.

"Having a big house doesn't make you happy necessarily, and neither does marrying the man you love. You have to be happy with yourself first," Estelle counseled. "When we were young, Oscar traveled all the time. Angelica and Sam were small and they fought like cats and dogs. If I didn't have my roses, I would have been miserable. You have to do what you love and throw the rule book out the window."

"I know." Rosie smiled. "I stole your line."

"Then apply it to yourself. Do you want to have fish taco shops all over the country?"

"It sounds exciting when Colby and Ryan describe it." Rosie wavered.

"Be certain that's your passion," Estelle instructed. "Then tell Josh your decision. It's up to him to see if it fits with his goals."

"What if he doesn't want to be with me if I accept the offer?" Rosie wondered.

"Then you weren't right for each other," Estelle said matter-of-factly. "I have to talk to Angelica. She mustn't interfere with people's lives; she could do some real damage."

"I think she already has," Rosie slumped in the armchair.

"If you love each other, you can fix it." Estelle patted Rosie's hand. "Take your time and think about what you want to do. Josh isn't going anywhere."

Rosie imagined Josh sitting in his kitchen, eating a turkey sandwich. She could almost smell the onions and the thick crusty bread. She wished she'd never heard from Colby and Ryan. She wished she were sitting beside Josh, asking him to pass the mayonnaise. They'd pile the dishes in the sink and go into the bedroom and make love on his lumpy mattress.

It was late afternoon and Rosie couldn't remember how long she had been sitting in the Pullmans' kitchen staring at an uneaten peanut butter sandwich. The brandy had made her nauseous and she needed to put something in her stomach. But the peanut butter stuck in her throat and the crusts seemed impossible to chew. She put the sandwich on the plate and rested her head on the table.

"I thought you'd be here," Morris said from the door. "I ran into Mrs. Pullman. She told me the whole story."

"I've messed everything up," Rosie groaned. "I chased Josh away."

"It sounds like Angelica had a hand in that." Morris set a basket of shirts on the table. "If Angelica was younger, Mrs. Pullman would have grounded her."

"You were right, Josh isn't a mind reader." Rosie lifted her head. "I should have told him how I felt in the beginning."

"Let me tell you a story. I first met Ryan when he came to one of Oscar's parties two years ago. He walked into the living room and I knew he was the one. We had a few nice conversations, but nothing was said." Morris paused. "At the end of the weekend, he packed his suitcase. I knew if I didn't say something he'd just drive away."

"What happened?" Rosie asked.

"Let's just say it took him a lot longer to pack," Morris said mischievously. "Tell Josh how you feel."

"Estelle said I can't do that until I decide what to do about Colby's offer," Rosie replied.

"It sounds like a fabulous opportunity." Morris nodded.

"I don't know if it's right for me." Rosie sighed. "I pushed numbers around at the studio and spent my days meeting with investors. I love having my own shop. The feeling of satisfaction of giving customers something they love. I even love being so tired at the end of the day I can barely drag myself into the bath. I feel like I've accomplished something."

"But Rosie's Fish Tacos would still be yours, only bigger."

"I know," Rosie agreed. "It all spins round and round in my head like a carousel."

"You need to go someplace quiet where you can think," Morris suggested. "If it was me, I'd take my basket of shirts to the laundry room and stand in front of a nice hot iron."

Rosie sat up straight and looked at Morris. She glanced at the clock on the wall and jumped up.

"You're brilliant!" She kissed Morris on the cheek and ran out of the kitchen.

Rosie entered the fish taco shop and found Patrick's sister, Mary, wiping the counter. Four teenagers sat on stools, eating tacos and drinking orange sodas. A family clutched bags of tacos and whispered at the signed picture of Colby hanging on the wall.

"You're supposed to take the whole day off," Mary said. "I'm sorry the place is a mess, I've been swamped."

"It looks great." Rosie glanced at the white-and-red floor, the gleaming counter, the stove piled with saucepans and skillets. "I'd like to close up, so you can go home early."

"Really?" Mary asked. "I'm supposed to meet two friends at the movies."

"Go on." Rosie nodded.

"You had a lot of happy customers." Mary peeled off her apron. "And three requests for your autograph."

Rosie tied an apron over her dress and stood behind the counter. She put a spoon in the guacamole and tasted it tentatively. She added a pinch of Hawaiian sea salt and stirred the bowl.

"Hi." A girl of about ten approached the counter. "I came in earlier but you weren't here."

"I remember you." Rosie smiled. "You were my first customer."

"You're really famous now," the girl replied. "I read you're going to marry Colby Young."

"Hardly." Rosie laughed. "Rumor has it he's taken, and I'm too old."

"I told my parents what you said about them having me in common." The girl rested her elbows on the counter. "We started playing a game of naming all the things they had in common. They stopped fighting and they're in Tahiti on their second honeymoon."

"That's wonderful." Rosie beamed.

"I'm here with my aunt and uncle," the girl continued. "They've been fighting too. I think they need some fish tacos."

"How many would you like?" Rosie spread out tortillas.

"Two for them and two for me," the girl said proudly. "I've grown two inches this summer. I eat all day long."

Rosie prepared the girl's tacos and slipped them in a bag with an extra side of guacamole. The girl skipped down the street and clutched the bag as if it was a present. Rosie chopped and sliced and rang up orders until the last customer left. She turned the sign to CLOSED and felt the delicious quiet after the hum of activity.

The store smelled of olive oil and onions and she realized she was starving. She spread lettuce and tomatoes on a tortilla and added grated cheese, grilled cod, and spoonfuls of guacamole. She scooped up the taco and bit into it, tomatoes and lettuce dribbling onto the counter.

Rosie had forgotten how good her fish tacos tasted. The guacamole was light and fluffy, the cod was seasoned just right. She made herself another taco, piling on shredded lettuce, juicy tomatoes, and adding a squeeze of lime.

She suddenly pictured the kitchen in their house in Santa Monica. She remembered sharing sandwiches with Ben: arranging layers of turkey, Swiss cheese, and Bermuda onions on French bread. For the first time, she didn't flinch when she thought about Ben. She pictured his expression when he told her about Mary Beth, and she wasn't heartbroken or angry.

Rosie collected taco baskets, realizing Ben was right to let her walk away. She didn't want the fast-paced life of a movie executive. She didn't want to wear well-cut suits and straighten her hair so she could flick it over her shoulders. Or sit in meetings and kiss up to producers and take lunches with drunken investors.

She wanted to stand in her own store, making delicious fish tacos. She wanted to count the money in the cash register and separate the bills with thick rubber bands. She wanted to go home to Josh and get up and do the same thing tomorrow.

Rosie grabbed her purse and locked the door. She would drive to Josh's house and tell him she was refusing Colby's offer. Her heart pounded and she walked quickly to her car. She would explain what she meant about not wanting to move in with him. Josh would wrap his arms around her and ask her to marry him.

"Rosie!" Rachel poked her head out of a shop door. "I have to show you something."

"Can it wait a little," Rosie asked. "I want to see but I'm in a hurry."

"Please, it will just take a minute." Rachel stepped onto the sidewalk. She wore a blue dress and a white leather belt. Her dark hair was curled and she wore her silver locket around her neck.

"You look very fancy." Rosie eyed her outfit.

"I've been to see the inquisition." Rachel rolled her eyes. "Come in the shop, I have to talk to you."

Rosie followed Rachel into the chocolate shop, breathing in the smell of cocoa and cinnamon. There were rows of pink marzipan, and orange-and-black chocolate pumpkins. A round table was devoted to a chocolate train with orange nougat cabooses.

"I can't believe I'm putting out Halloween displays already," Rachel groaned. "But tourists want to buy their Halloween candy before they go home."

"It all looks delicious." Rosie eyed a tray of dark chocolate truffles.

"Patrick proposed," Rachel announced.

"Congratulations, that's amazing news." Rosie gave her a hug. "Tell me everything. When, where, what did he say?"

"It was a complete surprise," Rachel gushed. "I was helping him make sandwiches at the delicatessen. He said wouldn't it be great to have a cafe attached to the deli: just a few tables where people could sit and eat. He took my hand and led me to the shop next door. It used to be a wine bar but the owner moved to San Francisco. He showed me where he could break through the wall and make it one big space. Then he handed me a blue velvet box." Rachel paused. "I opened it and I almost started crying. Inside was a key."

"A key to what?" Rosie wondered aloud.

"Patrick had already leased the space. He said he wanted a bigger income because he wanted to marry me and have at least four children. Then he got down on one knee and pulled this ring out of his pocket." Rachel displayed a round diamond in a platinum setting.

"It's gorgeous!" Rosie held it up to the light.

"I thought it would be some ancient ring belonging to his grandmother," Rachel continued. "But Patrick said when he called my father and asked for my hand, Dad insisted Patrick see a jeweler he knows in LA."

"Patrick called your father?" Rosie asked.

"It was the scariest thing he'd ever done." Rachel nodded. "But he said if the only thing stopping him from spending the rest of his life with me was a man who ate lox and bagels, he better learn to love lox. He overnighted my father a case of gefilte fish and they've been friends ever since."

"I'm so happy for you." Rosie smiled.

"We just came from his grandmother's." Rachel shuddered. "I thought she was going to put a curse on me. She held my hands so tightly they turned blue, and then she hugged me and started crying. She had been praying she'd live long enough to see a great-grandchild. She made me promise if it's a girl I'd call her Edna after her mother."

"I hope you kept your fingers crossed behind your back." Rosie laughed.

"I sort of like Edna," Rachel mused. "Now we have to find a rabbi and a priest who'll marry us, and whittle the guest list down from four hundred. The whole Gold clan is coming from New Jersey, and Patrick has twenty-three cousins."

"You'll be the most beautiful bride in Montecito," Rosie insisted.

"We can have a double engagement party," Rachel suggested. "You and Josh should join us."

"I'm not sure we're still together." Rosie flinched.

"Josh adores you. What happened?"

Rosie told Rachel about Colby's offer and Angelica's surprise appearance in the garage.

"I heard a rumor you were expanding Rosie's Fish Tacos," Rachel said. "Are you going to accept it?"

"I considered it. But I came to work this afternoon and realized I just want to stand in my own shop and sell tacos."

"I'm exactly the same. I never wanted to own department stores in five cities," Rachel agreed. "That's a recipe for headaches."

"Now I have to tell Josh." Rosie took a deep breath. "I'm afraid he won't see me."

"If I could face Patrick's grandmother, you can tell the man who adores you that you love him." Rachel unwrapped a toffee and popped it in her mouth.

"I have to try." Rosie nodded.

Rachel grabbed a box of fudge wrapped in gold tissue. "Take this to celebrate when you make up."

Rosie drove to Josh's house and felt a surge of adrenaline. If Angelica and Rachel could have happy endings, she could make it work with Josh. She pictured walking arm in arm on the beach, watching the waves roll in. She pressed her foot on the accelerator and drove faster. She had to reach Josh before he closed himself off, before the wounds became too big to heal.

Rosie punched Colby's number into her phone. She told him her decision, hoping she wouldn't hurt his feelings.

"You can't turn it down," Colby urged. "It's like turning down Santa Claus."

"It's a wonderful offer," Rosie assured him. "It's just not right for me. I don't want more. I just want what I have."

"Everyone wants more, Rosie," Colby argued. "It's as natural as breathing."

"I found what I want," Rosie said. "And it's all here in Montecito."

"If you change your mind, call me," Colby answered. "They're the best fish tacos I ever tasted."

Rosie parked across the street from Josh's house. Josh's car wasn't out front, and she debated driving to the beach to see if he was surfing. But she didn't want their reunion to be in front of other people.

She turned off the engine and suddenly felt light and happy. She was doing everything that Estelle and Morris suggested. She smoothed her dress and checked her makeup in the mirror. She rubbed on lip gloss and ran her fingers through her hair.

Josh's hatchback pulled into the driveway. Rosie opened her door to run and greet him but a young woman stepped out of the driver's seat. She was petite with an upturned nose and full red lips. Her long black hair fell down her back, and she wore platform shoes and a mini skirt with a sequined silver top.

Rosie froze and waited for Josh to open the passenger door. Her heart was beating so fast she thought it might explode. The woman took a bag of groceries out of the trunk. She opened the passenger door and scooped up a fluffy white dog. She walked to the front door, put a key in the lock, and disappeared inside.

Sixteen

Rosie stayed in bed all day and night. She stared at the ceiling, picturing the young woman with the long black hair and sequined top. Who could she be and why was she driving Josh's car? None of it made sense, and when she tried calling Josh's number it went straight to voicemail.

On the second day, there was a knock at the door and Morris entered carrying a tray and a vase of roses.

"Hi, Morris." Rosie opened the door. "It's nice to see you."

"I knocked but you didn't answer." Morris set the tray on the table. "I was afraid I'd find a dead body."

"I'm not feeling well. I wish I were dead," Rosie mumbled.

"Then these beautiful roses would go to waste," Morris admonished. "And Peg's chicken soup, guaranteed to cure anything including heartache."

"Tell Peg thank you but I'm not hungry." Rosie dropped back against the pillows.

"You haven't left the cottage in two days." Morris frowned. "You can't exist on cheese and crackers."

"I have the flu." Rosie closed her eyes. "All I need is sleep."

"That's funny." Morris walked around the room. "Not a single tissue in sight. You're pale instead of flushed, and there's an empty box of chocolate fudge on the bed."

"Please, Morris," Rosie begged. "I'll be fine, there's nothing to worry about."

"I paid a visit to your friend Rachel." Morris sat on the bed. "She said the last time she saw you, you were on your way to Josh's house."

"I don't want to talk about it." Rosie gulped.

"Tell me what happened," Morris instructed. "I'm a good listener, it goes with the job."

Rosie sat cross-legged on the bed and grabbed the box of tissues.

"I went to tell Josh I refused Colby's offer." She sniffled. "His car pulled up and a woman got out of the driver's seat. She took out a bag of groceries and a dog and went inside . . . with her own key."

"She could have been anyone." Morris shrugged. "She could have been delivering groceries."

"Driving Josh's car?" Rosie asked.

"He could have lent it to a neighbor. Maybe he twisted his ankle and she was being a Good Samaritan."

"Josh doesn't have any neighbors under the age of sixty, and Good Samaritans don't wear mini skirts and platform shoes."

"They could," Morris argued. "There's no dress code."

"She's probably an old girlfriend he called the minute he left me," Rosie declared.

"Has he ever mentioned a woman with long black hair?" Morris asked.

"He doesn't talk about women except the girl who dumped him in college," Rosie cried. "This woman was dressed as if she made one kind of house call, and it wasn't to deliver a carton of eggs."

"I knew you weren't dead." Morris grinned. "You still have your sense of humor."

"I don't, Morris," Rosie said glumly. "I don't have anything."

"You have Rosie's Fish Tacos, and you have Mr. and Mrs. Pullman, and you have me," Morris replied.

"I know that, and I'm incredibly grateful," Rosie said earnestly. "I arrived in Montecito with nothing and everyone has been wonderful." She looked at Morris. "But I'm falling for Josh and I don't know what to do."

"It's simple. You knock on Josh's door and ask him what's going on." Morris stood up and walked to the table. "The woman is probably gone, maybe she was a hallucination."

"You want me to check if she left her fingerprints?" Rosie demanded.

"I want you to be an adult." Morris dipped the spoon into the bowl of soup. "Now open your mouth and eat your soup like a good girl."

Rosie pulled up across from Josh's house. She turned off the engine and slouched in the seat, feeling like a character in a spy movie. She had driven off, seeing Morris' thumbs-up in the rearview mirror. But as she approached Josh's street, she began to shake. What if Josh and the woman were together inside? She couldn't bear the idea of Josh answering the door with rumpled hair and hooded eyes.

Josh's car was parked in the driveway and the living room window was open. Rosie flinched, remembering his words: "I don't want you to think I'm going to run every time we have an argument."

Rosie wanted to yell at him that he broke his promise. He ran right into the arms of another woman. But she was too scared to get out of the car. She was about to leave when a woman's figure appeared at the living room window.

Rosie rolled down the car window and listened. The woman was talking in a light, girly voice. She held her breath, waiting to see the familiar curve of Josh's chest. But the woman bent down to pick something up and disappeared.

Rosie drove away and punched Josh's number into her phone. She couldn't just appear at the door, she had to give him a chance to explain. But he didn't pick up and she tossed the phone on the passenger seat.

The gates of the estate opened and she pulled into the driveway. Her heart raced and there was a lump in her throat. She rested her head on the steering wheel and let the tears run down her cheek.

Rosie followed a strict routine. She was like a marathon runner, not allowing herself to think about Josh. Each morning she ran four laps around the lake and drove to the fish taco shop. All day she grilled fish and chopped onions and rang up sales. At closing time she made herself a taco and ate it in the cottage. Then she climbed in bed and forced herself to fall asleep.

By the fourth day the pain started to ebb, forced out by exhaustion. Her cheekbones were more defined and her eyes were void of color. But she could eat, she could breathe, and she could work. For now, that was enough.

"Hello, Rosie." Estelle entered the store as Rosie was cleaning up the lunchtime rush. Estelle wore a yellow silk dress and carried an ostrich-skin purse.

"I lunched with my gardening club and thought I must stop in." Estelle inspected Rosie. "Are you all right? Your cheeks are sunken and you look like you're recovering from the flu."

"Thank you for asking. I'm fine. I've been working a lot." Rosie swept plastic knives and forks into the garbage.

"Morris told me everything that happened." Estelle placed her hand on Rosie's shoulder. "You can't just work from morning to night."

"I don't mind," Rosie said. "The store has been busy and I don't want to lose customers."

"I'm having a dinner tonight," Estelle continued as if she hadn't heard her. "One of my dearest friends is in town. I'd like you to meet her."

"I'd love to, but I'm very tired." Rosie hesitated. "And I need to shower and change."

"We won't eat until nine, there's plenty of time for you to shower," Estelle continued. "I think you will really hit it off. You're two of my favorite people."

Rosie thought of everything Estelle had done: allowing her to stay in the cottage, hosting her grand-opening party, giving her the luxury of Morris and Peg.

"All right." Rosie nodded. "I'll be there."

Rosie crossed the lawn to the main house. She had been avoiding the house, afraid she'd see Josh coming or going from the garage. But the only car in the driveway was an old silver Bentley. It had lace curtains and an imposing silver grill.

Rosie opened the front door and stepped inside. The living room was empty except for the Irish setters lounging by the fireplace.

Maybe the dinner was canceled. She turned to go back to the cottage, and then she noticed an older woman standing in the dining room. She was admiring a Lladró statue of a boy playing the flute. Her hair was black and cut in a pageboy. Her eyes were large and smudged with kohl. She had long eyelashes and high cheek-bones.

The woman stroked the statue with long red fingernails. Rosie moved closer, certain it was Esmeralda, the most famous actress of her time. Esmeralda was a Hollywood legend like Grace Kelly and Marilyn Monroe. Rosie had studied all her movies at Kenyon, watched her mature from a wide-eyed child to a classical beauty.

Esmeralda played the title role in *Anya*, one of Rosie's favorite films. Rosie remembered the scene where Anya ran down a Greek hillside, trying to reach her fiancé before he sailed in a boat that Anya knew was doomed. She could still hear Anya's desperate plea, begging him not to go. But her only proof of danger was a fortune-teller's prophecy. Rosie knew, just by watching Anya's face, seeing her perfect mouth quiver, that her fiancé would never return.

Esmeralda was a Hollywood mystery, her personal life as intriguing as her film roles. Some accounts said she was born in Corsica; others said Brazil or Portugal. She blazed into the spotlight as a teenager and won her first Oscar before she was twenty-one. The critics called her "Lady in Black" because she always wore black in public, matching her glossy, black mane.

Rosie read countless articles about Esmeralda, but none said with certainty where she lived, whether she was married, or even her age. One of Rosie's wishes was to meet her idol in person. When she arrived in LA, she spent many afternoons sitting at the Beverly Hills Hotel waiting for her to pass by. But that was the year Esmeralda disappeared. *Variety* insisted it was a terrific marketing ploy. She would reappear in a blaze of publicity to launch her next film.

Esmeralda didn't return and there was no new movie. Eventually the paparazzi stopped hiding behind palm trees. The gossip columnists claimed she had a botched face-lift and was hiding in the South of France, or she had become a nun and was sequestered in a convent in Tuscany.

"I love Lladró." The woman turned to Rosie. "Henry gave me a statue after every movie—this is my favorite, such a beautiful young boy."

"I'm Rosie." Rosie moved towards Esmeralda. She felt like a schoolgirl; she didn't know what to say or what to do with her hands.

"Rosie!" Esmeralda fluttered long, dark eyelashes. "Estelle has told me all about you. Come sit with me, I've been traveling and I'm very tired."

Rosie and Esmeralda moved to the living room. Rosie couldn't help staring. Esmeralda's skin was stretched tight, and the kohl masked dark shadows under her eyes.

Esmeralda settled into the sofa. "Entertain me, tell me about yourself."

"I'm a huge fan," Rosie replied shyly. "I've seen all your movies."

"I thought that when I stopped acting, I'd die of boredom." Esmeralda sighed. "But life goes on, even if it's only to play backgammon. Henry said I should get a hobby, but I was very stubborn."

"Henry?" Rosie repeated.

Esmeralda glanced at Rosie as if she had forgotten she was there. "My manager and my husband, of course." Esmeralda raised her eyebrows. "It's all ancient history. If I flung myself on Sunset Boulevard no one would recognize me."

"You look exactly the same," Rosie protested.

"You are a kind girl." Esmeralda's eyes were suddenly bright. "What is your name?"

"Rosie!" Estelle called, hurrying down the staircase. "I was on the phone with the florist in Monte Carlo. It is not easy planning a transatlantic wedding."

"We've been getting to know each other," Esmeralda said. "I could use a drink. Do you have any of that lovely brandy?"

"I have some in the library." Estelle nodded. "Rosie, why don't you come help me."

"That really is Esmeralda," Rosie breathed when they reached the library.

"I told you I wanted you to meet someone special." Estelle smiled.

"But how do you know each other. Where has she been for the last ten years?"

"Esmeralda lived in Montecito for decades; no one knew of course. Esmeralda became famous so young she was terrified of growing old. Every year the studio held a big bash at the Polo Lounge to celebrate Esmeralda's twenty-ninth birthday. I don't think she even knows how old she is." Estelle took the bottle of brandy from the cabinet.

"She seems a bit forgetful," Rosie offered.

"She was diagnosed with early-onset Alzheimer's disease," Estelle explained. "It's terribly sad."

"When I moved to Hollywood, I spent weeks plotting to meet her. But she just disappeared," Rosie recalled.

"After Henry's death, she moved to Montreux, Switzerland. She couldn't function without him." Estelle took three shot glasses from the cabinet. "I visited her once. She had a beautiful home on the lake; we ate fondue and walnut torte."

"How did Henry die?" Rosie asked.

"He found Esmeralda in bed with Trevor Tate." Estelle poured brandy into the glasses. "Henry drove his car off the cliff, straight into the Pacific Ocean."

"Trevor Tate?" Rosie repeated.

"He's a wonderful actor but terribly young." Estelle frowned. "Much too young for Esmeralda."

"And she just disappeared?"

"We better go back." Estelle put the drinks on a tray. "I knew she'd like you, she loves young people."

Rosie followed Estelle into the living room. Esmeralda sat on the sofa, her hands crossed in her lap. There was a distant look in her eyes and she hummed a song.

"Tell me what I've missed in America." Esmeralda sipped her brandy. "By the time I get the gossip magazines, it's old news. Do you like movies, Rosie?"

Rosie blushed. "I was an associate producer until I moved up here."

"Hollywood will eat you up and spit you out." Esmeralda nodded knowingly. "I was so fortunate to discover Montecito: it's so peaceful, like a European village."

"Have you known each other long?" Rosie looked from Estelle to Esmeralda.

"We had children the same age," Estelle answered.

"I was a terrible mother, I kept them locked up like Hansel and Gretel." Esmeralda grimaced.

"You were a wonderful mother," Estelle soothed.

"It was impossible to be a mother and a movie star in those days." Esmeralda shrugged. "At least they had a lovely lawn to play on and all those trees to climb in. And the dogs! Do you remember the dogs, Estelle? We brought our dogs over and they chased yours around the lake. They scared the ducks so badly they almost flew away."

"I'll help Morris in the kitchen." Estelle stood up. "Why don't you two go into the dining room?"

Rosie followed Esmeralda across the hall. Esmeralda paused in front of the Lladró as if seeing it for the first time. "Don't you love this statue; it reminds me so much of Josh at that age."

Rosie stared at Esmeralda as if she was one of those crazy people who babble at street corners.

"The curly hair, the long legs, just like Josh when he was about twelve," Esmeralda mused.

"Who's Josh?" Rosie's eyes were wide.

"My son," Esmeralda explained. "I never let photographers take pictures of my children. Estelle took some years ago; I'll ask her if she has them."

"Where's Josh now?" Rosie asked in a strangled voice.

"I haven't talked to him in years," Esmeralda's mouth puckered. "But he was a beautiful boy: blue eyes and blond, curly hair. He took after Henry, and Yvette looked like me."

Rosie felt like her legs were going to give out. She sat down quickly, almost missing the chair. Her eyes blurred and her heart hammered in her chest.

"I was just telling Rosie I never let photographers in the house. God, I was stupid. As if we were going to live forever," Esmeralda said as Estelle entered the room. "Do you have any pictures of the children?"

"I do in the library." Estelle avoided Rosie's eyes. "I'll get them."

Esmeralda kept talking, but Rosie didn't hear her. Josh said both his parents were dead. How could he lie to her, how could Estelle not tell her?

Estelle returned with a leather photo album. She placed it in front of Esmeralda and flipped the pages.

"Here's one at Angelica's birthday party. Angelica and Yvette were so pretty." Esmeralda paused. "Josh and Sam were embarrassed to be at a party with a bunch of ten-year-old girls."

Rosie stared at the photo. Angelica's hair was in pigtails and she wore a pinafore dress. Next to her was a girl with long black hair and full red lips. Rosie picked up the album and studied it closely.

"Who's that?" She pointed to the girl.

"That's Yvette." Esmeralda smiled. "She was lovely at ten, but then she became a wild child. She almost gave her father a coronary when she scaled the fence and ran off with a boy in a band. I don't know how she did it, even the paparazzi couldn't scale that fence."

Rosie inhaled and tried to keep the air flowing through her lungs. She stared at the little girl with long black hair and knew she was looking at the woman getting out of Josh's car at his house.

"Here's one of Josh and Sam playing tennis." Esmeralda pointed to another photo on the page. "Josh hated it when Sam beat him."

Rosie pulled her eyes from Yvette and studied the picture of Josh and Sam holding tennis racquets. Josh wore a white polo shirt and white shorts. His eyes were pale blue and his hair curled to his shoulders. The room seemed to spin and she felt dizzy. She ran out the door and collided with Morris carrying a tray of steaming clam chowder.

"How could you not tell me Esmeralda was Josh's mother?" Rosie sat at the kitchen table, wrapped in a bath towel. Morris had been sent to the cottage to get her clean clothes, and Oscar was sipping cocktails in the dining room with Esmeralda.

"It wasn't my place to tell you," Estelle replied. "Few people knew that Esmeralda had a family. We met when we gave birth in the hospital; Josh and Sam share a birthday. Oscar and Henry became good friends: they both had classic car collections. We only socialized at home. In public Esmeralda surrounded herself with young people, so she never aged."

"How could Josh not tell me," Rosie persisted. "His mother was the most famous actress in the world."

"Josh is very private," Estelle said. "It wasn't an easy way to grow up. Josh and Yvette were very close; all they had was each other."

"What about Henry?" Rosie asked.

"Henry was the loveliest man you'd ever meet, tall and blond like Josh." Estelle handed Rosie a cup of herbal tea. "He grew up in Montecito. He discovered Esmeralda when she was seventeen. He put his career as a lawyer aside to manage her career."

"Why did she cheat on him?"

"At first Esmeralda just had little flings, always with her leading man. As she got older the men became younger: pool boys, golf caddies, tennis pros. She met Trevor Tate at a premiere. She told Henry she was leaving; Josh and Yvette were already grown. She thought they could remain friends, even business partners."

"What happened?" Rosie leaned across the table.

"Henry had just bought a classic Opal car. I remember Oscar was jealous; it was a real beauty," Estelle mused. "Henry was driving north on the Pacific Coast Highway. He missed a turn and drove into the ocean. No one really knew if it was suicide or if he didn't know how to handle the car."

"Oh, poor Josh." Rosie closed her eyes. She wished he were here so that she could hold him.

"Esmeralda was devastated. She closed up the house and checked herself into a sanatorium in Switzerland. Josh had just graduated from college; he moved in with Henry's mother. Yvette ran off with some artist to San Francisco."

"Yvette!" Rosie had forgotten about Yvette: scooping her dog from the passenger seat, carrying Josh's groceries. "Yvette is the woman I saw at Josh's house. I thought it was an old girlfriend, but it was Josh's sister."

"Yvette is here?" Estelle gasped. "We must tell Yvette that Esmeralda is in Montecito. Esmeralda came to see her children before she forgets them."

"I have to go. I should have knocked on Josh's door days ago." Rosie wrapped the towel around her and ran out of the house. "Give Esmeralda my apologies."

"Where are you going?" Estelle followed her.

"Josh is going to see me, even if I have to break the door down."

"Rosie," Estelle called. "You better put on some clothes."

✳

The woman who answered Josh's door didn't look much older than the girl in the photograph. Yvette wore a red mini skirt and a white blouse. Her hair fell to her waist and she had Esmeralda's long dark eyelashes and smoky eyes.

"Can I help you?" She clutched her dog, his tail waving furiously at Rosie.

"I'm here to see Josh." Rosie hesitated. Her confidence deserted her, and she wondered if he would talk to her. "I'm Rosie."

"Rosie!" Yvette eyed her curiously. "I heard about you. You're the girl who stole my brother's heart."

"I didn't mean to barge in." Rosie noticed a copy of *Glamour* and a bowl of caramel popcorn on the coffee table.

Yvette walked into the living room and sat cross-legged on the sofa. She picked up the bowl and passed it to Rosie. "Do you want some? It's not much of a dinner, but I'm a hopeless cook."

"No, thank you." Rosie shook her head. "Josh and I had a big fight. I came by a few days ago and saw you carrying in groceries." Rosie blushed. "I thought you were an old girlfriend and I fled."

"I asked Josh if I could crash for a while." Yvette munched popcorn. "An ex-boyfriend started showing up at my window in San Francisco every time I took a shower."

"Is Josh here?" Rosie inquired.

Yvette put the bowl of popcorn on the table. "He's in Carmel, at the Concours d'Elegance."

Rosie's eyes filled with tears. She had forgotten about the car auction. She should be sitting in a quaint bed-and-breakfast while Josh talked to car buyers. They would stroll the streets of Carmel and breathe in the foggy air. They'd eat at a cafe, sharing buttery crepes and drinking hot chocolate out of earthenware mugs.

"When will Josh be back?" Rosie asked.

Yvette studied her long red fingernails. "I'm not sure. I don't think he's coming back."

"What do you mean?"

"He got an offer to work at a classic car dealership in Carmel." Yvette looked at Rosie. "He's probably going to take it."

"I can't let him do that." Rosie got up and paced around the room. "He thought I told Estelle I didn't want to move in with him, but it was a mix-up. I meant I wanted to marry him." She stopped and her eyes glistened. "I'm in love with him."

"He didn't tell me exactly what was going on," Yvette said. "That's why I try never to fall in love. Someone always gets hurt."

"I didn't mean to hurt Josh." Rosie twisted her hands. "And now I don't know how to fix it. If only Angelica hadn't told Josh I didn't want to move in with him."

"Angelica and Josh have always gotten in each other's hair," Yvette said wisely. "When I was a teenager I had a crush on Sam, Angelica's brother. I confided in Angelica and she confessed she thought Josh was cute. We promised not to tell anyone, and I told Josh at a swim party." Yvette giggled. "She wouldn't talk to me for a week."

"What am I going to do?" Rosie crumpled on the sofa.

"Josh is complicated." Yvette scooped up her dog. "I'm sure he loves you, but he isn't good at relationships. Our parents had an unconventional marriage. They were terrible role models."

"I came to tell you about Esmeralda and I forgot! I feel terrible," Rosie exclaimed. "Your mother is in America. I had dinner with her; she's staying with Estelle. I recognized her, of course; she was the most famous actress of her time. Estelle told me the whole story."

"My mother is in Montecito!" Yvette's eyes widened.

"I'm sorry to be the one to tell you, but I thought you and Josh should know before you see her. Your mother isn't quite herself; she has early-onset Alzheimer's disease," Rosie said slowly. "She came to see you and Josh."

"But she's like Peter Pan. She never gets older, she can't die."

"Estelle said it's very early," Rosie offered. "Esmeralda remembers a lot about your childhood. She showed me a picture of you when you were ten."

"Josh wouldn't talk to our mother after our father died. She lost her two favorite men at the same time." Yvette sighed. "I'm a lot like her with relationships, but I try not to hurt anyone. I should call Josh and tell him she's here. Then I'll book him a flight so he can come and see her."

"You don't have to book him a flight." Rosie jumped up. She suddenly knew what she had to do. "I'm going to drive up the coast and get him."

"You're going to drive to Carmel?"

"Josh has to come home." Rosie grabbed her purse. "Everyone who loves him is in Montecito."

Seventeen

The waves crashed below her like cymbals in an orchestra. Rosie drove all night, her hands gripping the steering wheel. When she felt her eyes closing, she pulled over at a rest stop near Big Sur and curled up in the driver's seat.

Her car pulled onto the main street of Carmel in the early morning. The sky and the ocean were matching shades of gray, and the streets were slowly waking up. Rosie could smell eggs and bacon and longed to sit in the diner and drink a steaming cup of coffee.

She parked her car on Ocean Avenue and looked for the bed-and-breakfast where she and Josh were going to stay. Carmel resembled a medieval town. The streets were narrow and there were pubs and taverns and antiques shops stuffed with musty furniture.

Rosie climbed the steps of the Carmel Inn and rang the bell at the front desk. A man wearing a plaid shirt and slippers greeted Rosie sleepily.

"Check-in is at three o'clock," he said, and closed a magazine.

"I'm looking for one of your guests, Josh Fellows," Rosie replied. "Tall and blond, with surfer's hair and blue eyes."

"I remember him. He checked out an hour ago." The man shook his head. "His things are still in his room."

"Did he leave a note for Rosie by any chance?" she asked.

The man consulted the computer on his desk. "I'm sorry I can't help you."

"I really thought he'd be here," Rosie insisted. "His sister said he was staying in Carmel."

"It's not a very big town." The man shrugged. "There are only four intersecting streets, like a tic-tac-toe board."

Rosie thanked him and walked back to the car. She didn't want to call Josh. She had to talk to him in person. The coastal air was foggy and she wished she had brought a sweater. The cotton dress she had ripped out of Morris' hands as he crossed the lawn was too thin, and her sandals didn't keep her feet warm.

Rosie turned the heater in the car on high. If Josh wanted to see her, he would have left a note. Maybe she should give up and drive back to Montecito. She drove down Ocean Avenue and turned into the parking lot of Carmel Beach.

Josh was crouching on the cement, waxing his surfboard. He wore a black wet suit and his hair curled around his ears. He covered the board in long, easy strokes, not looking up as she raced towards him.

"Hi," Rosie said.

"What are you doing here, Rosie?" Josh jumped. His eyes darkened and his jaw was set in a firm line.

"I came to your house to tell you I didn't accept Colby's offer. I saw Yvette carrying in a bag of groceries. I thought she was an old girlfriend and ran away," Rosie said in a rush. "I went back to see Yvette last night and she told me you were here."

"You should accept Colby's offer; it's a once-in-a-lifetime opportunity." Josh kept waxing his surfboard. "I have to go. A bunch of the guys are waiting for me out there."

"I drove four hours straight," Rosie said. "Can we please talk?"

"We talked enough, Rosie." Josh didn't look up. "What's the point anyway? We're different people, we want different things."

Rosie crossed her arms over her chest. "You're not who you said you are. Your mother is Esmeralda."

Josh stood up, his back stiff. "Who told you that?"

"I met Esmeralda." Rosie gulped. "She's staying with Estelle."

"My mother is here?" Josh's voice softened.

"She was diagnosed with early-onset Alzheimer's disease," Rosie said quietly. "She came to see you and Yvette."

Josh's face crumpled. His eyes were suddenly wet, like those of a little boy who lost his puppy.

"She showed me a Lladró statue of a boy playing a flute. She said it looked just like you."

"My mother as good as killed my father," Josh said tersely.

"It was an accident. It's easy to lose control of a car on the Pacific Coast Highway," Rosie protested. "Esmeralda loves you, she wants to see you."

"I can't do this, Rosie. I'm not good at relationships. Maybe I'm too stubborn or I don't know how to communicate, but it never seems to work," he said, and there was anguish in his voice. "I was falling in love with you and you betrayed me. It's better that we end it before we hurt each other again." He looked at Rosie. "I've been offered a job at a classic car dealership in Carmel. I want to see my mother, of course. I'll fly down next weekend."

Rosie felt like the wind had been knocked out of her. "I didn't betray you and I would never hurt you," she begged. "You have to believe me. I never told Estelle I didn't want to move in with you."

"Then why did Angelica say you did?" Josh asked.

A line of surfers waited in the water. Rosie glanced at the surfboard on the ground. She took a deep breath. "I told Estelle I wanted to stand in a church and exchange vows. I want to marry you."

"Oh." Josh stood so close she could see the blond stubble on his chin.

"I was afraid you weren't ready to get married. I couldn't handle the rejection if you said no."

"I told you I wanted to live with you," Josh reminded her.

"I lived with Ben for eight years, and it took five minutes for him to get up and leave." Rosie's voice shook. "I want to be connected in so many ways it would take years to unravel us."

"My parents were married for thirty years and my mother still told my father she wanted to leave him," he responded.

"They lasted thirty years, and maybe Esmeralda would have changed her mind," Rosie insisted. "They had two beautiful children and a home. They invested in each other."

"I always felt my mother would rather be in Hollywood, sipping champagne at the Chateau Marmont," Josh replied. "She hid her husband and her kids because she was ashamed of us."

"She was terrified of growing old, of the public not loving her anymore. And she wanted to protect you and Yvette from the paparazzi," Rosie urged. "It's terrible to grow up with a camera pointed in your face."

"It still hurt. I was just a kid who wanted to be loved." Josh flinched. "I don't know how to forgive her, and it's hard to trust others."

"I love you and I'll never quit on you," Rosie whispered.

Josh looked at Rosie and touched her cheek. He pulled her towards him and hugged her against his chest. "You're shivering," he whispered into her hair.

"Can we get in the car?" Rosie asked. "I didn't dress for fog."

They got in the car and stared at the beach. A man walked his dog and carried a big stick. A couple walked arm in arm, wearing matching fisherman's sweaters.

"I sold the MG," Josh said. "I made a mint."

"I knew you would." Rosie beamed. "She was a beauty."

"I think I'll turn down the job at the dealership in Carmel. I don't really like it here. People say the waves in Carmel are awesome, but they break right onto the rocks," Josh mused. "It's not a good beach for surfing."

"I'm glad. It's so foggy." Rosie rubbed her hands together from the cold. "I heard you only see the sun in Carmel in October."

"And everyone eats organic food. There isn't a single diner that makes a decent cheeseburger with fries." Josh sighed.

"I'd do anything for something hot to eat right now." Rosie's teeth chattered. "Let's grab a bowl of soup and drive back to Montecito."

Josh turned her face towards his and kissed her. His lips were moist and salty. "There is something I want to ask you first. The front seat of a car isn't the ideal place, but if I don't do it now, I don't know when I will." He reached into his bag and took out a velvet box. "Rosie Keller, will you marry me?"

"You're asking me to marry you?" Rosie had never been more surprised in her life.

"I bought the ring after I asked you to move in with me." He snapped it open and revealed a small diamond on a gold band. "It's not much, but the jeweler in the village gave me a great deal." He stopped. "Marriage scared me, but I knew it was the right thing to do. You're everything to me and I don't want to be without you."

"But you never said anything." Rosie scanned her memory for any hint that Josh wanted to marry her.

"I was going to ask you the weekend that Angelica and Dirk came to visit, but we got into a terrible fight about their wedding."

He paused. "Then Angelica said you didn't want to live with me and I was so angry. But I'm asking you now. I'll spend the rest of my life making you happy. I love you, Rosie, will you marry me?"

Josh took the ring out of the box, and she studied it in the morning light. Her heart pounded and she took a deep breath.

"Yes, I'll marry you." She nodded. "But I have one request."

"What is it?" Josh looked up.

"It's only a small one." Her eyes danced. "I want to elope."

"Are you sure you want to elope?" he asked. "I thought you wanted a church wedding and a white poufy dress and a six-tier wedding cake."

"I thought I did, but all I want is to read our vows and the minister to pronounce us husband and wife," Rosie said. "Angelica is my best friend, and if we plan a wedding now it will interfere with hers. And if we wait, the date will be too far away. Besides, planning a wedding is as stressful as producing a movie. I don't want to spend my days choosing a site and creating budgets and overseeing vendors."

"But what about your parents and the dress and the cake?" Josh asked, rubbing his forehead.

"My parents got married at a registrar's office and their wedding cake was from Carvel. They'll understand." She shrugged. "We'll have a party next summer when Angelica and Dirk are back from Europe."

"Are you sure?" he asked, fiddling with the diamond ring.

"We can drive to Reno next weekend." Rosie nodded. "Maybe we'll stop on the way back and pick up a puppy. I'd love to start our life together with a dog."

Josh slipped the ring on her finger and kissed her. She kissed him back, and a shiver of excitement ran down her spine.

"Let's go back to my motel and get my things," he said hoarsely. "I'll show you how much I love you."

Rosie turned on the ignition and shifted into reverse.

"Rosie, wait!" Josh shouted and clutched the dashboard.

"What is it?" She froze, her hand on the steering wheel.

Josh ducked his head out the window and grinned. "You almost ran over my surfboard."

Eighteen

Rosie and Josh left the beach and picked up Josh's things at his motel room. They closed the curtains and made love. Afterwards Rosie stood in the motel shower, the hot water seeping into every part of her body. Her heart was so full she felt as light as the soap bubbles on her freshly washed skin.

They drove leisurely down the coast, the ocean changing from a dark gray to a shimmering turquoise. Their picnic of sourdough bread and Edam cheese was the best she ever tasted, and when they stopped at Point Lobos to watch the sea lions clambering over the rocks she never wanted to leave.

A warm breeze wafted in the window, and Josh kept his hand on her knee. He was like a schoolboy, showing her points of interest: inlets where he had surfed, taco shacks on the beach, colorful beds of flowers.

"When I was a kid, I was obsessed with California missions," Josh said as they approached San Luis Obispo. "I did my mission report on Mission San Luis Obispo. Did you know in 1772 there was a famine and the missionaries were starving? A group of men traveled to the Valley of the Bears and killed enough grizzly bears to feed four missions."

"I forgot you were a history buff." Rosie closed the window. It was early evening and the air was chilly.

"Do you mind if we stop here?" He waved at the low stone building. "I haven't visited the mission since I was nine years old."

Rosie was exhausted. The last twenty-four hours were a blur, like a car speeding on a racetrack. She wanted to sink into a bubble bath and then climb under the down comforter. She wanted to share a bowl of Peg's homemade soup, and eat a slice of chocolate cake for dessert.

"It's after five o'clock." Rosie checked her watch. "It's probably closed."

"I bet the church is open." Josh stopped the car in the gravel driveway. "Let's take a look."

Josh took Rosie's hand and led her down a stone path. "See the grapevines on the archway." He pointed to the trellis growing over the walkway. "The missionaries produced their own wine. It was the first wine made in California."

"It's very pretty." Rosie admired the lush rosebushes. "I'd love to take a quick peek."

"Let's go in the church." Josh pulled her towards a white building with a wooden door.

Josh opened the door and stepped inside. The church was one room with two pews separated by a narrow aisle. The floor was stone and the windows were set high in the wall. There was a beamed ceiling and yellow candles at the altar.

"It's beautiful." Rosie admired the stained-glass windows.

"There's a small room off the main sanctuary," Josh said. "When I was a kid I hid there after the tour ended. I got in so much trouble, I was grounded for a week."

Josh led her to a tiny room. There was a statue of Jesus and a painting of the Last Supper. A wooden altar was framed by a dozen candles, their flames flickering in the dark.

Rosie squinted in the darkness. A group of people huddled around the altar. Someone gasped and she made out the form of a woman in a yellow dress and a wide hat.

"Estelle?" Rosie recognized the opal dangling around Estelle's neck.

"Hello, dear." Estelle stepped closer. "It's lovely to see you."

"What are you doing here?" Rosie gasped. The faces in the group turned towards her.

"Colby, Ryan, Morris!" Rosie's eyes were wide. "Angelica, Dirk, Oscar, Yvette! What's going on?"

Estelle put her hand on Rosie's. "I had to bring the roses; we couldn't have a bare church." She led Rosie back to the main chapel and turned up the lights. There was a huge vase of white roses at the altar, pink and yellow roses tied to the pews, burnt-orange roses lining the aisle, and red roses scattered over the floor.

"I don't understand." Rosie felt shaky. Her throat was dry, and she couldn't swallow.

"I brought the champagne." Morris entered the main sanctuary. "It's in ice buckets in the back, but we can pop open a bottle now. You look like you need it."

"And I have the dress." Angelica stepped forward. "Thank god Dirk drives faster than a race-car driver, or we wouldn't have made it in time."

"We wouldn't miss it." Colby leaned forward and kissed Rosie on the cheek. "Josh called and told me you changed your mind."

"Changed my mind?" Rosie repeated in a daze.

"About Rosie's Fish Tacos." Colby grinned.

"I did?" Rosie turned to Josh.

"You did." Josh nodded. "It's a wonderful opportunity. We'll work out the details: if you have to travel for business, we'll go to-gether."

"Why is everyone here?" Rosie demanded, feeling like Alice in Wonderland tumbling down the rabbit hole.

"For your wedding." Esmeralda stepped out of the dark. She wore a floor-length black gown and red lipstick. Her dark hair was shiny, and she cradled a velvet box.

"Our what?" Rosie turned to Josh.

"This is a gift for both of you." Esmeralda handed Rosie the box. "I'd like you to open it now."

Rosie lifted the lid and took out a shiny brass key.

"It's the key to my house in Montecito." Esmeralda smiled. "I'd like you and Josh to live there and fill it with beautiful children."

"Thank you." Josh nodded, catching his mother's eye.

"Rosie!" A woman dashed through the door. She wore a heart-shaped pendant around her neck and clutched a red box. "Oh my god, I thought we'd be too late. Patrick's car doesn't go over fifty on the highway."

Rachel wiped the sweat from her forehead and handed the box to Josh.

"Rachel brought the wedding rings." Josh snapped open the box and revealed two matching gold bands. "You said you wanted to elope, but it didn't feel right to get married without our closest family and friends."

"But how did everyone know to come here?" Rosie wondered aloud.

"I called them while you were showering at the motel," Josh admitted. "Patrick is going to perform the ceremony. He got or-dained online. And Oscar will give you away; it's good practice for him before Angelica's wedding."

Rosie gulped and turned away, afraid she would burst into tears.

A hand touched her shoulder and she inhaled Angelica's perfume.

"Sometimes I'm not the easiest person to have as a friend, and I haven't been very supportive of your relationship with Josh," Angelica said. "But I love you more than anything and I know you're going to be happy."

Rosie gave Angelica a hug and wiped her eyes. "Your dress is in the back room." Angelica pointed to the door. "It's an Alexander McQueen crepe sheath with a sweep train."

"I'm going to do your makeup." Yvette stepped forward. "And Morris is going to style your hair."

"And I called your parents." Morris held up his phone. "We're going to FaceTime them when the ceremony begins."

Josh squeezed Rosie's hand and whispered in her ear, "You're going to be the most beautiful bride. I'll meet you at the altar."

Rosie curled her fingers around his. The candles flickered on the altar and it all looked so romantic. "I can't wait." She looked up and smiled.

Josh leaned close and kissed her. "Neither can I."

Epilogue

Rosie stood on the porch of the Pullman estate and couldn't believe it had been ten months since she and Josh got married. At first Esmeralda's house was overwhelming with its huge empty rooms and overgrown garden. But Estelle sent her gardener to help, and now Rosie had a vegetable garden and a rose garden and a lawn for entertaining. The dark wood floors had been replaced by a light oak, and Josh painted the walls yellow. Morris taught her how to dust in places she couldn't reach, and Rachel helped clean out the attic and stock the kitchen.

Her favorite things about the new house were Opal and Grace. The first thing Rosie and Josh did after they moved in was go down to the local animal shelter and pick out two dogs. Opal was a Labrador mix named after one of Josh's favorite cars and Grace was part English spaniel and loved to retrieve balls on the tennis court.

She tipped her face up to the sun and thought it was lovely to have a whole weekend to relax. There was always so much to do: projects around the house and approving Colby and Ryan's marketing plans and running the taco store in the village. And it was almost impossible to pull Josh away from the Classic Car Showroom. Sometimes she picked up a pizza and sat in his office while he mulled over his inventory and sales figures.

"Hi, Rosie." Estelle walked out onto the porch. "Aren't we lucky to have such perfect weather. The lawn looks gorgeous." She surveyed the long table covered with a white tablecloth and ceramic vases. Gold filigree chairs had pink cushions, and there were strings of colored lights. "I'm so glad we're finally holding a wedding here. I didn't think anything could top Angelica and Dirk's wedding in Monte Carlo, but it will be nice to have one at home. And Peg has outdone herself, with lobster and steak and three types of cheesecakes."

"It's beautiful," Rosie agreed. "Where are Angelica and Dirk? They'll miss the rehearsal dinner; it starts in three hours."

"Angelica called, they got held up at the studio and they're stuck in traffic." Estelle patted her hair. "I don't know how she juggles it all. She and Dirk are doing publicity for *To Catch a Thief* and she's in preproduction for her next movie. It's all hush-hush, but the leading man is supposed to be someone very famous."

At first when Rosie saw photos on Instagram from the set of *To Catch a Thief,* she couldn't help being envious. Even if she didn't have feelings for Ben she missed everything about making movies: watching the daily rushes and spending hours in the editing suite and the thrill of seeing the finished cut on the screen. She had lived and breathed cinema since Kenyon, and she hadn't realized how much she loved being surrounded by writers and actors and directors.

But she came home from a trip to New York with Colby, and Josh made her close her eyes and led her into the den. One whole wall was a movie screen and there were velvet-covered chairs and a library of DVDs. It was so much fun watching movies together. Rosie introduced Josh to classics like *A Streetcar Named Desire* with Paul Newman and *Butterfly 8* with Elizabeth Taylor, and they found they both loved current films from India and Brazil. Rosie even renewed her subscription to *Variety* and was so proud when Angelica was included among the hot new actresses.

"Where is the bride?" Rosie asked Estelle. "I haven't seen her all afternoon."

"Yvette is with Esmeralda in the cottage," Estelle replied. "I'm so glad Esmeralda is staying with us for a few days. It might be wishful thinking, but she seems better. The clinic in Switzerland is helping her memory."

"I can't wait to show her everything we've done with the house," Rosie responded as a yellow car pulled into the driveway. Dirk was driving and Angelica sat in the passenger seat, her hair hidden by a floppy hat.

"Rosie." Angelica ran up the steps and hugged her. "It's wonderful to see you, we have so much to catch up on. Don't you love Dirk's car." She waved at the car. "It's a 1965 Peugeot. Dirk found it in Cassis when we were filming and had it shipped to America. I feel like Grace Kelly driving along the Boulevard de la Croisette and Dirk is every bit as sexy as Cary Grant."

"You look beautiful." Estelle kissed her daughter. "Tell us all about the new movie, we're dying to hear the details."

Angelica took off her hat and adjusted her sunglasses. She wore a formfitting dress and white stilettos.

"It's a remake of *Pretty Woman*," she said. "Though I'll never manage Julia Roberts' smile, it's the best in Hollywood." She paused and her eyes danced. "We're in a mad rush to get the costumes sorted out because we had to move up the schedule. I'm pregnant!"

"You're pregnant?" Rosie gasped, noticing how Angelica's breasts were squeezed into her bra.

"We found out last week." Angelica beamed. "Dirk is already thinking of names; he wants something British: Rupert or Nigel if it's a boy and Tabitha or Beatrix for a girl."

"I'm going to be a grandmother," Estelle said and her voice cracked. "That's the best news in the world."

"Rosie has news of her own." Angelica glanced pointedly at Rosie.

Rosie looked at the ground and her cheeks turned red. She had confided in Angelica when she was in Los Angeles two weeks ago, but she asked her not to tell anyone.

"What is it, Rosie?" Estelle looked at Rosie inquisitively.

"Josh and I didn't want to say anything until after the first trimester. You never know what can happen." She fiddled with her ring. "We're having a baby. I'm due in December."

"A Christmas baby!" Estelle beamed. "How wonderful. Josh must be on top of the world."

"We're both excited and terrified." Rosie laughed. "Where is Josh? I haven't seen him since we arrived."

"He and the groom played tennis and they went to the pool house to change," Estelle said. "It's wonderful having everyone together. It reminds me of when they were children. Who would have guessed Sam and Yvette would fall in love and get engaged? I remember them playing cowboys and Indians and fighting over rafts in the pool."

Josh's sister, Yvette, and Angelica's brother, Sam, had started a whirlwind romance at Dirk and Angelica's wedding. Yvette said it was all because of her dog, Josie. Josie fell into the harbor in Monte Carlo and Sam fished her out and saved her.

"They seem like the perfect couple," Rosie agreed. "They both want to travel before they start a family. And Sam is teaching Yvette how to cook. They had us over for dinner last week and Sam made spaghetti marinara. He's a wonderful chef and the first time I met Yvette she was having caramel popcorn for dinner."

"Love is the strangest thing or maybe it's something about this house," Estelle said ruminatively. "All those years that Oscar lived above the garage, and it wasn't until he went away that we realized we were in love. Even Morris and Ryan fell in love in this house. I don't know why Morris kept it a secret for so long," Estelle said with a little smile. "Oscar and I are so thrilled. Morris deserves to be happy."

"I'm so happy for them." Rosie nodded. "I wish they were here for the wedding, but they're having a wonderful time in Europe. Morris sent us postcards from Ibiza and Sicily."

"You and Daddy are the best role models." Angelica hugged her mother. "Dirk and I hope to be half as good as parents. If you'll excuse me, I'm going to get a box of crackers and use the bathroom." Angelica turned to Rosie. "You know what it's like, Rosie. You can't go an hour without wanting to pee and if you're not eating saltines you feel like you're going to throw up." She squeezed Rosie's arm. "I can't wait to exchange food cravings and labor and delivery options. Dirk wants to have the baby in London like George and Amal Clooney. There are private hospitals, and they serve you hot chocolate and scones on a silver tray."

Angelica drifted inside and Rosie turned to Estelle.

"I'm sorry we didn't tell you about the baby sooner. I'm a little superstitious."

"I never told anyone until I was three months along," Estelle agreed. "But it's going to be fine. You and Angelica are lucky, there's nothing better than raising children with your closest friend. Esmeralda and I had so much fun when the kids were young. They were always running in and out of the house demanding Popsicles and getting pool water on the kitchen floor. Looking back, it was the best time of my life."

"I can't wait." Rosie nodded. "Angelica and Dirk will come up on the weekends, and we'll all play tennis and swim and go to the beach."

"I really can't think of anything better." Estelle noticed Oscar talking to the gardener. "Except of course, marrying the man you love."

Josh came out of the pool house and his hair was damp from the shower. He wore a sports shirt and slacks and he looked up at Rosie and waved. Rosie waved back and imagined what their child would look like: a little boy with Josh's blond hair or a girl with her dark hair and Josh's blue eyes.

They had already started talking about the things they would do as a family: get one of those baby backpacks and go hiking in Yosemite, teach him or her to swim early so they could accompany Josh surfing in Mexico. And one day they'd go to Italy and explore the Colosseum and the Roman Forum and eat gnocchi and gelato.

"Rosie, Estelle." Josh bounded up the steps. "Sam and I just played two sets of tennis and we're starving. We're going to raid the kitchen and Sam's going to make his roast beef sandwiches. You should join us, they're the best in Montecito."

The afternoon sun reflected on the lake and the air smelled of cut grass and roses. Rosie put a hand over her stomach and happiness bubbled up inside her. She touched Josh's arm and turned to Estelle.

"You're right," she said, and her face broke into a smile. "There's nothing better than marrying the man you love."

Guacamole with Cottage Cheese and Hawaiian Pink Sea Salt

2 ripe avocados, halved with pits removed

1 cup cottage cheese

juice of 2 limes

1 jalapeño pepper, minced (with seeds)

½ cup diced sweet onion

¼ cup fresh cilantro, chopped

1 teaspoon minced garlic

1 teaspoon pink sea salt to taste

½ teaspoon ground cumin

Scoop flesh out of the avocados and place it in a medium-sized mixing bowl. Mash the avocado well. Add lime juice to the avocado and mix well. Place cilantro, jalapeño pepper, onion, cottage cheese, cumin, and minced garlic into the mixing bowl; stir until the ingredients are combined. Sprinkle with Hawaiian pink sea salt to taste. Chill for at least one hour before serving.

Fish Tacos

1 pound cod fillets, cut into strips 2–3 inches in length
    by 1 inch in width
1 quart oil for frying
1 (12 ounce) package small flour tortillas
½ medium head cabbage, shredded

BEER BATTER

1 cup all-purpose flour
2 tablespoons cornstarch
1 teaspoon baking powder
½ teaspoon salt
1 egg
1 ¼ cup light beer (such as Mexican lager)

WHITE SAUCE

½ cup sour cream
½ cup mayonnaise
1 lime, juiced
1 jalapeño pepper, minced
1 teaspoon minced capers
1 teaspoon fresh cilantro, minced
1 teaspoon ground cumin
½ teaspoon dried dill weed

To make white sauce: Mix together sour cream and mayonnaise. Stir in lime juice until consistency is slightly runny. Season with jalapeño, capers, cilantro, cumin, and dill weed.

To make beer batter: In a large bowl, combine flour, cornstarch, baking powder, and salt. Blend egg and beer, and then quickly stir into the flour mixture.

Heat oil in deep fryer to 375 degrees.

Dip fish pieces into beer batter, and fry until crisp and golden brown. Place fish on paper towels to drain excess oil. Heat tortillas by placing 6 at a time between two wet paper towels and heat in the microwave until soft, about 30 seconds. To serve, place fried fish in a tortilla, and top with shredded cabbage, and white sauce.

Acknowledgments

Thank you to my brilliant agent and editor, Melissa Flashman and Lauren Jablonski, for their inspiration and dedication. Thank you to the whole team at St. Martin's Press: Brittani Hilles, Karen Masnica, Brant Janeway, Jennifer Enderlin, and Jennifer Weis.

Thank you to the friends who are always there for me—Andrea Katz, Traci Whitney, Sara Sullivan, Patricia Hull, Gary Fong, and Jessica Parr—and the biggest thanks to my children for everything they give me: Alex, Andrew, Heather, Madeleine, and Thomas.

About the Author

Anita Hughes is the author of *Monarch Beach; Market Street; Lake Como; French Coast; Rome in Love; Island in the Sea; Santorini Sunsets; Christmas in Paris; White Sand, Blue Sea; Emerald Coast;* and *Christmas in London*. She attended UC Berkeley's Masters in Creative Writing Program and lives in Dana Point, California, where she is at work on her next novel.